'A tragic accident, a dead friend and a fresh new voice in crime fiction... Wallace draws you into a deceptively ordinary world before she revels in the delicious horror beneath. Pure class'
Janice Hallett, author of *The Appeal*

'*Motherland* with murder! I haven't laughed so much in ages, then been struck speechless with horror... Funny, sad, wicked and very engaging'
Emma Curtis, author of *One Little Mistake*

'Darkly funny and deftly plotted'
Alice Clark-Platts, author of *The Flower Girls*

'A twisty-turny mystery with a brilliantly relatable protagonist, characters that leap off the page and a narrative voice that drew me in from the opening lines... A brilliantly entertaining and engaging read'
Philippa East, author of *Little White Lies*

'Had me rolling around with laughter on one page, and filled with empathy the next. *The Dead Friend Project* is hilariously brilliant, and Joanna Wallace is a rare talent'
J.M. Hewitt, author of *The Life She Wants*

'Supremely well plotted and often hilariously funny'
Leonora Nattrass, author of *Blue Water*

'Riotously funny, dark as anything, heartfelt and searingly observed'
Kate Simants, author of *Freeze*

'Darkly funny and touchingly observant, *The Dead Friend Project* is a page turner of an emotional thriller'
Alison Stockham, author of *The Cuckoo Sister*

'Wallace may have invented a new genre. Not cosy crime or comic crime, but clever crime'
Abbie Frost, author of *The Guesthouse*

'A wonderful antidote for anyone who's suffered the *Groundhog Day* torture of the school run! Perfectly observed and brilliantly funny'
Alison Belsham, author of *The Tattoo Thief*

'A perfectly paced and brilliantly executed murder mystery with a twist and a main character you can't help rooting for even at her most awful'
Sarah Lawton, author of *All the Little Things*

'A wickedly funny thriller that kept me guessing to the last page'
Dan Malakin, author of *The Box*

'Brilliantly dark... School gate conflicts degenerate into murder in this hilarious and fast-moving thriller'
Guy Morpuss, author of *Five Minds*

THE DEAD FRIEND PROJECT

JOANNA WALLACE

Joanna Wallace

First published in Great Britain in 2024 by Viper,
an imprint of Profile Books Ltd
29 Cloth Fair
London
EC1A 7JQ

www.profilebooks.com

Copyright © Joanna Wallace, 2024

1 3 5 7 9 10 8 6 4 2

Typeset by CC Book Production

Printed and bound in Great Britain by
Clays Ltd, Elcograf S.p.A.

The moral right of the author has been asserted.

All rights reserved. Without limiting the rights under copyright reserved above, no part of this publication may be reproduced, stored or introduced into a retrieval system, or transmitted, in any form or by any means (electronic, mechanical, photocopying, recording or otherwise), without the prior written permission of both the copyright owner and the publisher of this book.

A CIP catalogue record for this book is available from the British Library.

HB ISBN 978 1 80081 134 8
TPB ISBN 978 1 80081 135 5
eISBN 978 1 80081 137 9

For Marc, Grace, Charlie, Lucy, Sam, Star and Wilfred

Almost a Year Ago

The morning after an unexpected death – that's when the stillness arrives, ushering in the beginning of a forever she will never see. The sun is still here, the flowers, the milk she bought yesterday, her toothbrush – still damp – the spoon she stirred her tea with, where she left it by the kitchen sink. But there's stillness instead, in the place where she was.

And her family, they touch the toothbrush and the milk she bought yesterday. As if connecting with the things she most recently touched will somehow close the gap between where she stood then and where she is today.

And it sounds different – the home, the morning after an unexpected death. The wails of anguish, the quiet sobs. The visitors at the door. All saying the same words. Words that nobody spoke yesterday morning, when the radio played, and she danced around the kitchen and laughed. I can't believe it. I'm so sorry. I can't believe she's gone. Not Charlotte. The most alive person I've ever known.

All that aliveness. Joining the ranks of the dead.

And everyone wishes they could rewind time. To before it happened. To when she danced around the kitchen and took that milk from the fridge. And they would tell her. Don't go for a run this evening. Take a break from the marathon training. It's almost November, it's dark outside. Stay indoors and watch TV. You know about that bend in the lane. You warn your children about it every day. You know what could happen if a car comes around that bend in the darkness. If you run out into the lane at the wrong time.

And everyone's so busy rewinding the last twenty-four hours, no one pays much attention to Charlotte's youngest child. They cuddle him as they pass and bring him his sippy cup of juice, but they're too lost to look at what he's drawing. Maybe they notice the face and the arms and the legs, but it doesn't look like a monster, so no one knows it's the monster and he doesn't have the words yet to tell them. So, they cuddle him and kiss the top of his head and tell him it's a lovely picture. But it isn't a lovely picture, it's the monster – moving from his crayons to a locked room somewhere inside his developing mind. And maybe one day a clever therapist will unlock the door and Charlotte's youngest child will think again of the monster. But by then it will be distorted into something different. Twisted from memory into something he thinks he imagined or maybe he dreamt. The lady in the yellow coat. Banging at the front door and waking him up. The lady in the yellow coat. Pulling Mummy out the house and making her scared. The lady in the yellow coat. Chasing Mummy into the road. The monster who didn't look like a monster.

Making his mummy be dead.

1

The school bell is loud but almost goes unnoticed, underneath the chatter of parents standing out here in the playground.

'Mum! Can I go and play at Noah's house?'

'Not today, Jack,' I say, flicking my eyes to the seven-year-old child looking up at me – marvelling at the mystery for which I'm never quite fully prepared. How someone so recently released from a classroom can look like they've spent the day playing with a cement mixer.

'But Mum . . .'

'It's a bit early for playdates, isn't it? I mean, it's only the first day of school.'

Those grey trousers, so spotlessly clean when he put them on this morning, are already scuffed with dirt. And that navy-blue school jumper is covered in . . . what is that? Paint? And wasn't he wearing a tie this morning?

'But Mum . . .'

'No, Jack!' I start to walk from the playground.

'But why not?' he asks.

'Oh, come on, Jack, put on your listening ears, I've already told you. The school year has only just started. Give me a few weeks at least to ease back into playdates and all that . . . crap.'

I say the last word under my breath. His little freckled face, looking pleadingly up into my own, is flushed red – his hair slicked back neatly with . . . what is that in his hair? More paint? Hopefully it's paint.

'But Mum, I really want to—'

'And I really want to grab you and your brother and go home. Where is Freddie anyway? Oh look, there he is – on the climbing wall. Go and get him, please.'

'But why can't I go to Noah's? His mum says it's OK. Look, she's coming over.'

'No, Jack, not today! Go get your brother and—'

'Hello Beth. How was your summer?'

'Hi Emily,' I say, staring into a face that can only be described as an exclamation. Huge bright eyes, razor-sharp cheekbones – there's an almost other-worldly quality to attractiveness as combative as that. She's wearing trainers, Sweaty Betty leggings and a Sweaty Betty sports bra – no coat, even though it's cold today, and there's not even the suggestion of frizz escaping from her long, elegant ponytail. A couple of Minions rucksacks are draped casually over one of her delicate shoulders, a yoga mat is slung over the other, a dispenser of hand sanitiser is clipped to her waistband and there's a Tupperware container of chopped vegetables clasped in her manicured hand.

'It seems the boys have their hearts set on a playdate,' she says, popping a slice of carrot into her mouth. 'I don't mind Jack coming round to ours for his tea. You know me. The more the merrier.'

'That's very kind of you, Emily, but I don't know. It's the first day back—'

'She said it's too early for playdates and all that crap,' says Jack, demonstrating the remarkably selective superpower of his listening ears.

'Beth.' Emily's taking a step towards me and whispering, suddenly serious. 'I hope this doesn't sound preachy—' Oh God, am I in trouble? 'It's just that I've been a mum for a very long time now. Nineteen years, can you believe it? Georgina's off to university in a few weeks . . .' She always does this; the same irrelevant information dropped into every conversation. 'And little Tobias – not so little any more! He'll be sitting his A-levels next year! Anyway, like I say, I'm not being preachy,' beginning to sound a bit preachy, 'but something I've learnt during my nineteen years of being a mum . . . Beth?'

'Yes?'

'Do you know what happens every time you swear in front of your child?'

'No,' I reply. 'Does a fairy die?'

'You reduce yourself in their eyes,' she continues, ignoring my last words. 'Every time you swear, you become smaller and smaller to the people who look up to you most.'

'I want to become smaller and smaller.'

'Right,' she says, taking a step back and appraising me with those enormous, freakily intense eyes. Does she ever blink? I'm not sure I've ever seen her blink. 'Well, baby weight can be difficult to shift, can't it?' she continues. 'How old is Hope now?' she asks, looking at the small human in my arms.

'She's eighteen months,' I reply. 'Jack, stop hitting my leg with your book bag.' My voice is raised, irritation seeping in.

'Why don't you grab a couple of after-school snacks, Jack, and go over to play on the climbing wall?' says Emily, holding the Tupperware pot out to my child. As well as carrots, there is chopped up cucumber in there and red peppers and what's that? Is that a courgette? Who chops up a courgette and brings it into the school playground? And then has the audacity to call it an after-school snack?

'Thanks, Emily, but Jack refuses to eat vegetables,' I say, just as Jack grabs a handful of chopped vegetables and shoves them into his mouth before running towards the climbing wall.

'Isn't it lovely watching children having fun together,' she's saying, gazing around the playground, her smile verging on eerie. 'So important for them to let off steam. That's why I think playdates are important. It would be so lovely if Jack could come back to our house today, it will be good for Noah to have someone his own age to run around with and he seems to love playing with Jack. Poor Noah has been so busy lately. We only got three weeks away in the house in Tuscany and he spent the rest of the summer working with his tutor.'

'Why's Noah got a tutor?'

'So he can pass the exam to get into a decent secondary

school,' she says, offering a mushy piece of courgette to my daughter.

'But that exam isn't for another . . .'

'Three years, I know. We probably should have started the tutoring earlier.'

'Earlier?' I say, as Hope kicks her legs and wriggles in my arms. She's laughing, yelling 'More!' and reaching out for more of the mushy, green stuff.

'Well, secondary school is so important, isn't it?' Emily says, picking out more courgette for my daughter. 'If Noah doesn't get into a good one, he probably won't do well in his GCSEs and A-levels, which means he won't get into a good university,' she says, smiling at Hope. 'And then he won't get a good job,' she adds, in a sing-song voice.

'Right,' I say, reaching out towards the Tupperware container. I want to understand all this fuss about the courgette. I drop a piece into my mouth. As I suspected. Gross.

'Emily! Emily, I just heard something really interesting.' If Emily's face is an exclamation, Danielle's is a question mark. The woman always looks anxious and confused. She's running towards us wearing Sweaty Betty flowery leggings and a flowing yoga top. It's a decent attempt but she's not carrying off the look anywhere near as effortlessly as Emily. Less Sweaty Betty chic. More . . . sweaty.

'You'll never guess what,' she's saying to Emily, after directing a nervous but friendly nod towards me. 'I was just speaking to Kylie, you know Kylie – Finn's mum. You know Finn? The kid with the eyepatch. Well, his mum Kylie is the Australian woman who works in the school office, and she was saying—'

'That Australian mum is called Kylie?' I say with a smile. 'That's brilliant. I can't wait for her to throw a few shrimps on the barbie.'

'Have you become friends with Kylie, Beth?' Emily asks, smiling back at me. 'I must say, I think that's the most wonderful news.'

'Why?' I ask, looking from her to Danielle.

'Can I be honest?' Emily asks, clipping the lid shut on the Tupperware container and dropping it into one of her bags. 'I've been so worried about you. We all have, haven't we?' she adds, glancing at Danielle, who does more of that peculiar head nod. 'We remember what you used to be like. The life and soul of the party! Always making us laugh with your hilarious jokes.'

'Hilarious,' agrees Danielle.

'But for the last year,' Emily says, taking a step towards me, 'you've been keeping yourself to yourself. And it's perfectly understandable, you know, what with . . .' She's looking towards Danielle again who's looking anxious. 'You know, what with . . . everything that happened.' She reaches her hand out towards me. 'You've been through so much, all we want is for you to be happy again. So, I'm so pleased to hear you're making new friends.' She squeezes my arm. 'I think it's great that you're meeting up with Kylie for a barbecue.'

'What are you talking about?' I ask, taking a step back and shaking her hand from my arm. 'I'm not meeting up with Kylie. I literally just found out her name.'

'So, why were you talking about her barbecue?'

'I was making a joke, that's all! About her being so . . . you know, Australian.'

Not a great joke, I admit, and certainly not hilarious, but I don't think it warrants this tumbleweed.

'So, what was she talking about?' I ask Danielle, when the silence becomes unbearable.

'Who?'

'Kylie. The Australian mum who works in the school office. You said you were talking to her and heard something interesting.'

'Oh yes,' says Danielle. 'Kylie was saying that a new family is joining the school this term and guess what? They've moved into Charlotte's old house.'

'Oh, that is interesting,' says Emily, unclipping the hand sanitiser from her waistband.

'How does Kylie know?' I ask.

'She works in the school office,' says Emily. 'Kylie knows where everyone lives.'

'But addresses are confidential,' I say. 'Surely she shouldn't be passing personal information around?'

'Oh, no one cares about things like that, Beth! Chill out and go with the flow,' laughs the woman currently micromanaging every step of her child's life journey – from *Minions* to billions and every overachievement in between. 'I wonder whether the new family know,' she's asking now, rubbing antibacterial gel between her fingers and into her palms. 'You know, what happened to Charlotte? I wonder whether they were told, before they bought the house.'

'My second cousin is an estate agent,' says Danielle, 'so I know there are very specific rules about this. I think it's in their code of ethics.'

'Estate agents have a code of ethics?' I laugh. 'What's that written on, a postage stamp?'

'Emily, guess what?' Suddenly Fara appears and I know I'm looking as dumbfounded as Danielle because it's a mystery to me why someone as brilliant as Fara remains so utterly devoted to Emily. She's got more degrees than children, and Fara has a lot of children. Four or five, at least. And she never shouts at them, even the annoying one, she always speaks calmly and uses interesting, intelligent words, which isn't surprising because I heard she's descended from a long line of brilliant people. Her dad is a top politician in Nigeria and Fara has clearly inherited all his brains and charm. Yet here she is, desperately vying for Emily's attention. I don't get it. 'Guess what?' she's saying again. 'That's the new mum, over there – the one who's just moved into Charlotte's old house.'

We all turn in the direction of Fara's pointed finger, to gawp at the new mum who's just moved into Charlotte's old house. She's holding a small child, who I guess must hear a lot of swear words because the new mum is tiny. She looks young and athletic, with gorgeous dark curls tumbling over her shoulders. She's wearing blue jeans and a black fitted jacket and looks like she may just have stepped out of an advert. One of those weird perfume adverts on TV that never seem to have any discernible storyline but do, I suppose, provide an opportunity for the insanely attractive to hang out with their own kind for a while.

'I think she looks lovely,' Emily says, after a moment. 'Very warm, and friendly.'

'I agree,' says Danielle, 'I think she'll fit in really well.'

'I concur,' says Fara.

Concur? There's my word of the day and now it's definitely time to leave. I look over to the climbing wall and start to wave, trying to attract Jack's attention.

'Still makes me shiver,' Emily says, running her hands up her bare arms. 'Even though it's been almost a year since . . . it happened, I don't think it will ever stop feeling weird, standing here in the playground, without Charlotte.'

'I know,' says Fara. 'And it must be so tough for you, Beth,' she adds, looking at me. 'What with you and Charlotte being such good friends.'

I nod, straining my eyes, trying to see my two sons. From over here, all the children on the climbing wall look the same.

'Have you stayed in contact with them?' Fara asks.

'Who?'

'Charlotte's family,' she says. 'Bill and the children. Do you still speak to them?'

'No,' I reply. 'Not since they moved away.' They're all staring at me. 'And I've been busy . . .'

'Of course,' Fara says, smiling.

'We're still in contact with Bill,' says Emily. 'I speak to him on the phone every so often. He's incredibly strong, doing everything he can to help those children. But . . .' another shiver, 'I'm not sure he'll ever forgive himself.'

'For what?' Fara asks, as I spot Jack's laughing face amongst all the others on the climbing wall. I stand on my toes, waving, and call out his name.

'For not being with her,' Emily says. 'That night. At the end.'

'But he can't blame himself for that,' Fara says. 'How could he have possibly known what was going to happen?'

'He couldn't,' Emily agrees. 'But you know what it's like with hindsight. I think he regrets coming to my party that night. I think he wishes he'd stayed at home with them. If only I hadn't had that party . . .'

'Oh, come on, Emily,' says Danielle. 'You can't think like that. Everyone was at yours that night; we'd all been looking forward to it for ages, especially the children. It was a fabulous evening, until . . .' Her voice tails off and I'm about to shout out to Jack again when something stops me. Something I just heard. Something that didn't sound right.

'What did you say?' I turn towards Emily.

'When?'

'About Bill.'

'How we still speak on the phone occasionally. How he's so strong, doing everything he can for—'

'No, after that. What did you say about hindsight?'

'How I think he regrets coming to my party that night.'

'And?'

'How I think he wishes he'd stayed at home with them.'

That's it. 'What do you mean, *them*?'

'Them,' she says simply. 'Charlotte and Leo.'

'But little Leo was at your party, wasn't he? I remember his sisters Amber and Poppy being there.'

'No, he stayed at home with Charlotte.'

'Why?'

'I don't know,' Emily says. 'Obviously he wanted to stay at home with his mum.'

'Are you sure?' I ask, staring at her.

'Yes,' she replies.

'Why didn't I know that?' I ask. 'Did you know that?' I add, looking from Fara to Danielle.

They nod but Emily answers. 'Well, it's like I said earlier, Beth, we haven't seen much of you since it happened. You've kept yourself to yourself. That isn't a criticism,' she says, taking a step towards me. 'It's perfectly understandable. What with everything that happened to Charlotte and then, you know, all the other stuff—'

'Right,' I say, interrupting. 'I just want to make sure I understand this correctly. Charlotte was at home with Leo on the evening that she died?'

'Yes.'

'How old was he then? Around two?'

'Two and a half, I think,' Danielle says. 'I remember Charlotte had a lovely party for him in the Easter holidays.'

I ignore this. 'Was anyone else with them?' I ask Emily.

'No, Bill, Amber and Poppy were at the party.'

'So, why did she go out for a run?' They're all staring at me. 'That's what everyone said happened. She went out for a run in the dark and got hit by a car coming round that blind bend. But Charlotte would never leave her kid in the house on his own.' I close my eyes for a moment, trying to focus. 'It doesn't make sense—'

Suddenly I see Jack running towards me and as soon as I see his face, I feel sick. From the moment I gave birth to Jack seven years ago, there has only ever been one of two expressions plastered onto his face. Happy. Or pissed off. Never anything in between. But this look is completely different. Fear. I think I might scream.

'Mummy, Mummy! Freddie fell off the climbing wall and now he can't move his arm.'

Passing my daughter to Danielle, I run towards the climbing wall and he's there. Lying on the ground and crying. Freddie. Five years old and usually so boisterous. Now curled up into a terrifying ball of pain.

'This is why children aren't supposed to play on the climbing wall unsupervised. All you parents standing around and nattering, not paying any attention. I knew something like this would happen again one day. I said as much—'

'Not helpful, Carl,' I snap at the grumpy school caretaker, before helping Freddie to his feet. Grabbing my daughter from Danielle, I strap Hope into the pushchair while pleading with Jack.

'No, Jack, please! You can't go to Noah's for a bloody playdate because you're coming to the hospital with me. Why can't I ever just walk into this bloody playground, collect you two and just *leave*?'

And now I'm running towards the exit, aware of other people staring in my direction and panic pushing the occasional swear word from my mouth. So, it's strange, the silence I fall into as I approach her. That new mum who's just moved into Charlotte's old house. And even stranger that, I'm fighting a peculiar urge to warn her . . . but of what, I'm not entirely sure. Freddie whimpers: he's injured, and there's no time for thinking. I put down my head and run faster.

2

'Mummy! My arm isn't hurting any more. Can I go back on the climbing wall?'

'No, Fred. We need to go to hospital and get you properly checked out.'

'But I don't want to go to hospital,' he shouts, kicking his feet into the back of the driver's seat.

'See, he's fine. Now can I go and play at Noah's?'

'No, Jack!' I say, glancing at my eldest child. He's sitting in the passenger seat beside me and looking angry. 'We need to get a doctor to look at Freddie's arm.'

'That sounds boring! How long is it going to take?'

'As long as it takes.'

'Mummy?'

'Yes, Fred?' I ask, staring into the rear-view mirror at my two youngest children strapped into their car seats – securing everything in place, other than smiles.

'Have you got any Haribo? Green ones. I only want green ones.'

'I don't think I have, but I'll try to get some after we've got you checked out.'

'Where are you going to get green Haribo?' asks Jack.

'I don't know. The supermarket, most probably.'

'What?' he says, as I keep my eyes locked on the road ahead. There's no need to look at his face. 'We have to go to hospital and *then* we have to go to the supermarket? This is going to take ages.'

'Ow! My arm hurts again!'

'OK, Freddie,' I say, squeezing the steering wheel tightly. 'Not long now. Oh, look at that big bus! Let's sing "The Wheels on the Bus"!'

'No.'

'OK, Jack. How about you, Freddie? We could sing it for Hope.'

'Mummy? If you can't get green Haribo, can you get me the red ones?' asks Freddie. 'They're my second favourite. I like them nearly as much as the green ones.'

'You can't buy just green or red Haribo, you idiot!'

'Jack! Don't call your brother an idiot.'

'He *is* an idiot.'

'But Mummy,' says Freddie. 'I only want the green or the red ones. Or maybe those other ones but I can't remember what colour the other ones are.'

'See, he is an idiot.'

'Jack!' I say, slowing down at the traffic lights. 'Oh, look at that. Another red light. Red is a lovely colour, isn't it? I know, why don't we all take turns to tell each other our favourite colour? Who would like to start? Nobody? Well, I can go first. My favourite colour is blue. No, maybe it's green. You know what, I think my favourite colour is bluey green.'

'Is this why Daddy went away?' asks Jack. 'Because you're so boring?'

'Look at that!' I say, my knuckles white on the steering wheel. 'A sign for the hospital. Not long now. Who wants to play a game?'

'What kind of game?'

'I don't know. I-spy maybe?'

'You're so boring!' Jack shouts.

'Right, who wants to listen to the radio?' Red light to amber. 'This is a nice song, isn't it?' I turn the volume up. 'I really love this song, don't you?' Amber to green. 'I tell you what,' foot to the floor. 'Why don't we all sit quietly and listen to the radio for a while?'

3

She would never leave a two-year-old child alone in the house to go out running. Not Charlotte. Her children were her life, she took a break from her high-flying career to care for them, there's no way she'd have left Leo on his own.

'Mummy, look what I've found.' Freddie's sitting on the floor in the middle of the Paediatrics A&E waiting area, playing with a large toy spaceship.

'That's great, Freddie,' I say from my seat in the corner. 'How's your arm?'

'It's good,' he replies, as a light on the top of the toy starts flashing. Maybe I'm wrong. Maybe it isn't a spaceship. Maybe it's a lighthouse. Could I be wrong about Charlotte, too? Maybe she did leave her son in the house on his own.

'That's great, Freddie,' I say again, reaching forward to remove Hope from the pushchair, who kicks her legs and squeals with excitement at the prospect of being freed.

'We're just going to wait here until you can see the doctor, OK?'

He doesn't answer because he's stopped listening. Too busy taking toy animals out of the intergalactic lighthouse. Why are there animals in there? Hope is batting at my face and wriggling desperately to get down, so I place her on the floor, before checking briefly on Jack, who has found a collection of small cars and seems happy lining them up in rows before pushing them along the floor. I turn back towards Hope who is holding something in her hand, waving it in the air, laughing manically and . . . oh my God! It's one of the toy animals from the lighthouse and now she's banging it on someone's foot.

'No, Hope!' I say, grabbing her back up into my arms, before apologising to a smiley woman with beautiful red hair, seated in the chair closest to mine. 'I'm so sorry,' I say, 'I hope she didn't hurt you.'

'Oh no,' the lady replies, glancing down at her feet, encased in bright green, sturdy-looking leather lace-ups. 'I didn't feel a thing.' Lucky she isn't wearing flip-flops. Returning her smile, I place my wriggling daughter back on the floor.

'I bet it's hard work with three little ones,' she says.

'Yes, sometimes it is,' I agree, back on my feet, shadowing Hope who has pulled herself up and is slowly cruising between chairs.

'How did your son hurt his arm?' Redhead asks, nodding towards Freddie.

'He fell off the climbing wall in the school playground. It's my fault,' I add, 'I should have been watching him.'

'Well, we don't have eyes in the back of our heads, do we? More's the pity,' she adds. 'I took my son to the park after school and only looked away for a moment. The next thing I know he's falling out of a tree.'

'Oh, my goodness,' I say. 'Is he OK?'

'Well, he said his leg hurt, so I rushed him straight here. It caused quite a stir in the park and everyone was so lovely, a couple of people even helped me carry him to the car. Anyway,' she says, 'he seems fine now, thank goodness. That's him,' she adds, pointing towards an excited little boy scoring goal after goal on the football table. With his feet. He looks a similar age to Jack – seven or eight years old – and he's wearing a red school uniform.

'Ollie! Get off the table! You're not supposed to be up there,' she shouts before turning back towards me. 'The problem is he's great at climbing up things but not so good at getting back down. Always seems to be falling from a height, my Ollie.' She gets up to try to coax her son down, and I turn my attention to the wall, covered in posters and leaflets – a patchwork of medical information. *Top Tips for Managing Stress* catches my eye and I'm halfway through the list when chatty Redhead returns to her seat. 'At least it isn't too busy in here today,' she says, looking around the waiting area. 'Hopefully we won't have to wait too long. It's not a bad day to come to A&E,' she adds, 'the first day back at school. It never seems to get too busy on the first day back.'

'Really?' I ask, turning to face her.

'Oh, yeah. I mean, obviously there are certain days of the year you definitely don't want to be here. Fireworks Night – that goes without saying – and Halloween. I think it's all the sugar – sends everyone doolally. We were here one Halloween when Ollie was a toddler, and it was horrendous. There were all these children running around in scary costumes, a woman literally collapsing in that corner over there, a small child literally dying over there, and all these kids puking into their trick or treat buckets. It was carnage. I told Ollie, I'm never bringing you here at Halloween ever again.'

'Christmas is just as bad,' I say, remembering. 'A few years ago, Jack, that's my eldest, he was so excited to open his presents, he slipped on the stairs and almost knocked himself out. My husband and I,' another glance at those stress-busting tips, 'I mean, my ex-husband, we were beside ourselves with worry. Luckily, Jack was fine, but we had to wait so long to see a doctor, I thought we'd be here until Boxing Day.'

'Thank goodness you weren't,' she says. 'Boxing Day is one of the worst days. Almost as bad as Christmas Eve. I think it's all the excitement. And the sugar, which never helps anything. Nor does tiredness. Have you ever been here on New Year's Day?'

'No,' I reply, after thinking about it for a moment.

'That's good,' she says. 'Try to keep it that way, because believe me, it's awful here then. All the kids have been up so late and when they're tired, of course they're going to slam their fingers in car doors and get their heads stuck in saucepans or what have you. We were here one New Year's Day, and it was rammed – standing room only – and I said to Ollie, never again.' I glance over at her son. Luckily he hasn't clambered back onto the football table because he clearly has a death wish, or maybe he just enjoys spending his holidays with NHS staff. He's sitting on the ground with Jack now, helping to set up an elaborate car race.

'It's relentless, isn't it?' Redhead says. 'The things us parents have to deal with. We try our best, obviously, but you can't watch them every second of every day, can you? It's like when we were in the park earlier, I didn't think I had to keep my eyes on him constantly. I mean, why would I? We've been to the park hundreds of times, we're always there – it's his favourite place in the world.'

My eyes move back towards the overloaded wall of information. There are a few posters about breastfeeding, but I skip over them. Been there, done that.

'And of course there's Easter Sunday!' She's talking. Again. 'If you're going to throw that amount of sugar into a competitive version of hide and seek, you're asking for trouble. Personally,' she adds, 'I think everyone should sign a disclaimer before setting off on an Easter egg hunt and as for the summer holidays . . .'

I'm still listening but find my eyes keep moving away from the talkative lady with beautiful red hair who seems completely obsessed with sugar intake. I glance towards Freddie, who still looks fascinated with that peculiar toy. Jack and accident-prone Ollie are lying face down on the floor, playing demolition derby with the little cars. Hope is sitting by my feet, knocking two building blocks together, and my eyes are drawn back to the wall. It's a very haphazard display of information, with random posters covering every spare inch; a mish-mash of fragmented advice. *Seven Silent Symptoms of Sepsis* has been pinned at a weird angle, partly covering something else, and I've nearly finished reading the list, when I recognise her smile. Almost completely obscured by silent symptoms, but not quite.

Redhead is still talking, recounting all the ways young children can break a bone on a beach, when I excuse myself and walk towards the wall. Peeling back the leaflet about sepsis, she's there. Charlotte. She looks so happy, her mouth turning upwards into a smile, her eyes sparkling. So alive. She's got that look on her face, that look she always has – just before she's about to laugh. I wonder what she's about to laugh at.

Bright green, sturdy-looking leather lace-ups appear next to my shoes and Redhead is there at my shoulder.

'Who's that?' she asks, sounding distracted, before turning to check on her son. She's probably terrified he's going to hurt himself. The poor woman really does need eyes at the back of her head.

'Her name was Charlotte,' I reply. 'She used to be a doctor here. She was killed last year. Hit by a car.'

'Oh, that's awful,' she says with a shiver.

'Yes,' I agree. 'I knew her,' I say, still staring at the poster. 'You may have seen her, actually, one of the times you came here with Ollie. She was so great with kids.' I feel tears in my eyes and wipe them away.

Redhead looks uncomfortable at my sudden outburst and sticks her hands deep into her pockets.

'That's really sad,' she says. 'But I don't think I remember her. There are a lot of doctors here.' She turns to check on Ollie, who thankfully hasn't dislocated anything in the last ten seconds, giving me time to wipe my eyes again.

'She was my friend,' I add. 'We met at toddler group and our children went to the same school.'

'What school was that?' she asks. 'St Michael's?'

'Yes.'

'I thought so,' says Redhead, seeming relieved to get back onto less emotionally soggy ground. 'I recognised your children's uniform. My Ollie used to go to St Michael's, but I moved him to Pond Street Primary because, to be honest, I didn't like the attitude of some of the staff there and, also, I found the St Michael's mums to be quite snooty. No offence. Not the mums like you, obviously. The other ones. The posh ones.' We stand in the briefest moment of silence. 'So, why is your friend on a poster?' she asks.

'I'm not sure,' I reply, squinting to read the words under Charlotte's face. 'I think it's about her charity work. Yes,' I say, reading, 'it talks about how she was training for the London Marathon when she died, raising money for meningitis research. People can still donate money in her name. Typical Charlotte.' I take a step back and stare at her face. 'Raising money for good causes even after she's gone. She was an incredible person, and the most brilliant mum, somehow finding time to train for the Marathon and . . .' the lump in my throat is immediate, 'be my best friend.' And certainly not the kind of person to leave a two-year-old kid in the house on his own. But if she wasn't out running that night, what was she doing in the road? Why was she there?

'Freddie?'

A nurse with a kind face has appeared in the waiting area, calling my son's name.

'Hi, this is Freddie,' I say, pointing towards him. 'He had a fall in the playground earlier and hurt his arm, but he seems fine now. I'm sorry if I'm wasting your time.'

'Not at all, Mum,' the nurse says, with a kind smile. 'It's like I always say – where there's doubt, check it out.'

'Yes,' I say, glancing back at the image of Charlotte. 'I think you're right.'

4

An hour or so later, I'm turning the car into our road when Jack sees him first.

'Daddy! Daddy's here.'

Rowan is pacing up and down outside the house looking tanned and concerned. Wearing a Superdry hoodie I bought him years ago for his birthday. I park outside the house and as I get out of the car, his eyes lock onto mine and that concern is replaced with annoyance.

'Beth, why the hell don't you ever answer your phone?' he asks.

'I left it at home,' I reply. 'I thought I was only going to be out for ten minutes or so, collecting the boys from school. What are you doing here?'

'Emily called me. She said Freddie fell off the climbing wall and hurt his arm. I was worried.'

'Daddy! Daddy!' Jack's out the car and looking happy. 'Are we sleeping at your house tonight?'

'Hi buddy,' Rowan says as Jack jumps into his arms. 'What's this?' he asks, ruffling Jack's hair. 'It's on your jumper too. Is that paint?'

'I think so,' Jack smiles, as Rowan lowers him to the ground. 'I think we did painting today, but I can't remember. School was ages ago. Are we sleeping at your house tonight?' he asks again.

'Hello Daddy,' shouts Freddie, clambering out the car, and as soon as I see his face, I find myself thinking about happiness. How it doesn't need any invitation to arrive. No fanfare, no applause – when happiness wants to show up, it's just there. 'Hello Daddy,' he says again, running towards my ex-husband.

'Hi Fred,' says his dad, 'how's your arm?'

'It's fine,' I say. 'Nothing broken, the doctor said. He's fine.'

'That's good news,' he says, carefully lifting Freddie for a cuddle, before placing him down and taking a step towards me. 'So, what happened?'

'When?'

'How did Freddie hurt his arm?'

'Like Emily said. He fell off the climbing wall in the school playground.'

'But *how* did it happen?' he asks. 'Weren't you keeping an eye on him?'

I open my mouth to answer but it's easier to become distracted by his eyes. Almost blue, nearly green – same eyes I stared into on our wedding day, just before I grabbed the microphone and started to talk. People said it was unconventional for the bride to make a speech and I laughed. Why wouldn't I stand up and tell everyone how much I loved my new husband? How he meant everything to me. This man with the most beautiful eyes. Eyes the same colour as the ocean, that day on our honeymoon when we went scuba diving off the coast of Mexico. I was so nervous that day, terrified that something would go wrong with my oxygen supply, that I wouldn't be able to breathe. But once we fell into the water, it was magical. Almost as though time didn't exist any more and there was nothing else, just me and Rowan. Holding hands and exploring a whole new version of life together. A better version of life; a life cocooned in my favourite colour. Almost blue, nearly green, where everything unfolds at its own pace, in its own time and . . .

'It could have been really serious, Beth,' Rowan says. 'What if he'd hit his head? Why weren't you keeping an eye on him?' Irritation, like happiness, doesn't need any invitation to arrive.

'I do my best, Rowan,' I say quietly. 'And I've been doing my best all summer, keeping *our* children safe, while you've been gallivanting with your new family.'

'Mummy!'

'Ssshh, Jack. All I wanted to do this afternoon was pick the boys up from school and come home. Instead, I've been in the hospital, waiting and worrying for hours.'

'Mummy, please don't start fighting with Daddy!'

'I'm not, Jack,' I say. 'I'm just trying to explain something to Daddy because he doesn't collect you from school very often, does he? So, maybe he doesn't understand that everyone lets their children play on the climbing wall. Even perfect people, like Emily.'

'Please, Mummy, don't start a fight,' Jack says again.

'It's OK, buddy,' says Rowan, pulling our eldest son towards him. 'You don't need to worry about any of this. Look, Beth,' he says, flicking those eyes back towards me. 'I'm sorry, OK? That was out of order. I've just been worried, you know? It must have been horrible at the hospital. Why don't the kids come back to stay with me tonight? Give you a break.'

'Yes!' shout Jack and Freddie. 'Can we, Mummy? Can we?'

'But it's not your day to have them,' I say, raising my voice to be heard.

'I know,' says Rowan. 'But you've had a tough day and you're right, you have had them most of the summer.'

'I don't know . . .'

'Please, Mummy,' say Jack and Freddie. 'Please can we go back with Daddy?'

'OK,' I say to Rowan as our sons start to cheer, 'but call me if you're worried about anything. The doctor said we should keep a careful eye on Freddie after his fall and take him back to the hospital if he starts acting weird.'

'How will we know the difference?'

'Jack! Do you want me to pack their overnight bags?' I ask. 'Clean school uniform for the morning?'

'No, don't worry,' he replies. 'They've got pyjamas and toothbrushes at mine, and Jade . . .' I wince at the sound of her name. Did he notice? '. . . and I, we'll wash what they're wearing, ready for tomorrow.'

'Will Jade make that dinner we like?' asks Jack.

'Will she, Daddy?' adds Freddie. 'The macaroni and cheese?'

'We'll see. Now, say goodbye to Mummy while I get my little princess out of the car.'

'Are you taking Hope too?' I ask and then I cough. Why does my voice sound weird? 'I thought you'd just take the boys.'

'I'll take all three,' he says, taking our daughter into his arms and giving her a kiss. 'Give you a complete break, OK?'

'Of course,' I smile. Hollow smile. Hollow voice. 'I just assumed, that's all.'

'Assumed what?'

'That you'd leave me with Hope.'

'Make the most of the peace and quiet,' he says, strapping our daughter into his car. 'They'll all be back before you know it.'

I stand and wave until his car is completely out of sight and then I turn the key in the front door. Our yellow Labrador Wilfred is there instantly, wagging his tail and jumping up to kiss me. 'Hello Wilfred,' I say, as he knocks over the umbrella stand with his tail, 'sorry to leave you on your own for so long. Looks like it's just you and me tonight.'

I take him for a long walk and when we get home, I feed him, hoover downstairs and sort out a load of washing. In the bathroom I look at my reflection in the mirror. If I wasn't me, how old would I think I was? What kind of life would I think I lived? I think I'd notice my eyes first. The amber flickers escaping from dark pools of burnt wood, suggesting an intensity that never seems to fade. Brown eyes shining out from the midst of dark shadows, surrounded by a myriad of fine lines and tiny thread veins and what's that on my chin – is that a spot? That wasn't there when I looked in the mirror this morning. *Did* I even look in the mirror this morning? Aren't I too old for spots? Hardly seems fair – spots and wrinkles cohabiting on my forty-year-old face. I look tired. Exhausted, even. Maybe I should light a scented candle and run a bath. I'm sure I won some bath salts on the tombola at the school Christmas fair. Have I still got them or did I donate them back to the tombola for the summer fair? It's too late to go out and buy anything now. I glance at my watch. Twenty past eight. The evening is slipping away, why am I wasting my precious free time staring into the mirror?

I wander down to the kitchen, flick the light on and glance at the large poster on the wall. *Turn that frown upside down.* What a stupid message. Why did I ever think it was a good idea to frame that thing? I take a bottle of white wine from the fridge and reach into a cupboard for a plastic mug when I remember. There are no children here. No manic scampering or footballs bouncing off walls. Replacing the plastic mug, I open the bottle and pour wine into a proper wine glass.

I take a gulp and another and she's there again, staring at me from the collage of photos on the fridge door. We're standing together, and I can remember exactly when and where – the first school run after Hope was born. She's cradling my baby daughter in her arms, and we're laughing.

I know I was happy then, back when Charlotte was still alive. This photograph has been on the fridge for the last year and a half, but I feel like I'm looking at it for the first time. It's not the face of a woman who would leave a child alone in the house. But then what was she doing in the road, standing in the path of that car? Another gulp of wine and a promise. Spoken out loud and made by me to my dear, dead friend.

'I don't think you went out for a run that night, Charlotte, and if there's doubt, check it out. I'm going to find out what happened to you.'

Eighteen Months Ago

'Oh Beth, she's heavenly,' Fara says. 'Congratulations!'

'Thank you,' I smile.

'Is that your new baby?' Emily shouts, rushing over. 'Oh, she's beautiful,' she says, giving me a hug.

'Thanks, Emily.'

'Yes, she's very cute, Beth.'

'Thanks, Danielle.'

'Where's this gorgeous baby I keep hearing about?' booms Charlotte, charging through the playground towards us. Her son Leo is fast asleep in his pushchair clutching a toy Spider-Man as Charlotte reaches us and peers into the pram. 'Oh wow, what a sweetheart. Well done, Beth,' she says. 'How are you feeling?'

'Bit sore,' I say, 'but over the moon!'

'I'm so happy for you,' Charlotte smiles, her face radiant. Her hair scraped back into a messy bun. 'Have you decided on a name yet?'

'Hope.'

'Oh, that's lovely,' they all say, a chorus of nodding heads and approval.

'It's perfect, Beth,' Charlotte smiles, putting her arms around me. 'Really perfect,' she adds, diluting my self-doubt, making me stand tall. 'Beth's had her baby!' Charlotte calls to someone over my shoulder. 'A beautiful little girl called Hope.'

'That's wonderful news.' Miss Lane briskly approaches our huddle. 'Many congratulations on the new arrival,' her words delivered with just the right combination of headteacher authority and charm. 'Charlotte,' she adds, 'just checking you're still OK to represent the PTA at the governors' meeting next week? You did such a good presentation at the last one.'

'Yes, that's fine,' Charlotte says, smiling.

'Do you need me to come too, Miss Lane?' asks Emily. 'I'm happy to help with the PowerPoint.'

'I don't think that will be necessary,' says the headmistress, before turning back to Charlotte. 'And are you still OK to be . . .' Her voice trails into silence.

'Oh, yeah,' says Charlotte. The headmistress smiles approvingly before turning and walking away.

'What was that about?' I ask.

'They want me to dress up as the Easter bunny again,' Charlotte says, lowering her voice. 'You know, in the school parade.'

'Bloody hell,' I laugh. 'Is there anything you can't do?'

'Well, I'm not very good at decorating!' she says with a smile. 'I've spent most of the afternoon fighting with Spider-Man wallpaper, but I'm determined to get Leo's room finished by the end of the day.'

'Congratulations, Beth.' I turn and see my friend Jade. 'I

got you a little something. It's not much,' she adds quickly, as I take a small parcel from her outstretched hand.

'These are beautiful,' I smile, unwrapping and studying two matching pendants.

'They're for you and Hope,' she says. 'Aquamarine is her birthstone.'

'You're so thoughtful,' I say, reaching out for her. She's so tiny, I make sure I don't hug her too hard. 'Thank you.'

'You're welcome. It's a very calming crystal,' she adds. 'Good for anxiety and nerves.'

'Have you got any going spare?' laughs Emily. 'I could do with some of that. What with Tobias sitting his GCSEs in a couple of months,' she says, unclipping her hand sanitiser from her belt, 'and Georgina studying four A-levels, my nerves are shot!'

'How are they feeling about the exams?' asks Fara.

'Both very confident,' Emily says, rubbing antibacterial gel into her palms. 'Their predicted grades are excellent, but that only adds to the pressure, in a way. Believe me,' she says, looking at each of us in turn. 'If you think it's tough now, wait until your children are teenagers. I've been a mum for eighteen years, and it never gets any easier.'

'It must be such hard work,' says Danielle.

'It is,' Emily says, nodding. 'And I think that's why it's so important to put in the time and the work when they're young. Do you know, since I started doing extra story time with Noah every day, he's moved up four reading levels in less than a term. At this rate,' she adds, clipping the hand sanitiser back onto her belt, 'he'll be a gold level reader by the end of Year Three!'

'Four reading levels in less than a term? That's a Herculean achievement,' says Fara. 'Congratulations to you and Noah.'

I make a mental note of Herculean – today's word of the day – and lift my murmuring baby daughter from the pram.

'Oh, look at her,' says Danielle, nervously stepping towards me. 'You forget how tiny they are, when they're newborns, don't you? She's so cute.'

'Would you like to hold her?'

'Oh no,' she says, almost tripping over her feet as she steps back.

'I'll have a cuddle,' says Charlotte. 'How does Rowan feel about having a daughter?' she asks, staring into Hope's tiny face. 'I bet he's already smitten with his little girl.'

'Yeah,' I reply, 'he seems happy enough when he's with her, but to be honest, he hasn't been around much since the birth. Having another mouth to feed means he's always out working and I'm not complaining, it would just be nice to see him a bit more.'

'It's so good to catch up with you, Beth, but I better get going,' says Jade. 'I'm interviewing new staff for Tea and Tots in an hour. Congratulations again.'

One by one they all round up their children and leave until only Charlotte and I are left.

'Jade's doing really well with that parenting group, isn't she?' Charlotte says, gently rocking Hope, as I call out to Jack and Freddie and tell them it's time to go. 'She's turning it into quite a success.'

'Yeah,' I reply.

'Are you OK?'

'Just a bit irritated, that's all.'

'Well, you have *just had a baby.'*

'No, it's not that. It's Emily. She annoys me.'

'Really?'

'Yeah, why does she always have to tell us about her brilliant children?'

'Oh, I think she's just proud.'

'Well, I think she's a show-off. Going on and on about Noah moving up four reading levels? Why did we need to know that?'

'I don't think she was going on and on . . .'

'I do, and I bet she was only saying it to make me feel bad.'

'What do you mean?'

'Jack's only moved up one reading level this term.'

'So?'

'So, it felt like she's judging me because I don't have time to do extra reading with him.'

'Of course you don't, you've just had a baby.'

'And it's not like I'm getting much help at home. Rowan's working so late these days, he doesn't get back until the boys are in bed.'

'If you ever need any help, you know you only have to ask. And as for Emily, I honestly don't think she was trying to make you feel bad. She's just proud of her children, like we all are. Carl!' she shouts towards the school caretaker, standing by the gate. 'I know you're waiting to lock up the playground, but can I be cheeky and ask you a massive favour?'

'What is it?' he asks.

'I really want to get a photo of me and Beth while I'm holding her beautiful baby,' she says, passing him her phone. 'Would you mind?'

'OK,' he says.

'And what's the big deal anyway?' I ask, getting into position next to Charlotte. 'Even if Noah does become a gold level reader by the end of Year Three, who cares? Sure, he may excel at reading at the age of six but what happens if he becomes a drug addict when he's older? Or a bank robber? What if he goes off travelling, gets stoned and comes back with swear words tattooed all over his face? How good is gold level reading going to look then?'

'I don't think he's going to become a drug addict or get swear words tattooed on his face,' Charlotte says, putting her free arm around me.

'So, you're not ruling out bank robbery?' I ask and with that, we both start to laugh.

'There, I took it,' says Carl, handing back her phone.

'Oh, that's a great photo,' she says, smiling at the screen. 'Thanks, Carl. I'll get this printed out for you, Beth. Oh, and Carl . . .'

'Yes?'

'The Treasure Island Garden outside the Year One classrooms looks fantastic! Well done, you've done a great job with that.'

'Thank you,' he mumbles. 'No rush to leave the playground,' he adds, walking away. 'Take your time.'

'Thanks.' Charlotte places Hope back into the pram before calling to her children.

'What Treasure Island Garden?' I ask.

'The one Carl's been working on for months,' she replies. 'We literally walk past it every day,' she adds, as I stare at her blankly. 'You really are the least observant person I know, Beth. You don't notice anything, do you?'

'I notice you're always nice to Carl the Snarl.'

'Don't call him that,' she says quietly, checking over her shoulder, making sure he can't hear. 'He's a lovely man who works really hard.'

'He isn't a lovely man,' I say, as we walk out of the playground, our children trailing behind. 'He's the grumpiest school caretaker in the world.'

'Well, lucky for you, I like grumpy people.'

'Sorry,' I say. 'I just don't understand why she has to turn everything our children do into a competition.'

'Who?'

'Emily.'

'Oh God, are we still talking about this?'

'It shouldn't be a race, should it? To see which child gets to gold reading level first.'

'It isn't a race, Beth. I'm not sure why you're obsessing about it.'

'Emily's the one with the obsession! Obsessed with her children coming first, even in stupid competitions that nobody else cares about because it's completely irrelevant to the rest of their lives. It's not like they're going to be asked the date they became gold level readers in job interviews, are they? Or have to put it on passport application forms.'

'Assuming they can read the passport information forms,' she says, sniggering. 'Oh, come on, that was a joke!'

'Well, I'm not laughing.'

'Look,' Charlotte says, putting the brake on her buggy and turning to face me. 'From one mother of three to another, you're allowed to lose your mind and your temper every so often, that's to be expected. But please, don't lose your sense of humour.'

'There's nothing funny about feeling judged.'

'Beth,' she says gently. 'Listen to me, I'm saying this because I love you. You've just had a baby and you're hormonal and tired, but let's get things into perspective. You've got two incredible sons,' a glance towards Jack and Freddie, 'a great husband and now the most beautiful daughter. Try to let go of all the nonsense swirling around inside your head and focus on what's important – your wonderful family and your health. Because believe me . . .' Her eyes cloud over for a moment. 'Nothing else matters. And let's not forget the biggest news of today,' she says, peering into my pram, 'this little one just survived her first school run without crying. What a superstar! I predict great things for you, baby Hope,' she says, leaning towards my daughter and giving her a kiss, before standing and meeting my eyes with a smile. 'I predict great things for us all.'

5

I wake up on the living room floor. My face squashed into the carpet and my hand on something cool and white, a large sheet of paper. Wilfred is barking and my phone is ringing from somewhere behind me. I'm not sure I can raise my head, but if I keep it close to the ground, I should be able to crawl. I inch towards the ringtone, my hair tickling my face, and find my phone on the sofa.

'Hello?'

'There you are! How did you sleep? Do you feel rested?'

'Yes.'

'That's good. Freddie seems fine after his fall yesterday, so we're in the car on our way to school. Jade washed their uniforms last night, but we couldn't find Jack's tie. I'm not sure whether he was wearing it when I collected him yesterday. Do you have a spare? Beth?'

'Yes?'

'Great! We'll swing by now on the way to school to collect it and I'll drop Hope off. She's already yawning, bless her heart. I think she's ready for a nap.'

'Right.'

'Actually, I'd like to have a quick word with you about her when I get there.'

'OK.'

'I know you stopped taking her to the parent and child group after, you know – everything that happened, but I just wondered whether you'd consider giving it another try.'

'Right.'

'I know it's difficult, what with Jade running the place, but she doesn't do Tea and Tots on a Tuesday because that's when she does her crystal healing.'

'OK.'

'So, I wondered whether you'd take Hope next Tuesday. Beth?'

'Yes?'

'Social interaction is important at her age, isn't it? Look, I'll be with you in a minute. We can talk about it when I arrive.'

'What? You're coming here? Now?'

'Yes, to collect Jack's tie. I'm just turning into your road—'

It repulses me suddenly, all of it – his voice, this conversation, the phone – so I drop it back onto the sofa and heave myself up to standing. Wilfred is barking for his breakfast and he wants to be let outside. The ground shifts jerkily as I stumble towards the kitchen, pour out dog food and open the back door. Something about the kitchen doesn't look right but my focus is diverted by Rowan fast approaching the front door and my outfit of yesterday's crumpled clothes. Closing the kitchen door behind me, the banister is my friend as I drag myself up the stairs. It feels nice having support – makes me want to cry. I change into a polo neck jumper dress, pulling it painfully over my head and instantly feeling too hot. I gargle mouthwash and toothpaste, splash water onto my eyes and bundle my straw-like hair into a ponytail. And there's the knock, as I'm making my way carefully down the stairs, leaning heavily on the banister again. Trying to absorb its quiet reliability through my hand.

'Hi!' I say, as I open the door. Too loud. Too keen. Too unlike me.

'Are you OK?'

Why is he looking at me like that?

'Yes, I'm fine.'

'You just look a bit . . .'

A bit, what? Hungover? Ugly? Fat? Mad?

'I guess I thought you'd look a little more rested,' he says. Almost blue, nearly green eyes tunnelling into mine. I look away. His car is parked on the road directly outside the house. In my parking space. I can see Freddie and Jack's faces at the car window. Freddie's sitting in the middle seat at the back, leaning across Jack to be seen. They're both smiling and waving at me, vying for my attention. Hang on. Why is Rowan's car in my parking space?

'Where's your car?' he asks. How do I get him out of my mind?

'What?'

'Your car. It's normally parked outside the house.'

'I don't always park it there,' I shrug. 'Sometimes I park it . . . elsewhere.'

'Right,' he says, gently rubbing his right temple. Does he have a headache too? 'So, do you know where it is?'

'Of course I know where my car is.'

'No, Jack's tie. That's why I'm here. Have you got it?'

'Yes, one sec.' I turn back into the house and hear scratching. Wilfred. He's shut in the kitchen and as soon as I let him out, he jumps up to kiss me before bolting towards the front door.

'Hello Wilfred, hello gorgeous,' my ex-husband says. 'It's so good to see you.' I climb the staircase and wonder how it would feel to be the recipient of a fraction of that love. 'I know, I know boy. I miss you too.' I'm at the top of the stairs, imagining Wilfred jumping up to kiss him – a flurry of tail-wagging and positivity. It hurts to think about it – causes me physical pain. I guess even unconditional love can be weaponised when it's directed with wild abandon at the wrong place.

I'm in the boys' room now, opening the wardrobe. Do we even have a spare school tie? And where the hell is my car? I know I parked it outside the house when I got back from the hospital yesterday. Has it been stolen?

I rummage through clothes. If I was an organised person, where would I keep a spare school tie? And who would steal my car, anyway? A shabby car, parked outside a shabby house on a shabby street – who would go to the trouble of stealing it? Especially when we're surrounded by nicer streets. There's an Audi parked on every driveway outside the big, detached houses on Herrywell Lane. If I was a car thief, I'd go there. What's Rowan going to say when I tell him I don't know where the car is, and I don't know where the spare school tie is, and I don't even know if I have a spare school tie and bloody hell! I'm searching for something I'm not even sure exists. What am I doing? How long am I going to spend up here, rummaging through grey trousers and Batman pyjamas and Peppa Pig leggings and hang on, these are Hope's leggings. What are they doing in here? I've been looking for these leggings for ages – I really need to sort out this wardrobe and what's this? I can't believe it! Curled up at the bottom of the wardrobe, underneath a Captain America costume and a Storm Trooper mask, is a spare school tie! Success.

I run towards the stairs and then I realise running is a mistake. I feel suddenly nauseous. I'm thinking about the pain as I carefully descend each stair, wondering whether this is what it feels like to be shot in the head. And then I think about the flipside, the total absence of pain. When there's nothing left to feel. Just the end.

Rowan is standing at the door, holding Hope in his arms, giving her a kiss before passing her over. Our hands brush slightly as he takes the school tie and I feel it – familiarity, gone wrong. Carved into something dangerous by betrayal.

'Thanks for this,' he says, indicating the tie. 'Are you sure everything's OK? Is there anything you need?'

To make this stop. To be shot in the head.

'Everything's fine,' I reply.

'Good,' he says, rubbing his right temple again. 'So, what do you think about Tea and Tots?'

'Yeah, I'll take her.'

'Because I know it's a difficult situation, but I think it's in Hope's best interests. She still isn't walking, is she? And when the boys were her age, I remember them running all over the place. I mean, she's doing well – cruising around our sofa like a champ – but maybe being around other kids her age might give her some encouragement. Because you know, she's eighteen months—'

'I said I'll take her.'

'Oh, right, that's great.' Relieved smile. 'And are Tuesdays OK for you?'

'Yeah, but why do I have to go on a Tuesday? Isn't Tea and Tots on most days each week?'

'Yes,' he replies, smile vanishing. 'But like I said, Jade does crystal healing on a Tuesday so that's probably the best day for you to go.'

'Fine,' I say. 'We'll go this morning.'

'Oh,' he says, looking alarmed. 'I meant *next* Tuesday. Maybe don't go there today.'

'Why not? It's Tuesday.'

'Yeah, but Jade's going to be there today.'

'What about the crystal healing?'

'She's starting that next week.'

'I see.' We stare at each other for a moment. 'Well, like you said, Rowan,' his right temple must be hurting again, 'social interaction is very important.'

'Right,' and the left temple too. 'Goodbye Hope,' he adds, giving her another kiss. 'Goodbye Beth.'

'Dada,' Hope says solemnly.

'Bye,' I say, ushering Wilfred back inside the house

before closing the door behind me. I stand still because I don't think I can move, not until the world starts to settle. I breathe in my daughter's scent, innocent and pure, and that's when I start to remember. Two smiling faces at the window, desperate to be seen, waving at me, vying for my attention. I open the front door and run back outside – *I'm here boys! I see you. I love you.* But there's nothing left to vie for, just an empty parking space. And everything that's already gone, I wave it goodbye.

6

The poster's gone from the kitchen wall, which is confusing. How am I going to remember to turn my frown upside down? And the table is covered in Haribo. I wonder what happened here last night. While I was passed out on the living room floor, did a burglar break into a shabby house on a shabby street, steal a shabby poster and a shabby car and ... bring sweets? And then what? What kind of intruder sits at a kitchen table, empties packets of sweets and starts dividing them into colours? Because there's a small pile of green sweets over there and a red pile here and ... oh my God, Freddie was talking about green Haribo yesterday on the way to hospital. Did I do this? But where did they all come from? I don't remember ...

'No, Wilfred! Get down!' The dog jumps up at the table and tries to reach the sweets. I push him back down but not before he snaffles a couple, which can't be good for a dog, can it? After a panicked search for my phone, I find it on the sofa in the living room and ask the one person I can always rely on. 'Siri, is it dangerous for a Labrador to eat Haribo?'

'I found this on the web,' Siri replies, presenting me with a bunch of articles I don't have time to read. I'm too hungover for all these details. I just need a vague response.

'Siri, is it dangerous? Yes or no.'

'I'm sorry,' Siri replies. Sorry for what? Too vague now, Siri. Far too vague.

Hope lowers her head and snuggles into my shoulder.

'Mama, Mama,' she says sleepily.

'Come on, darling,' I say gently. 'Let's put you down for a nap.' Once she's settled upstairs, I return to the kitchen, gulp down a pint of water and two Nurofen, scrape sweets into a salad bowl, collect wrappers from the floor, find my handbag, car keys and a crumpled receipt. It was just before midnight when I bought all these sweets, from the twenty-four-hour supermarket. I couldn't have walked there, it's on the other side of town, but a scroll through my call history shows no contact with cab firms.

I study the receipt again. Three bottles of wine, a ton of Haribo and a final farewell to the person I used to be – all for the bargain price of thirty-two pounds and sixty-five pence. And she's remarkably calm, the vile drink-driver I am now; blithely wiping kitchen surfaces before the police arrive to arrest her. Maybe they'll find the car embedded in a tree, or the side of a house. Maybe they'll find casualties. What they won't find is my defence because that doesn't exist, other than Freddie wanted green Haribo and

I wanted more wine – it will be better for everyone when they throw away the key.

I move into the living room, open curtains, let in air, check outside – no sign of police officers yet. Two green bottles are sitting on the floor and if one green bottle should accidentally be full . . . no, they're both empty; discarded next to a large sheet of white paper. The photo of Charlotte and me from the collage on the fridge has been stuck in the centre, surrounded by scrawled words I can't read. Is that my handwriting? I can just about make out *What Happened to Charlotte?* at the top of the sheet, but the rest is illegible. Clearly I was trying to crack the case while too drunk to hold a pen. I'm sorry, Charlotte, I made you a promise last night, but I haven't got very far. Maybe they'll let me work on it in prison.

Picking up the sheet of paper, I realise there's something printed on the other side, inviting me to turn my frown upside down. No chance. I roll up the poster and chuck it into the corner of the room – where I find the frame the poster had been in, discarded and cracked along one edge where I clearly opened it far too violently – and pick up the empty wine bottles.

Another glance through the window – no police cars. I go back to the kitchen. Fresh air greets me like an old friend as I open the back door, walk towards the shed at the end of the garden, place the empty bottles on the ground and hunt for that rock that isn't really a rock but looks so much like all the other rocks that it's always impossible to find. Here it is, the fake rock concealing the key to the padlock on the door of the shed. I go inside and throw the empty bottles into the nearest box. Glass onto glass, remnants of a secret life – hidden away and piled high inside an ordinary-looking shed. Something huge scuttles towards me and I scream, polo neck digging into my throat, suffocated by a terrible choice of outfit. It's only a spider. Closing the door behind me, I lock the padlock, hide the key in the rock, walk into the house and peer out the living room window. Still no police.

I head upstairs to check on Hope – sleeping soundly – then have a shower, scrub my hair and change into clothes that don't make me feel claustrophobic. I stare into the mirror and try not to cry. Is this what I looked like when I spoke to Rowan earlier? Those dark shadows under my eyes have swirled into something sinister – bottomless pits devouring all but the occasional flicker of amber. And gorging on white wine hasn't been kind to my skin. In fact, it seems to have fed that spot on my chin – turned it into a monster. I grab my makeup bag and smear foundation over my face, managing within moments to make myself look even worse. The Nurofen isn't kicking in yet, I'm dehydrated and need to lie down, so gulp another glass of water by the kitchen sink and then collapse onto the sofa. Wilfred jumps up next to me and I stroke his head, closing my eyes. Try to forget everything I can't remember.

An hour or so later, Hope wakes and starts to cry, so I change her and get ready to leave the house. The police still haven't turned up and with the hideously named Tea and Tots starting soon, I need to look for the car. Heading in the direction of the supermarket with Hope protesting loudly about being in my arms, I'm halfway down the street when I see the gang of teenage boys who live on our road and used to be such cute children when they knocked on our door every Halloween. Dressed as skeletons and ghosts, they would always pretend to scare me, and I would always pretend to be scared. Now they're all taller than me, none of them ever seem to go to school, and there's no need for anyone to pretend any more – to be scary or to be scared.

'So, how was it?' one of them asks, as I approach.

'Sorry, what?' I stop. 'Are you talking to me?'

'Yes,' he replies, flicking his eyes towards the others. He's got a little beard and a wispy moustache. 'Your Haribo and Vino party,' he says. 'How was it?'

'What are you talking about?'

'Last night, you said you were having a Haribo and Vino party.'

'You saw me last night?'

'Yes. Can't you remember?'

'Of course I can.' I can't. So many evenings a black hole in my memory.

'So, how was the party?'

'It was good. It was really good. I don't suppose you've seen my car anywhere, have you?'

'You think we stole your car?'

'No! I never said that. I'm just not sure where—'

'Why would we steal your car?'

'I never said you stole my car.'

'Your car's well old. And shit. Why would we steal that?'

'Exactly. And I never said—'

'If we steal a car, we steal a decent one. From outside one of the big houses on Herrywell Lane.'

'That makes sense. That's what I would do too. If I wanted to steal a car.'

'Can't you remember what happened last night?' My scream is silent. 'Are you OK?' he asks, a scary man-child with sickening concern in his eyes. 'You were so happy last night, laughing and joking with us, and now you seem . . .'

'Yes?'

'Sad. And confused.'

I am sad, kind scary man-child. And confused. Wondering why your concern is making me want to cry.

'I'm fine,' I say, turning away from them. 'I just need to get my daughter to Tea and Tots.'

'Your car is down there,' he says, pointing towards the end of the road. 'You said it was OK for me to park it there.'

'Sorry, what? You drove my car last night?'

'You said you needed to get to the supermarket, but you'd been drinking, so you said I could drive your car. I've only just passed my test, but you said I'm already a better driver than most of the idiots on the road.'

'Right. So, *you* drove me to the supermarket?'

'Yes. I waited in the car while you did your shopping and then I drove you home. You gave me a tub of Haribo. Don't you remember?'

'Of course,' I say, squinting towards my car. It's there! Not embedded in a tree or the side of someone's house. Simply parked further down the road. 'Of course I remember! I don't know what's wrong with me today,' I say with a smile. 'Must be old age!'

I lower my head to Hope's cheek as I walk away, trying to block out the laughter and raised voices. A comment about 'the size of that thing on her chin' reaches me and I move faster, but not before I hear the kind one telling the others to 'shut up'.

There's a large scratch down one side of my car, but other than that it looks fine, and for all I know the scratch could have been there already. I strap Hope into her seat and take my place at the steering wheel, then I take a moment. To collect my thoughts, which is a curious phrase because what do people do with them once they're collected? And whose thoughts am I collecting anyway? Mine? Or the woman who sat in this car last night and asked a stranger to drive her into the darkness? Because that wasn't me, not really. It may have looked like me and sounded like me and made decisions for me, but it wasn't me and I can't collect thoughts that aren't mine.

I wonder what she thinks about – that woman, every time she walks around in my body and takes control of my mind. Maybe she ponders the temporary nature of her existence. How she can disappear at any moment, leaving me to deal with her decisions, her mistakes. A life without responsibility and consequence. No wonder she's laughing with car thieves in the middle of the night.

7

Tea and Tots is held inside a large, soulless building that calls itself a church even though there isn't a stained-glass window or crucifix in sight. There isn't even a fearful reverence for the Almighty, just the ever-constant worry that someone may appear at any moment with a tambourine.

'Hello! Welcome! Did you manage to find a space in the car park, Mum?' asks a woman in her fifties, wearing black leggings, a black T-shirt and a plastic tiara. She's standing at the door of the church welcoming parents, and has just watched me park my car in the enormous car park outside.

'Yes,' I reply, confused. There are about a hundred empty spaces in the car park.

'Car!' Hope says helpfully.

'Good, good. You wouldn't believe it, Mum, but some people park out there when they shouldn't, making it difficult for our mums and dads to find a space. Commuters,' she adds with a scowl. 'They don't want to pay to park at the train station, you see. Come in, make yourselves at home. If you need any help with anything, look for a fairy,' she says, turning to show Hope and me the sparkly wings on her back. 'All the helpers are dressed as fairies today.'

'Why?' I ask, but she's no longer listening. Too busy asking the person behind me whether they managed to park.

I walk inside and quickly scan the perimeter. It's been almost a year since I was last here, but everything looks the same. As usual the painting tables and ball pit are the most populated areas but there's only one woman sitting in Story Time Corner. The perfect place for my hangover. I settle Hope onto the floor next to some toys, then glance at the other woman. We don't know each other. Perfect. In fact, the only way this scenario could get any more perfect would be if neither of us acknowledges the other and nobody starts to talk.

'Hello, I'm Sally Jones,' she says, extending her hand towards me.

'Hi,' I say, shaking her hand and wondering when Tea and Tots became so formal. 'I'm Beth.'

'She's gorgeous,' Sally says, glancing at Hope, who is bashing a stuffed Peppa Pig with a plastic rubbish truck.

'Thank you.'

'How old is she?'

'Eighteen months,' I answer, returning her smile.

'That's my daughter over there,' she says, pointing towards an adorable little girl pushing a toy buggy across the room.

'She's adorable,' I say.

'Thank you,' says Sally. 'She's called Freya. She's eleven months old.'

'She's lovely,' I say.

'Freya's been walking for six weeks now.'

'That's great.'

'Isn't your daughter walking yet?' she asks.

'No,' I reply, vaguely aware of movement inside the depths of my hangover. A mental image hurtling towards my attention, shoving dehydration and pain to one side. An image of me and Sally jostling for position at the start line, straining to hear it – where is it? Where is the sound?

'She's great at crawling and cruising along the coffee table, but we're still waiting for proper walking,' I say. 'She's a bit late but the GP said it's nothing to worry about.' Why do I feel the need to explain this? 'She'll do it in her own time.'

'I see,' Sally says, and there it is – the starting pistol. She pretends she doesn't hear it, but I know she hears it. People like Sally Jones always hear it. The people for whom all of life is a competition. And this race is about to begin. 'So she's only crawling and cruising?'

'Yes,' I say.

'Oh right,' she says, her face stretching into a smile. 'Well, they all get there in their own time, don't they?'

'Yes.' I just said that.

'Some children bum-shuffle first, don't they?'

'Yes,' I say again, staring at Peppa. That toy has definitely seen better days.

'Freya didn't need to – bum-shuffle, I mean. She was

able to pull herself up onto her feet at a very young age. I think it's because she's got very strong bones.'

'That's great,' I say, still staring at Peppa. Some of the stuffing has been knocked out of her and her face looks faded and worn. I can relate.

'Probably gets it from me and her dad. We've all got very strong bones.'

'Wow! Family Jones with the strong bones!' I say with a smile. Silence. I've misjudged the conversation. Wrongly assumed that someone with a strong humerus could handle the occasional joke. I close my eyes. There's no way Charlotte would have left her son alone in the house that night, so what was she doing outside?

The obvious person to ask is the driver of the car that hit her. I remember hearing that he was only eighteen years old and was traumatised after the accident, as were his passengers. One of them was Tobias, Emily's eldest son. I'm sure I remember someone telling me that Emily was getting him therapy to help him recover from the shock and—

'So, this is Story Time Corner, Mum,' the voice is booming, forcing me to open my eyes. The middle-aged woman in the tiara is talking to a young-looking woman on her right – long dark hair falling in curls over her shoulders, screaming child in her arms – where have I seen her before? 'This is a good place for little ones to come to calm down, you know, when they need a little quiet time. Oh, hello Mum,' she says to Sally with the strong bones. 'I've just seen Freya pushing the buggy, so confident on her feet. Isn't she doing well? And she's not even a year old yet, is she?'

'She's eleven months,' replies Sally. 'But she's been walking for six weeks now.'

As Sally and Fairy continue talking, the young mum turns towards me. 'Is your little boy OK now?' she asks, her voice barely audible over the screams of the child in her arms. 'I saw you in the playground, yesterday,' she says. 'You were . . . swearing.'

'That sounds like me,' I say with a smile. The playground! That's where I've seen her before. 'Of course! You're the new mum who's just moved into Charlotte's old house.'

'Yes, also known as Ana,' she says, readjusting her grip on the screaming child who I've just noticed is brandishing a paintbrush while aiming kicks with impressive precision, fully focused on struggling to get free.

'Hi Ana, nice to meet you. I'm Beth.'

'Hi Beth. I'm just going to put Willow down before she stabs me in the eye.'

Willow looks just like her mother with long curly dark hair and huge brown eyes. As soon as Ana lowers her to the floor she stops screaming and toddles towards the battered-looking Peppa Pig, which Hope has already grown bored of. She grabs hold of it, stares at it and for a moment I think she's going to hug it but no – she's hurling it at the wall. Poor Peppa. Looks like her day is about to get even worse.

'Willow!' shouts Ana, 'stop throwing toys.'

Hope sits quietly, watching Willow. Now Willow toddles back over and sits down opposite, watching Hope. They stare at each other, two little girls connected by silence, and I wonder what they're thinking about. It's so serene after all that screaming – I feel cushioned by the quiet, it's comforting. And when my eyes start to close again, it's enticing – the idea of simply drifting away.

'So, how is your son now?'

I open my eyes. Ana is looking at me.

'It must have been terrifying,' she adds, 'when he fell off that wall.'

'He's fine, thanks,' I say. 'No broken bones.'

'That's good. You must have been so worried. No wonder you were swearing so much.'

'Was I? To be honest, it's all a bit of a blur.'

'You were swearing quite a lot, yes,' she says, 'but I mean, who could blame you? I'm sure no one minds and it's not like you used the C-word. That would have been a lot worse.'

'Well, yes. Especially on the first day of term. I tend to leave it a few weeks before throwing that around.'

She laughs, glancing towards Fairy and Sally who seem to have moved on from raving about Freya and are now discussing the non-existent parking problem in the over-sized car park.

'The woman who says she's a fairy,' Ana says quietly, 'told us to come sit over here. Willow got into a fight at the painting table with another kid over a paintbrush. But look at her now.' I watch as Willow collects building blocks and places them in front of Hope before they both take turns to place one block on top of another. 'She's lovely, your daughter,' says Ana. 'What's her name?'

'Hope,' I reply.

'Beautiful,' smiles Ana. 'She's such a good influence on Willow. Look how nicely they're playing together.'

'They're a good influence on each other,' I say, watching my daughter smiling and chuckling as both girls take turns to knock down the tower of building blocks, both babbling frantically with the occasional recognisable word rising to the surface. 'So, where are you from, Ana?' I ask. 'I don't recognise your accent.'

'Romania,' she replies.

'Ooh, Romania,' booms the woman who says she's a fairy, tuning back into our conversation. 'How exciting! The home of vampires.'

'What?' I say, laughing. 'Why is Romania the home of vampires?'

'Count Dracula,' whispers Fairy. 'He lives in Transylvania.' Why is she whispering?

'Yeah, but Transylvania isn't a real place, is it?' Why am *I* whispering?

'Yes, Transylvania is a real place,' bellows another voice. Strong bones don't whisper. 'It's in central Romania.'

'Really?' I ask.

'Yes, she's right,' replies Ana.

'Wow,' I say. 'I never knew that.'

'Well, Mum, as I always say,' says Fairy, 'it's not just the little ones who learn something new at Tea and Tots. Can I just ask?' she says, turning to Ana, 'did you manage to find a space in the car park?'

'Of course,' says Ana, sounding puzzled. 'There were loads of spaces.'

'Good, good. You wouldn't believe it, but some people park out there when they shouldn't . . .'

And that's when I see her, over Fairy's shoulder. She's

standing in the middle of the room and I'm back in those waters, off the coast of Mexico. Rowan's reaching out towards me and I'm nervous at first but then I swim towards him, towards my new husband with the most beautiful eyes. And it's so magical, how could I have possibly known that we'd already reached it? That this was it – the deepest depths of our love. And my memories of that day, they're mine forever, but that woman over there – she's taken everything else. Even my favourite colour. Almost blue, nearly green. Jade.

8

Jade's tan is the same as Rowan's tan. Matching his-and-her tans. How sweet. She's dressed as Snow White, her tiny yoga-toned arms on display in short white sleeves, and her hair's grown over the summer. It looks lighter. Highlights? She's wearing that amethyst bracelet her children bought her for Mother's Day a few years ago. It's her birthstone – amethyst – and her favourite crystal too. I know this because we used to be friends.

   She's talking to someone and smiling but as her face turns towards mine, the smile vanishes from her eyes, and she moves her hand to the bracelet. She always fiddles with it when she feels uncomfortable. How *dare* she feel uncomfortable. She turns away from me and that's when I see the sparkly wings on her back. Why is she wearing wings? Snow White doesn't have wings. It's irritating, all of it. Her tan, those wings, the yoga-toned arms, all that fiddling with the bracelet . . .

'So, tell me,' Fairy's saying, still talking to Ana. 'Have you ever seen any?'

'Any what?'

'Vampires?'

'I don't come from Transylvania.'

'Right. But I'm sure they'd travel to the surrounding areas.'

'Actually, I'm sure they'd travel rather more extensively than that,' says Sally. 'I mean, you would, wouldn't you? If you had all the time in the world.'

'Yes, that's a good point,' smiles Fairy.

'They're not real, you know,' and as soon as the words leave my mouth, I'm aware of the tone – too sharp, verging on abrasive. 'Vampires,' I add, 'you do realise they're not real?'

'I do know that, yes,' Fairy replies, her smile disappearing. 'Right,' she says, 'I'm just about to host a pre-phonics workshop over by the ball pit, if any of you would like to join me,' she asks, looking from me to Ana and Sally. 'It's light-hearted and fun but very informative. I think you'll find it useful.'

'Sounds great,' says Sally, scooping up Freya and following Fairy.

'Are you OK?' asks Ana, as I pick up the battered-looking Peppa Pig.

'I'm fine, just get a bit irritated sometimes.' She's still looking at me. 'With other people,' I add. 'Sometimes they really irritate me.'

'Me too,' she says. 'Especially that fairy woman. She was quite rude when she told me and Willow to come over here. I mean, I know Willow flicked some paint but she's two years old! That's what two-year-olds do. She made me feel like a bad parent. She was really . . . what's the word in English? Sorry, I can't think of it.'

'Don't apologise. Your English is far better than my Romanian.'

'Thank you,' she says, smiling. 'I've lived in England for a long time. But what I was saying? She was very . . . I can't think of the word, how she was looking down at me. Like I was wrong, and she was right.'

'Judgemental?'

'Yes, that's it! She was judgemental.'

'Well, everyone loves to judge the parent of a screaming child.'

'But all children scream sometimes, don't they? Which means that somebody is always being judged. I wish I'd been warned about it before I had kids.' She smiles. 'Surely the midwife could have said something.'

'Like what?'

'I don't know. "*Congratulations. Here's your new baby. Now prepare to be judged. By everyone. Everywhere. Forever.*" Something like that?'

I laugh. 'You should work for Hallmark.'

'I'll be judged if I work.'

'You'll be judged if you don't. Mostly by other parents. They love to judge, almost as much as they love to compete, and everything becomes a competition once you have children, have you noticed that? You know the woman I was talking to before you came over? I've never seen her before, but she was very quick to dish it out.'

'About what?'

'Walking. Her daughter's been doing it for six weeks, you see, and mine isn't.'

'But who cares whether she's walking?' Ana says, staring at Hope. 'She's a wonderful little girl, so calm and well-behaved. Such a good influence on Willow.'

'I know, but in the walking competition of life, all that matters is that all-important "date of first step" and because Hope can't compete with Freya and her extraordinarily strong bones, I'm made to feel like a failure.'

'But why does it matter?' she asks, wrinkling her delicate forehead into a frown, which in my experience usually dilutes a person's attractiveness but, in Ana's case, does nothing to diminish her beauty which is so natural and real, it's almost unnatural. Unreal. Sitting so close to her, to her glossy hair, perfect figure, flawless skin, I'm more aware of my flabby tummy and my hair still wet from the shower, tied back hurriedly into a messy bun. And that spot on my chin, which has started pulsating – has it developed its own circulatory system?

'Who cares what age babies walk?' she says. 'As long as they do eventually?'

'Other parents,' I say, pulling Peppa onto my lap – not entirely sure why. If I'm trying to hide my insecurity, I'm not sure a battered-looking Peppa Pig is up to the job.

'Do you know the date of your first step?'

'No.'

'Exactly! Because nobody bloody cares!'

'Ow!' I say, laughing.

'What's the matter? Are you OK?'

'Yes,' I reply, 'it's just this spot on my chin, it really hurts when I laugh.'

'What spot on your chin?' she asks. 'I don't see anything.'

For a moment I think she's being serious but then I see the corners of her mouth twitch into a smile and we both start laughing again.

'I mean it! Stop making me laugh!' I say. 'It really hurts.'

'How do you think that spot feels? Do you think it knows it has a woman attached to it?'

'Ana!'

'I'm sorry,' she says, still smiling. 'It's just that spot is magnificent! I honestly think it might be the most impressive spot I've ever seen.'

'Thank you, I'm very proud.' I laugh, looking around the room. 'This feels strange.'

'What?'

'Laughing.'

'You don't like to laugh?'

'No, I love it! Well, I used to, but it feels like I haven't laughed, not for a very long time. And certainly not here,' I add, glancing around the room again. 'I haven't been to Tea and Tots for ages.'

'Why not?'

'Well, you know what I said about other people? About them irritating me?'

'Yes?'

'Look around,' I say, vaguely waving my hand across the length of the room. 'What do you see?'

'Children,' she says, scanning the room. 'Lots and lots of children. Why?' she asks. 'What do *you* see?'

'I see dead people.' She looks scared, and then confused when I start laughing. Bloody hell, this spot – combined with a killer hangover – is causing me considerable pain. 'Only kidding! I don't really see dead people.' She still looks confused, and a little scared. 'Not sure why I said that, to be honest. No, what I see when I look around this room is people, and every single one of them, they all irritate me.'

'But why? What are they doing wrong?'

'Oh, nothing.' I pull at a loose thread by Peppa Pig's eye. The thread starts to unravel. I stop pulling. 'I know I'm being unfair. Truth is, there's only one person here who irritates me, and that's her,' I add, gesturing towards Jade. She's lurking in between the pre-phonics workshop over by the ball pit and the painting tables. Smiling at parents and children while surveying her kingdom, and still fiddling with that bracelet.

'Who?' Ana asks, following my gaze. 'The one dressed as—?'

'Snow White. Her name's Jade and she runs this place. We used to be friends.'

'But not any more?'

'No, not since she started sleeping with my husband. They're still together. He left me for her.'

'Right,' she says, her eyes flicking towards Jade once again. 'Well, I can understand why that would stop you laughing.'

'Yeah,' I agree. 'Before that I used to love coming here and meeting up with my friends.'

'I see.'

'But now I've grown distant from them.'

'That's a shame.'

'I haven't brought Hope here for almost a year.'

'That's understandable.'

'Maybe, but I feel bad about it.'

'Why?'

'Well, social interaction is important at their age, isn't it?' I say, nodding my head towards Willow and Hope. 'I always took my older kids to toddler groups. That's where I met Charlotte.'

'Charlotte?'

'Yes, Charlotte. The Charlotte who used to live in your house. I met her at toddler group. Must have been about five years ago.'

'I heard that she died.'

'Yes, she was hit by a car. Ran out into the road without looking, by all accounts.'

'What was she like?'

Not the kind of person to run out into the road without looking, I think but do not say, focusing on that loose thread by Peppa's eye; twirling it around the length of my finger before I reply. 'On the face of it, Charlotte should have irritated the hell out of me.'

'Why?'

'Because she was Super Mum and Wonder Woman combined. Seriously, it was ridiculous – how good she was at everything.'

'In what way?'

'Well, first of all – she was clever.' I place Peppa on the

ground and give Ana my full attention. 'She was a doctor for years and then took a career break to concentrate on her family. Her mothering skills – they were off-the-scale.'

I glance over at Hope. She's sitting on the floor, holding a building block in her hand, and babbling. Willow's sitting opposite, listening and nodding her head. It looks really important; whatever they're talking about.

'Charlotte had endless patience and enthusiasm for kids' activities. Always busy with the arts and crafts. She even let her children loose with glue guns and she never seemed to mind about mess. Charlotte seemed to enjoy the mess!'

'Wow!'

'I know, and somehow she always kept her house, sorry, I mean – your house – spotlessly clean. And on top of having an incredible career, three wonderful children, a loving husband, and an immaculate home,' I'm counting all her achievements on my fingers, 'Charlotte ran marathons for charity, collected clothes for the homeless and somehow found time to be chair of the school's PTA. She was beautiful, kind, compassionate,' I'm getting into this now, 'and on top of all that, she was humble – never talked about herself, and everything she did, she put loads of effort into it, you know?' It's nice, talking about Charlotte, almost distracts me from feeling hungover. 'Like the Easter egg hunt she organised every year, she'd dress up as the Easter bunny for that, and on Bonfire Night she always put on the most amazing firework display. Even the presents she bought for the teachers at the end of term – no Amazon gift cards or bottles of wine. Everything was personalised. One Christmas, she even got something engraved for the miserable old lollipop lady who never speaks! I mean, how did she know her name? *Nobody* knows her name. The more I'm talking about her, the more I realise . . .'

'What?'

'Charlotte was insufferable. But . . .'

'But what?'

'She was also funny. Hilariously funny, with a wicked sense of humour and . . . She was my friend.' I unravel the loose thread from around my finger. 'I liked her, and for some reason, she seemed to like me. But now she's gone and I feel . . .' *I feel that something isn't right about the night she died . . .*

'No, Willow!' Ana is up on her feet and running towards her daughter, who is standing at the wall, brandishing the paintbrush again, which is now dripping bright green. 'How did you get paint?' shouts Ana, and as she scoops Willow up into her arms, I see the wall. That's a terrifying amount of swirly green paint. Oh dear. At least Hope never . . . oh no! Where's Hope? Has someone moved her? Taken her?

Willow is screaming, wriggling furiously in her mother's arms, waving the paintbrush around and pointing towards some beanbags. Something is emerging from behind them. Someone. It's the toy buggy that strong-boned Freya had been pushing before she moved on to phonics. But it's not Freya pushing it now. It's Hope! She's on her feet, pushing the buggy along with fierce determination. It's not walking but it's damn close.

'Hope!' I shout, rushing towards her. 'Look at you! You're pushing a buggy all on your own! Ana, look!'

'Is that good?' she shouts, over Willow's screams.

'Good?' I say. 'It's bloody marvellous!'

'Beth!' I turn at the sound of my name. And there they are. Emily, Danielle, Fara, Jade. Emily's standing in front of the others, massaging sanitiser into her hands, her face an exclamation, razor-sharp cheekbones slicing into this – my most marvellous of moments. 'Beth,' she says again. She takes a step towards me, those alien eyes unblinking. 'Aren't you going to introduce us to your new friend?'

9

All of us sit in Story Time Corner, except Ana and Jade. They're wiping green paint off the wall. Jade is telling Ana not to worry. She's saying these things happen and Willow is clearly a very artistic little girl. Ana is saying she feels awful about not keeping a closer eye on her and hopes no permanent damage has been done. Jade says the green paint is coming off nicely, and she's sure the wall will soon look as good as new. Now she's smiling at Ana, telling her again not to worry, how the wall looks even better than before. Snow White with wings dishing out forgiveness. What a bitch.

'Beth.' Danielle's staring at me, looking anxious. 'How did you get on at the hospital yesterday? How's Freddie?'

'He's fine,' I say, pulling at that loose thread by Peppa's eye again. 'No broken bones.'

'Thank goodness for that,' she says, and I wonder why she still looks so anxious. Maybe I'm not the only one who finds it awkward – sitting here with the old gang after so long, for the first time since they all chose to remain friends with Jade. 'Were you at the hospital all evening?' she asks.

'No, only a couple of hours,' I reply. 'Luckily there were decent toys in the waiting room, so the kids were happy.'

'That's good. It's not too bad in Paediatric A&E, is it?' says Danielle. 'That's where I had my most serious anaphylactic shock. Six years ago now. Have I ever told you about that?'

'Yes,' I reply, as Ana sits down beside me.

'I was just saying to Beth,' says Danielle, 'it was in the hospital – that's where I had my worst ever anaphylactic shock. I was there with Zac, that's my son,' she explains to Ana, 'because he'd tripped over a pumpkin on someone's doorstep and I thought he'd broken his wrist. Anyway, we were waiting to see the doctor, and that's when it happened.'

She pauses at this point, and I take the opportunity to close my eyes. The pain inside my head is extraordinary. If I didn't know for certain that I'm hungover, I think I'd take *myself* off to A&E.

'You see, I'm allergic to most nuts and someone in the waiting area opened a bag of trail mix and, my goodness, it was terrifying how quick it happened. One minute I was OK and the next my throat started closing up and I couldn't speak, couldn't breathe. I don't even remember collapsing. If I hadn't already been in the hospital, I might have died!'

I open my eyes. It's interesting how Danielle always looks like she's wearing glasses because her brow is forever furrowed in confusion so there's a constant line across the top of her nose. Despite the panic in her eyes, they're a nice colour and she's got a nice nose, nice mouth, nice figure, even her hair's quite nice, despite its occasional tendency to stick out at weird angles – almost as though distancing itself from whatever's going on inside that anxious mind. But none of the nice things about Danielle are memorable, because they're overshadowed by her constantly confused expression. Maybe that's why it doesn't matter how many Sweaty Betty ensembles she wears, or how many cashmere scarves she drapes herself in. To me, Danielle will always have the look of a deranged scientist, desperately trying to work out why her latest experiment isn't going to plan.

'And so, to cut a long story short,' she's saying now, 'that's why I never go anywhere without my EpiPen.'

'Ana,' says Emily, sitting forward in her seat, signalling silence. There will be no more talk about nuts from Danielle. 'Where are you from? I don't recognise your accent.'

'Romania.'

'Oh, how nice. And obviously we've met your lovely daughter, Willow. How old is she?'

'Just turned two,' Ana replies.

'She's gorgeous.' Emily smiles. 'Certainly got a lot of get-up-and-go, hasn't she? And you have another at school, don't you?'

'I have an older daughter, called Summer. She's five.'

'Oh, has she just started in Year One? I think I might have read with her yesterday at school.'

We all turn towards Fara. She's sitting on the floor, leaning up against a beanbag. Just an ordinary-looking beanbag but with Fara leaning up against it, suddenly chic.

She's wearing cream trousers, neutral-coloured trainers, a creamy brown striped top and a thick yellow shawl and is looking, as always, perfectly coordinated and . . . what the hell is she doing? Lifting up that creamy brown top, unhooking her bra, reaching into her shawl, retrieving a baby and moving it towards her breast. Why is Fara breastfeeding a baby?

'Fara, why are you breastfeeding?' I ask.

'I always breastfeed,' she replies with a smile. 'Oh,' she says, suddenly serious. 'I hope that didn't sound sanctimonious. I know some people struggle to breastfeed or choose not to and when I said that I always do, I wasn't being supercilious – honestly, I wasn't. It's just that for me, personally, I find breastfeeding easier than making up bottles.'

'Right,' I say, taking a mental note of 'sanctimonious' and 'supercilious' before deciding on 'supercilious' as my word of the day. 'I'm sorry, I didn't realise you'd had another baby.'

'That's OK, Beth,' Fara says, smiling again. 'I gave birth to him over the summer.'

'Congratulations.'

'How could you not know that?' asks Emily, providing an impromptu masterclass on how to sound sanctimonious and supercilious all at the same time. 'Fara was pregnant all last term. *And* she was carrying her baby yesterday in the playground when we were all talking.'

'Was she? Were you?' I ask, turning back to Fara. 'I'm so sorry, I didn't notice.'

'Well, to be fair,' says Fara kindly, 'when I saw you yesterday, this little one was fast asleep in the sling,' she says, tapping at her yellow shawl, 'which is the exact same colour as my coat. So, that's probably why you didn't spot him.'

'Right. Well, congratulations,' I say again, before falling into silence. How on earth does she do it? I can't even get in and out of that playground without swearing. Fara's camouflaging babies and smuggling them in and out.

'Thanks, Beth,' she says with another smile.

'I don't know how you do it,' I say. 'You're amazing, Fara. I mean, you've literally got millions of children but you're so serene. And sane.'

'I've only got six,' she laughs.

'Six?' I exclaim. 'Bloody hell! I didn't know you had that many. And you're wearing cream-coloured trousers! How on earth do you do it?'

'Well . . .'

'And you've got loads of degrees, haven't you?'

'Well, I've got two degrees.'

'And you work in the City, don't you? As one of those hedge . . . hunter things.'

'Well, right now I'm on maternity leave,' she says, smiling. Even her kindness is accomplished. 'That's why I was in the school yesterday, reading with some of the children. Your daughter, Summer,' she says, turning her attention to Ana, 'she's a clever little girl, isn't she? Already reading purple level books.'

'Thank you,' says Ana. 'Can I ask, what does that mean? Purple level books? They used a different phonics system at Summer's last school.'

Fara opens her mouth to answer but Emily gets there first. 'That's a great question,' she says, spotlight illuminating those cheekbones. Chosen specialised subject about to begin. 'So, what happens,' she says, coffee mug clasped in manicured hands, 'is that all the reading books are divided up into different groups, depending on difficulty.' Imagine if people were divided up depending on difficulty. I wonder which group I'd find myself in. 'And then each group is assigned a colour. So, the books your daughter brings home to read, you'll notice each of them has a little colour taped onto the spine.' Look at her, immaculate and knowledgeable Emily. Delivering little nuggets of information, dressed in a jumpsuit that looks designer and trainers that have never taken a step outside. 'The children are regularly assessed to make sure they're reading at the correct level.'

'I see,' says Ana. 'And purple level, is that good?'

'Oh yes, that's good for Year One,' says Emily. 'My youngest, of four, yes – I have four children. Not quite as many as Fara,' she adds with a wry smile, 'but still quite a brood. And Fara, you had your children quite close together, didn't you? Whereas I chose to space mine out, so, you probably won't believe this,' she says, returning her focus to Ana, 'but I've been a mother now for nineteen years! My eldest, she's nineteen years old. I know, crazy, right?'

She seems to be expecting Ana to gush about her youthful complexion, but Ana just smiles politely, which makes me want to jump out of my seat and punch the air.

'Anyway, Seraphina, that's my youngest, she's in Year One – quite the character, isn't she?' Emily's looking round at the rest of us. Is anyone still listening? 'Well, Seraphina had her reading assessment yesterday, and she was moved up to lime green, which is phenomenal for her age.' She smiles smugly. 'Two levels above purple. At this rate, she may become a gold level reader by the end of Year Two!'

I'm mid eye-roll when Emily turns her head towards me. What is it with hungover eye-rolls? Why are they so bloody slow?

'Do you have any other questions about the reading levels, Ana?' Emily asks, flicking those alien eyes from mine.

'No,' Ana replies.

'Great,' smiles Emily. She arranges her face into a serious expression. 'In that case, I'd like to speak to you all in my official capacity as PTA chair, get the ball rolling. I was in the storage shed at the school yesterday, and there's an astonishing amount of stock left over from the summer fair. So I think we should have a start-of-term tombola to raise funds for the school.'

'People buy any old crap at the summer fair,' I say, returning my focus to the loose thread by Peppa Pig's eye. Twirling it again around my finger. 'If you couldn't flog it there, it's because it belongs in a tip. Not on a tombola.'

'But that's the beauty of a tombola,' Emily says. 'People don't care what they win. They just get excited about pulling out a winning ticket. It's the gambling aspect, you see,' she says, turning towards Ana. 'People love to gamble. And that's what we need to encourage.'

'Sounds perfectly ethical.' I need to stop pulling at this thread. Peppa's eye is about to fall off.

'There's a PTA meeting scheduled at my house tomorrow morning,' Emily continues, 'which will give us a chance to sort out the stock and stick raffle tickets onto prizes. I live on Herrywell Lane down from you, Ana,' she adds.

'You've probably seen my house. It's the one with the big white gates outside. You should come tomorrow; it will be a good chance for you to meet everyone properly, including my eldest two. Georgina doesn't start at university for a couple of weeks, she got into Oxford,' she adds as an aside, 'and Tobias isn't back at sixth form until Monday.'

'I'll come tomorrow, Emily,' I say, raising my head.

'What?' She almost splutters the word. 'Well, that would be lovely, Beth, though you haven't been part of the PTA for ages. Certainly not since I've been running things. What's made you want to get involved again now?'

'Why not?' I shrug.

'I'll come along if Beth's going to be there,' says Ana. 'It will be lovely for Willow to see Hope again. Look how nicely they're playing together.'

'Of course,' says Emily, before turning back to me. 'I'm just wondering why now, after all this time—'

She visibly flinches as Willow lets out an extraordinarily high shriek and as I pull the loose thread free and Peppa's eye pings away, I think about Emily's house. The bleached surfaces inside a spotless, germ-free zone, and the arrival of get-up-and-go Willow. That will definitely be fun to watch. But my main motivation for going is Emily's son Tobias. He was there that night. A passenger in the car that hit Charlotte on Herrywell Lane. I need to find out what he saw.

'I won't be able to join you,' says Jade, fiddling with her amethyst bracelet. I hadn't realised she was standing nearby. I stare at her but she won't meet my gaze. At least she has some shame. 'Thanks so much for the invitation, Emily, but I'm working tomorrow morning.' She checks her watch. 'Talking of which, I'm just about to host an everyday dangers discussion over by the painting table, if anyone's interested? Just a relaxed chat, really.'

'What do you mean?' asks Danielle, looking anxious. 'What kind of dangers?'

'Just the everyday stuff we all have inside our homes,' Jade says with an irritating smile. 'You know, things that look safe but can be lethal.'

'Like what?'

'Well, fridge magnets, for example. And hair straighteners, dishwashers, pen lids, dressing gown cords ... you know, the everyday objects that don't look dangerous but can so easily cause choking, scarring, brain damage, paralysis and death. It's all going to be very light-hearted. And if there's time, I might throw in a quick comparison quiz about bio and non-bio washing detergent, just for fun. Would anyone like to join? Ana?'

'No, thank you,' says Ana with a smile. 'I think I need to get Willow home for her nap and besides, she doesn't care which washing capsules I use. Bio, non-bio – she's not fussy. She'll eat either.'

'Ha, that's funny,' says Jade. How much fiddling can one bracelet take? 'But you do know that Willow shouldn't be eating any washing detergent? Even non-bio.'

'Yes, I know,' smiles Ana. 'It was just a joke.'

After that, Ana and I spend a few minutes trying to separate new best friends Willow and Hope, who cling to each other and scream 'No, no, no,' before scrambling towards the nearest toys and flinging them at us. Hope's face is screwed up in anger as she hurls building blocks at me with all her might. I don't think I've ever felt so proud.

'It's OK, Hope. It's OK,' I say, scooping her up into my arms as one-eyed Peppa Pig flies through the air and makes contact. Ouch. Even with one eye, that spot on my chin is a large enough target. 'You'll see Willow again tomorrow at Emily's house. Won't that be nice?'

As Ana and I head towards the exit we pass the painting table where Jade is standing in front of a group of parents, telling them that toddlers don't care whether the washing capsules we use are bio or non-bio. They'll eat either.

There's laughter as we step outside into the car park. Bloody Snow White. Stole Ana's line. Stole my husband. Fairest in the land? I don't think so. And that's when I feel it. Because it's everywhere, suddenly, and recognisable just as fast. I've felt this before. In the days running up to Charlotte's death. A sense that something has been triggered, a chain of events set into motion. Something awful about to happen. Sinister and already set in stone.

And then I hear Ana giggle. There's a man dressed in a business suit, holding a briefcase, sprinting across the car park. He looks terrified. Chasing him is a middle-aged woman wearing a tiara. 'You're not supposed to park in here!' she's shouting. 'Bloody commuters. What's wrong with you? Can't you read the signs?'

I turn to Ana. We're both laughing now and it feels good. Standing in an oversized car park, with Hope in my arms and joy swirling all around, rushing towards that sense of foreboding. Diluting it, destroying it until only laughter remains. And doubt. Because that thing that I felt that was sinister, maybe it was never there.

10

I'm always trying so hard to remember the last time I felt happy. The last time I felt loved. Because if I can go back in my mind to that exact moment, maybe I can reconnect with who I was then – the loved, happy version of myself – and if I can find myself there, maybe I can unthink what I thought. Unsay what I said. Do what I didn't do, to stop that moment from developing into this one. It's got to be somewhere – that exact moment in time, hidden amongst all the random scraps of information, piled so high inside my mind. And if I can find it, maybe I can point it in a different direction, towards a different today. A different tomorrow. A future where I'm happy and loved and I don't have to waste any time trying to remember the last time. The last time I passed through these ridiculously huge, white gates. The last time I was here, on that day almost a year ago. The day Charlotte died.

'Beth, are you aware there's a dreadful-looking scratch down one side of your car?'

'Yes, I am. Fully aware, thank you, Emily.' Why is she standing in her own driveway wearing a bright yellow high-vis jacket and holding a pencil and notebook in her manicured hands?

'Right, well, I hope you don't think I'm being pedantic but I'm going to make a note of that scratch,' she says, turning a page of the notebook and starting to write. 'I just don't want there being any suggestion that your car was damaged while parked on our land,' she adds, glancing at me with a concerned smile. 'So,' she says, closing the notebook, 'to enable everyone to park considerately, I've opened up a second parking area down by the orchard.'

'A second parking area?' I say, even though I know I should probably keep my thoughts to myself. 'Bloody hell, Emily! It's a PTA meeting, not Glastonbury.'

'We need to keep the traffic moving,' she says, flicking her eyes towards a car turning into the driveway behind me, 'so if you don't mind, please go and park in the orchard.'

'That's not traffic,' I say, checking my rear-view mirror, 'it's just Danielle.'

'Ah, good. Danielle's arrived,' Emily says, opening the notebook again. 'She can park in the orchard too. I'll tell her to follow you.'

'Follow me where? I didn't even know you had an orchard.'

'Down there,' she says, pointing towards the side of the house. I drive in the direction of her pointed finger and park my car between two trees. Danielle pulls in behind me, gets out of her car and looks confused.

'Hello Beth,' she says, with an anxious nod. 'What beautiful trees!' she adds, looking around. 'I don't think I've ever parked in an orchard before.'

'Oh, come on, Danielle,' I say, unstrapping Hope from her seat in the back of the car. 'This isn't an orchard, is it? It's just some muddy grass. And two trees.'

'Apple trees,' she says, staring up into the branches. 'The kind you'd see in an orchard.'

'If we were in an orchard,' I say, as we trudge up the muddy track towards the house. 'Which we're not.'

'Welcome, welcome,' Emily says, opening the front door. High-vis jacket retired from duty, notebook and pencil still firmly in hand. 'I was just telling Ana about our orchard.' She smiles. 'Not a real one, obviously,' she adds with a gentle laugh. 'Just a joke, really. More a suggestion.'

'I'm sorry, I don't understand,' says Ana, who doesn't appear to be in the mood for jokes. She's standing behind Emily, holding Willow in her arms – mother and daughter both looking seriously bored.

Emily seems pleased to have an excuse to explain. 'Well, we have two magnificent apple trees, and whenever I need to clear my head I go and stand between them and close my eyes.' Maybe I need to take a wander down there and close my eyes because I'm starting to feel irritated. 'I listen to the rustling leaves and imagine myself in the middle of a huge orchard with rows and rows of apple trees.'

Perhaps I'm irritated at Emily and Ana. Both so slim, glowing with health, each ridiculously beautiful in their own way. Emily's way looks like it takes a lot more effort than Ana's but who cares? The result is the same. Both infinitely better-looking and better at living than me. I feel suddenly huge and frumpy, ugly—

'I know it sounds silly,' Emily continues, 'but taking a few minutes out of a busy day to stand between those trees, it's so relaxing. Almost magical. Because life can be difficult sometimes, can't it?' Her voice splinters slightly. Is she blinking away tears? 'I know it's only an imaginary orchard but for a place so alive in my mind, I'm never certain. Is it there? Or isn't it there? Who can ever know for sure? Anyway,' she says, manicured hand dabbing the corner of her eye. 'That's enough of me being daft!'

Everyone's staring at their feet. This weird monologue moved from irritating to awkward very fast.

'Could I ask you all to please leave your shoes at the door,' Emily says, staring down at our feet too. 'With little ones crawling around,' a glance up towards Hope in my arms, 'best not to risk mud on the floor.'

'Mud mud mud,' Hope adds helpfully.

'It's magical mud, Emily,' I say, glancing again at my grubby trainers. 'From the magical orchard.' Maybe a joke will lighten things up. 'Is it there? Or isn't it there? How can we ever know for sure?'

'Beth!' And she's back. Eyes reset. Smile fixed. Composure regained. Total reboot.

'All right, all right,' I say, kicking my shoes off.

'Hello Beth.' If Emily's face is an exclamation, her husband's is an apology. An attractive man, burdened by intimidating intelligence, Nigel always looks and sounds desperately sorry for the rest of us, struggling through life with our average IQ. 'It's been a long time,' he's saying now, as the others remove their shoes and follow Emily into the kitchen.

'Yes, it has,' I reply. 'How are you, Nigel?'

'I'm fine. More importantly, Beth, how are you?'

'I'm OK,' I say, glancing down at my socks. It's quite disarming – genius and compassion combined.

'Must have been the Halloween party last year. Yes, that's right. Last time I saw you, you were standing right here with Rowan . . .' He tails off. 'Shouting at him.'

'Well yes,' I say, glancing back down at my socks. 'I tend to do that when I'm angry.'

'I don't blame you,' he says. 'Not after what Rowan did. But when you stormed out, well . . . I was just worried,' he says. 'You'd had a few drinks – we all had,' he adds quickly. 'It was a party, wasn't it? But the thought of you walking down the lane on your own in the dark when you were so . . . upset . . . When I first heard that someone had been knocked down and killed out there, I thought it was you – Georgina!' He's looking towards the top of the staircase and checking his watch. 'What's the emergency? You're out of bed and it's not even midday.'

'Very funny, Dad,' says his daughter, gliding down to join us. She's wearing leggings and a tiny crop top, her long hair tied up on the top of her head in a messy bun. 'That's a cute kid,' she says, nodding towards Hope, who is gazing at Georgina while sticking a finger up her nose. I'm gazing at her too, wondering what life is like for people like that. While the rest of us are standing in front of the mirror miserably trying to find clothes that make us look good, I wonder what people like Georgina do with all that extra time. 'You've got so tall,' I find myself saying, classic middle-aged mantra. 'How old are you now?'

'Nineteen.'

'Wow! I can't believe you're all grown up. What are you doing these days? Are you still modelling?'

'Yeah, that's what I've been doing in my gap year, but I'm starting university in a couple of weeks.'

'Oh yes, your mum said you got into Oxford. Congratulations!'

'She tells everyone that,' Georgina smirks. 'It's embarrassing.'

'I think she's just proud.'

'It's embarrassing,' she says again. 'And she's roped me into helping with this PTA thing,' she says, turning towards the kitchen. 'Are you coming?'

'Of course,' I say, before flicking my eyes back to Nigel. 'Nice to see you again.'

'You too,' he says, with a kind smile. 'Look after yourself, Beth. You've had a tough time.'

'I concur,' I say with a nod.

'Concur?' Another smirk from Georgina.

'What about Tobias?' I ask, following her towards the kitchen. 'Will he be joining us?'

'Oh God, no!' laughs Georgina, over her shoulder.

'Pity.' Was coming here a waste of time?

'That geek at a PTA meeting? Like putting Einstein on *Love Island*. Awkward for everyone involved and probably not even that interesting to watch.'

Talking of islands, Fara, Danielle and Ana are perched at one that is probably the same size as an actual island in the centre of Emily's enormous kitchen, surrounded by clear, gleaming surfaces as far as the eye can see. Not big enough to have border control and its own currency but certainly one that a couple of castaways could quite happily live upon. Fara's baby is sleeping soundly in the car seat as I carefully pull out a chair. There's a lot to choose from. Where's everyone else?

'I must apologise for the mess,' says Emily, scooping up a pair of socks and a needlework box from the work surface, which are the only two items on display. Where does she keep everything? Where's her kettle? Her toaster? Where's her Sellotape? Everyone has Sellotape. I bet everything's squashed into a drawer somewhere. I'm beginning to feel a bit happier about the state of my own house when she opens a drawer and I spot her Sellotape in its own little section next to the Blu Tack section and the clothes pegs section. She places the socks and the needlework box into yet another section before stepping away from a drawer that's not only immaculate, it seems to know how to close itself, requiring no help from Emily at all.

'Sorry about that,' she says. 'I was just embroidering Noah and Seraphina's names into their school socks before you arrived.'

'Why?' I ask, still staring at that drawer. How did it know when to close?

'Well, primary school children are always getting their socks muddled up, aren't they?' says Emily. 'Especially after PE lessons.'

'Yes,' agrees Danielle. 'My children are forever wearing the wrong socks home from school.'

'Mine too,' smiles Fara.

'Can't say I've ever noticed,' I say, dragging my eyes away from the drawer. Emily has hiked down one side of the island and is opening the huge oven, which is filled with baking trays. Something smells incredible. 'I had a meeting with Miss Lane and the governors at the end of last term,' she says, removing a tray of muffins. 'Miss Lane,' she adds as an aside to Ana, 'is the headmistress. You probably met her when Summer joined the school. Anyway, we've decided on our next fundraising goal. It was my idea, but we all agreed that what the school most desperately needs is waterproof shading for the playground. It's frightfully expensive,' she adds, arranging muffins decoratively onto a plate before heading back down the island towards us. 'But it means the children will be shaded from the sun on hot days and sheltered from the rain when it's wet.'

'But why don't the kids just wear sun hats when it's sunny?' asks Ana, reaching for the plate of muffins. 'And stay indoors or put their hoods up when it rains?'

Nobody speaks. Instead everyone eats very intently. Just one more mouthful and then I'll say something. Stop this silence from accelerating towards awkward.

'Is this your first PTA meeting, Ana?' asks Georgina, breaking the silence before I do.

'Yes.'

'Ah, that's why you don't know the rules yet. See, what you said just then, that's what we call "common sense". But the thing is,' she says, smiling, 'nobody wants common sense at a PTA meeting. Just entrenched views, a total unwillingness to listen, and a ton of passive aggression.'

She's almost laughing, and I have to bite my lip. 'Don't get me wrong, feel free to make as many suggestions as you like but any containing common sense will be ignored.'

'Georgina!' snaps Emily. 'If you want to be helpful, why don't you settle Willow and Hope into the play area I've set up for them in the living room? On the soft carpet.'

'Why do we have any other kind? Carpet should always be soft. That's the whole point.'

'Right,' says Emily, ignoring her. 'Let's make a start. What I think might work best is if we divide into two groups. Fara and Danielle, if you work with me, we can start sorting through the prizes and Beth and Ana, you can start—'

'Hang on a minute,' says Georgina, dropping the last of a muffin into her mouth. 'Is no one else coming?'

'This is everyone, for now,' says Emily, staring down at her hands. Which is odd, because Emily's eyes are always open wide and forward-facing. That's what makes her face such an exclamation. With downcast eyes, she doesn't look like Emily at all.

'Bloody hell, Mum!' giggles Georgina. 'Only four people turned up? You're so extra,' she adds, laughing. 'I think the orchard parking might have been overkill!'

I think of the high-vis, the notebook, the pencil, the second parking area, the blueberry muffins – not the ones we're eating, the other ones. The trays and trays of them still in the oven, and when I look at Emily, I feel sorry for her.

'Many people expressed an interest yesterday at drop-off,' she says quietly, still staring down at her hands. 'They may still turn up.' A quick glance at her watch. 'They're probably just running late.'

'They're not running late,' says Georgina. 'If they're not here now, it means they're not coming.'

'How can you be so sure?' asks Emily, raising her eyes to face her daughter.

'Because the people who come to a PTA meeting at ten o'clock in the morning on the third day of term are the kind of people who are never late for anything,' Georgina replies. 'Because they're the people with fuck all else to do. No offence,' she adds, glancing down our side of the island.

'Georgina!' Emily's eyes look less alien for a second, authentic almost, and then she blinks. Another reboot. She's back. 'That may be how they're talking on the catwalks these days, but please mind your language in here. Actually,' she says with a smile, 'maybe I should set up a swear jar. Knowing us lot,' she adds, glancing towards me, 'we'll have enough money for waterproof shading by the end of the day.'

'Seriously, Mum,' says Georgina, grabbing another muffin. 'How many parents send their kids to that school? Four hundred? Five? And only four turn up to a PTA meeting? It's pathetic.'

'It's very early in the term, Georgina,' says Emily. 'I didn't have time to advertise properly . . .'

'Bollocks!'

'Georgina! Swear jar!' she says, pointing, I guess, towards an imaginary jar on the island.

'There is no swear jar,' her daughter says, 'and you did advertise. You put it all over the school's socials. Has it always been like this?' she asks, looking at me.

'Like what?'

'Such a pathetic turnout. Was it like this when your friend was in charge?'

'Charlotte?'

'Yeah, did people come to the meetings then?'

'Er—' I think about the question for a moment as my mind flits back to PTA meetings of the past. The packed venues, standing room only and Charlotte at the front, making everyone laugh . . . 'I think there may have been a slightly bigger crowd back then,' I say, focusing solely on Georgina, 'but you know Charlotte,' I add, glancing towards the others, 'she was always good at rallying the troops.'

'And micromanaging them,' says Danielle, her confusion tinged with something I can't place. Annoyance? Anger? 'Charlotte always made sure she knew what everyone was doing, didn't she? Just so she could be the one to swoop in and save the day.'

'Well, she certainly saved the day *that* day, didn't she?' I say, staring at Danielle. Why's she being so mean about Charlotte? 'That day in the hospital when you had your anaphylactic shock. Charlotte was the doctor on duty, wasn't she? She saved your life.'

'She did her job,' Danielle says, her face frozen. Each word a block of ice. 'And she never let me forget it.'

'I think we can all agree that there are many different leadership styles,' says Fara. 'And Charlotte was certainly very punctilious when she ran the PTA.'

'Right,' I say, when it becomes clear she's not going to say anything else. 'What does that mean?'

'Good attention to detail,' Fara explains. 'Charlotte was extremely meticulous in her note-keeping and planning of events. If I'm honest,' she says, glancing briefly towards Emily, 'I found her leadership style rather autocratic. Perfect for a corporate setting, perhaps, but a PTA meeting? All the charts and colour-coded lists and updates – probably unwarranted.'

'Right,' says Emily, tapping her manicured nails on the counter, her face forcing into a smile. 'Shall we make a start? Beth, have you got your Sellotape?'

'What? Why would I have Sellotape?'

'To get the prizes ready for the tombola. It would have been helpful if you'd brought Sellotape with you, in your bag.'

'Who brings Sellotape with them, in their bag?'

'I've got Sellotape,' says Fara, rummaging inside her huge bag. 'Where is it? I know it's in here somewhere.' And now she's placing nappies and wipes and keys and notebooks onto the counter before finding Sellotape and passing it over. 'Here you are, Beth.' She smiles at me. 'I've got everything in this bag. Well, you know what it's like with a newborn, got to be ready for any contingency.' With Sellotape? 'I've got my whole life squished up inside this bloody bag! Oops. Where's the swear jar?'

Lovely Fara. Providing swearing solidarity and a vast array of words of the day. What is it about her I find so difficult to trust? And why doesn't Emily let me use her Sellotape? I saw a whole section of it, inside her perfect drawer. Didn't I? Maybe I didn't. Maybe it's all an illusion, like the imaginary swear jar and orchard. Maybe imaginary Sellotape is what Emily uses to stick it all together, all the imaginary pieces of her imaginary perfect life. Let's hope no one ever turns up with a big pair of imaginary scissors. Chops the whole fucking illusion up.

11

The carpet in the enormous living room is fantastically soft. Georgina is tuning the TV to CBeebies as Ana and I carry Willow and Hope to the play area. Soft toys, musical instruments and jigsaws – the perfect balance of educational fun. Get-up-and-go Willow heads straight for the mini drumkit and as I catch Ana's eye, we both smile.

'Looks like it's going to get loud in here, Toby,' says Georgina. 'You might want to go somewhere else.'

'All right,' says a voice from the corner of a sofa so large, I didn't notice him sitting there. Tobias is wearing a blue hoodie and tracksuit bottoms and staring intently at the Rubik's Cube in his hand, his fingers moving manically – the rest of his body completely still. 'Just give me a minute,' he says, without looking up.

'He's obsessed with that thing,' says Georgina. 'Always trying to beat his personal best.'

'Shut up, George,' he says, 'you're putting me off.' He slams the cube onto the sofa beside him and raises his head, then stares at Ana and me through his thick, floppy fringe, looking a bit startled. I don't think he expected to see anyone other than his sister standing here. I feel elated at the sight of him. Maybe Sellotape Gate will have been worth it. But I'll have to tread carefully.

'Hi, Tobias,' I say, sitting on the sofa beside him. 'I'm not sure if you remember me. I'm Beth, your mum's friend.'

He snorts something I can't decipher and picks up the Rubik's Cube again. 'And this is Ana,' I say. 'She's your new neighbour. She's just moved to Herrywell Lane.'

'Whereabouts?' asks Georgina.

'Charlotte's old house,' I reply, turning back to face Tobias. He's looking at Ana, his face reddening as she settles herself down on the soft carpet. 'Talking of Charlotte,' I say, raising my voice as Willow hits a drum with extreme force, 'I can't believe it's almost a year since she died. I was here that night,' I say, looking from a bored-looking Georgina to an awkward Tobias. 'Your parents had a big party. I remember there was huge cauldron full of dry ice over there, in the bay window. It looked amazing.'

'Yeah, it was a good party,' agrees Georgina, sitting down next to Ana. 'Mum got so stressed in the days running up to it, do you remember?' she asks her brother, who nods, glances at Ana and turns an even deeper shade of red. 'The trouble with Mum is that she always wants everything to be perfect and ends up trying way too hard. It was a good party, though,' she says again. 'Even the old people had decent costumes. I can't remember, what were you dressed as, Beth?'

'Big Bird.'

'Yeah, I know. But what were you dressed as?'

'Big Bird.'

'Oh, come on, be more body positive. You can't do anything about your natural build and besides, you'd probably just had your baby, hadn't you?'

'No, I mean I was dressed as Big Bird. From *Sesame Street*.'

'Oh, my bad! Sorry,' she laughs. 'Is that why you were wearing that big fluffy yellow coat?'

'It wasn't a coat! That was my costume.'

'Oh, right. It looked like a big coat.'

'Why would I wear a big fluffy coat inside?'

'I dunno. Hormones? But I'll say this for you,' she adds, smiling, 'you were bloody entertaining. She got absolutely hammered,' she says to Ana. 'I didn't notice at first because you seemed OK,' talking to me again, 'until you nearly fell headfirst into the cauldron! It was hilarious. Then later you started screaming at your husband, calling him all kinds of names. Mind you, he probably deserved it, didn't he? Yeah, you really livened things up. Shame you stormed out because it all went downhill from there.'

The memories arrive as jagged snapshots, each accompanied by a new beat of the drum. The cauldron. A skeleton, laughing. A ghost. Another ghost. Rowan's face. Tears. Shouting. Jade. Devil's horns. The ground underfoot. Enormous white gates.

'And how about you, Tobias?' I ask, turning back to face him. 'Did you enjoy the party?' He lifts his head and turns his face towards me. Behind his fringe, his eyes are enormous, and he has a few teenage spots, together with razor-sharp cheekbones, just like his mum.

'I wasn't at the party,' he says.

'Weren't you?' I feel cruel, leading him like this.

'No,' he replies, and there's silence as he stares again at the cube in his hands. 'I was at chess club,' he says eventually.

'Don't you remember?' asks Georgina. 'Toby was in the car that night. The car that hit Charlotte.' She looks at me with pity. Old people are so forgetful.

'Was he? Oh my God, Tobias,' I say. 'I did know that, but I'd completely forgotten. I'm so sorry.'

'It's OK,' he mumbles.

'I feel awful,' I say. 'What a dreadful thing to go through.'

'It's OK.' Another mumble.

'I can't imagine how awful that must have been,' I say. 'Especially for the driver. How's he doing?'

'James?' he asks. 'He's OK.' More fiddling with the Rubik's Cube. 'I mean, it wasn't his fault.'

'Of course not,' I say. 'I just wonder . . .'

'What?' His eyes peering up at me through his fringe.

'Whether he thinks there's anything he could have done differently,' I say, pushing my socked toes into the soft carpet. 'I should imagine it still haunts him. If it was me, I'd replay it over and over again in my mind.'

'He couldn't have done anything differently,' Tobias says, meeting my eyes with his, unblinking. 'There wasn't time.'

'Yeah,' says Georgina, 'and the police were there. He was breathalysed and drug tested—'

'It's not like the places you go, George,' Tobias snaps,

whipping his head towards his sister. 'There's no getting pissed at chess club.'

'I'm not suggesting there is,' she says, with a rather dramatic but well-practised eye-roll. 'Can't imagine you or your geeky chess mates doing anything interesting.'

'Shut up!' he snaps, pushing himself up from the sofa.

'So, you know James from chess club?' I ask, placing my hand on his arm.

'Yeah,' he says, glancing at my hand before sitting back down. 'And from school,' he adds. 'He was in the year above me.'

'Did he always drive you home?'

'No, normally Mum or Dad picked me up but I got a lift that night because of the party. And before you ask,' he says, raising his eyes to meet mine, 'James was eighteen and had only just passed his test, and no – he wasn't speeding or driving like a lunatic.'

'I wasn't going to ask that.'

'Most adults do.'

'Well, not me. Personally, I think young drivers are often a lot better than most of the idiots you see on the road.'

'Yeah,' he says, nodding. 'Well, anyway, James drove the whole team home that night. There were four of us, including him. He was going to drop me off first.'

'What happened, exactly? Do you remember?'

'I was sitting in the back, giving directions, because James had never driven to my house before and I remember telling him that after the bend in the lane he should carry on for a couple of minutes then look out for white gates on the right. I was almost home when . . .' He pauses, closes his eyes for a moment. 'I heard the screech of brakes first, then James screaming, then we felt the thud. And he wasn't speeding,' his eyes open and back on mine. 'He was slowing down around the bend when she just appeared, out of nowhere. It happened in less than a second.'

'It must have been awful.'

'It was,' he says, staring at something on the immaculate, soft carpet. 'We all got out of the car and ran to the front, and there she was, lying on the ground. She was wearing running clothes,' his eyes back on mine, 'and someone told me afterwards that she'd been training for the marathon. I guess she must have been distracted and forgot to check for traffic—'

'Yeah,' I say. 'That's the part I find strange.'

'What do you mean?' asks Georgina.

'Well, her two-year-old son was at home when it happened and the Charlotte I knew would never have left him alone to go for a run.'

'Maybe that's who she was talking about,' Tobias says.

'Who?' I ask.

'Charlotte,' he replies. 'When she was lying on the ground, maybe she was talking about her son.'

'She was talking?'

'Yeah, we all heard her. We told the police.'

'What was she saying?' I ask, holding my breath.

'Just the same words, over and over again. "*That poor boy. That poor boy.*" Maybe she felt bad about leaving him in the house on his own,' he says, fiddling with the Rubik's Cube. 'Maybe she felt guilty.'

'Maybe,' I say, my eyes moving involuntarily towards my

youngest child. Willow's hitting the drums and Hope is smiling, clapping her hands, babbling 'More, more, more!'

'Charlotte had three children,' I say to Ana, who's staring at the girls too. 'Her youngest, Leo, he was only a little older than Willow when Charlotte died. Did she say anything else, Toby?' I ask, turning back towards him.

'I'm sorry.'

'You don't have to apologise. This must be so difficult for you, going through it all again—'

'No,' he says, 'that's what she said. Right at the end, just before she closed her eyes, *"I'm sorry. I'm so sorry."* Like it was her fault.'

'Well, Toby darling, it *was* her fault.'

We all jump at the contrast. Tobias's voice soft and gentle, his mother's reinforced with steel. Emily enters the living room at speed, followed by Fara and Danielle, and squeezes herself in beside me on the sofa, enveloping her son in her arms. 'Charlotte was obsessed with training for that blasted marathon, my love,' she says, 'and she chose to go out when it was far too dark. It was her decision to run out into the lane without looking, my darling. The people in the car could have been hurt. *You* could have been hurt. What if James had swerved to avoid her and hit a tree? You could have been killed. I'm not surprised she was saying sorry. It was her fault—'

'Yes,' I say, standing up from the sofa. 'The woman who made colour-coded lists and micromanaged everyone and took meticulous notes . . . that woman, that organised, *punctilious*,' a glance towards Fara, 'woman just decided one night to run blindly out into the middle of the road.'

'What are you saying?' asks Emily, steely voice moulded into something sharp. 'Are you saying my son's lying?'

'Of course not! But I do find it strange.'

'It *was* strange.' A soft voice. Gentle.

'What was, Toby?' I say, crouching down at his feet.

'When she was . . . dying . . .' He's staring down at his socks. They're red. Jaunty. 'We were all with her, all four of us got out of the car, but . . .'

'But what?'

'I kept looking around, into the darkness.'

'Why?'

'Because I kept expecting to see someone. It felt like there was someone else there. Watching.'

He stares up into my face. Really stares. Really sees me.

'Who was it, Toby?' I ask. 'Who else was there? Who did you see?'

He stares at me for a moment longer and then his eyes flick towards the other people in the room. Fara, Danielle, Ana, Georgina, before settling on his mother. They look at each other for a long moment, unblinking.

'I don't know.' He's staring back down at his hands. 'It was too dark. Maybe there was nobody there.'

'Oh, Toby,' says Emily, wrapping her arms around him even tighter. 'Please don't upset yourself. Why don't you go up to your room and play your PlayStation for a while? Try to take your mind off it.'

'OK,' he says, getting up from the sofa and leaving the room, red-socked feet padding gently across the soft carpet. Rubik's Cube clutched in his hand.

'That poor boy,' Emily says, as the living room door

closes behind him. 'It was bad enough for him at the time. It's horrible when he has to go through it all again.'

'I'm sorry,' I say quietly, but I don't think she hears as she turns away from me, following her son out of the room. Leaving me with the echo of Charlotte's last words.

That poor boy. I'm sorry.

12

'It's not fair!' Jack shouts, slumping down onto the sofa. 'Why was Hope allowed to have a playdate at Noah's house? She's a baby.'

'Why are you still going on about this? It was yesterday and it wasn't a playdate,' I say, scooping up toys and dropping them into random toy boxes. 'It was a boring PTA meeting, you would have hated it, and anyway, you were at school.'

'I wouldn't have hated it!' he shouts, glaring at me. 'Noah's big brother's got a PlayStation 5. It's brilliant round there. It's much better than here.'

'Don't say that. You've got loads of toys—'

'It's more fun at Noah's house,' he says, getting to his feet. 'And his mum always makes nice cakes and biscuits.'

'Well, I can't argue with that,' I say, feeling under the sofa for little toy cars. 'She made the most incredible blueberry muffins. I should have asked her if I could bring some home.'

'Yes, you should,' he says, starting to jump on the sofa. 'They're much nicer than the muffins you make.'

'I've never made blueberry muffins in my life!' I laugh. 'All our cakes and biscuits are bought from the supermarket, Jack. There's a couple of packets in the kitchen if you want one?'

'No, they're disgusting!' he shouts, jumping higher.

'I tell you what, why don't we build something with all this Lego?'

'I've already built everything,' he says, picking up one of the sofa cushions and throwing it up into the air. 'I don't want to play with it any more.'

'How about tidying it up then?' I ask, risking an optimistic smile. 'There's Lego all over the floor, Jack. If Hope puts a piece in her mouth, she could choke.' I gesture at his sister, who is happily cruising along the edge of the sofa yelling 'Bear now!' at the top of her lungs.

'That's her fault for being disgusting!' he shouts, lobbing another cushion. 'Why does she put everything in her mouth? And why's she always shouting out stupid words?'

'Because she's a toddler. And please stop throwing cushions, I'm trying to tidy up. Freddie!' I call to his younger brother, 'could you help me put these toys away? I want to get you all to bed nice and early tonight because you're staying at Daddy's house this weekend and I think he's got lots of fun things planned. Won't that be nice?'

'Yeah!' both boys shout, and with Jack momentarily cheered up, even he starts throwing Lego into the nearest toy box.

'What will you do all weekend, Mummy?' Freddie asks, his face suddenly concerned.

'Oh, I'll be fine,' I say, planting a kiss on the top of his head. 'I've got plenty of work to be getting on with.'

'What work?' he asks. 'I didn't know you did work, Mummy.'

'Very important work,' I say with a smile, giving him another kiss.

'Are we getting a dolphin, Mummy?' he asks, staring at me.

'What?'

'We are, aren't we? We're getting a dolphin!' he shouts, jumping up and down. Lego flies in every direction, other than into the toy box. 'Thank you, Mummy!' he says, hugging me. 'I've always wanted a dolphin. Jack! Jack! Mummy's doing very important work so we can get a dolphin.'

'What are you talking about?' I ask him.

'That's what they said. Daddy and Jade. I heard them talking about it.'

'When?'

'The day we went to the hospital. We stayed at Daddy and Jade's house.'

'Right. And what did you hear them say?'

'They said that if you get a job you'll get a dolphin.'

'What?' I laugh. 'That doesn't make any sense.'

'Don't laugh at me!' No more jumping up and down. 'I'm not lying.'

'I'm not saying that, Freddie. It's just a very strange thing for Daddy and Jade to say.'

'Well, that's what they said. They might not have said you'd get a dolphin, but that's what they meant.'

'You're such an idiot,' says Jack, attempting keepy-uppies with one of the sofa cushions.

'Jack! Don't call your brother an idiot. He made a mistake, that's all. Everyone makes mistakes.'

'No, Mummy! It wasn't a mistake,' says Freddie. 'I asked Miss Ford about it, and she showed me a picture on the computer at school. Looked just like a dolphin.'

'She showed you a picture of what?'

'A porpoise. Daddy and Jade said work would give you a porpoise and that's what you need, but I didn't know what it was, so I asked Miss Ford and she showed me a picture. And it looked just like a dolphin. Why will work give you a porpoise, Mummy? Is it easier to look after than a dolphin?'

'We're not getting a porpoise – or a dolphin,' I add, before he has a chance to ask.

'Of course we're not,' says Jack. 'We never do anything fun.'

'How would having a dolphin be fun, Jack?' I ask, turning towards him. 'Think about it. Where would we put a dolphin? In the bath?'

'At least it would give us something to do,' he says, as the cushion bounces off his foot and hits the TV. 'It's so boring here. I wish I lived at Daddy's house all the time. He's got a PlayStation 5, same as Noah's brother.'

'But, Mummy, if we're not getting a dolphin, why did Daddy and Jade say it?'

'They didn't say porpoise, you idiot,' says Jack. 'Work

will give her purpose, that's what they said. That's what they always say. It's a different word.'

'What's that, Mummy?'

'It's something I already have,' I reply. 'You. And Jack, and Hope. Being your mummy, that's my purpose.'

'Jade has children to give her purpose,' says Jack - more keepy-uppies, different cushion, 'and *she* has a job at the tots thing. And she does something with magic stones.'

'Well, Jade's children are all at school,' I say. 'So, she has time to have a job.'

'But we're at school most of the time,' he says.

'Hope isn't though, is she?' I ask. 'I can't work because I look after Hope. Talking of which,' I say, glancing at Hope who is rubbing her eyes, then at my watch, 'bedtime. Now.'

An hour or so later, the children are tucked up in bed and I'm in my bedroom. *Turn that frown upside down* is back to front, unfurled across the floor, with the photo of Charlotte in the centre. I'm sitting next to it, drinking white wine from Hope's Little Miss Sunshine plastic cup, wondering what I think I'm doing. Scribbling on the back of a poster like a school art project, trying to find the reason my friend died. Because there has to be a reason, doesn't there? A better reason than just 'life is random and shit'.

I spent yesterday evening doing this too. Gathering my thoughts and trying to write down everything I can remember Tobias saying about the night Charlotte died. There's something at the corner of my mind but I can't grasp it. Something he said that didn't make sense.

I lay my head down on the scratchy carpet. I wonder how Charlotte felt that night. Lying in the cold and the dark on a hard road, hurt and bleeding. Knowing she was about to die. Knowing that everything was about to slip away. No more worry. No more struggle. How would I feel? Happy. Relieved. But what about Charlotte? I sit up and raise the plastic mug to my lips. Little Miss Sunshine. I lay my head back down and close my eyes.

'That poor boy.' That's what she said right at the end. Spending those last few moments thinking about her son. Imagining his journey through life without her, perhaps? 'I'm sorry.' Sorry for what? What were you sorry for, Charlotte? Leaving him alone in the house? 'That poor boy.' Why is that wrong? Why does that feel wrong?

'Who are you talking to?'

'Jack!' I say, sitting up. 'You made me jump!'

'Why are you lying on the floor? Are you pretending to be a porpoise?' he adds with a smile. 'A big porpoise?'

'Why aren't you in bed?' I ask.

'What's this?' he asks, pointing at my project. 'What . . . Happened . . . To . . . Charlotte?' he reads out each word phonetically. 'What are you doing?'

'Why aren't you in bed?' I ask again.

'I can't find my goalkeeper gloves. Freddie's probably put them somewhere. He's always moving things.'

'So?'

'I need them.'

'No, it's bedtime. You need to go to sleep.'

'Daddy said we can play penalties in the garden this weekend. I need to pack my gloves.'

'We'll find them in the morning.'

'No, we won't!'

'Jack, stop shouting! You'll wake the others. I promise you; we'll find your gloves before you go to Daddy's.'

'But it's Friday tomorrow and Daddy's picking us up from school so we need to find my gloves now.'

'No, we don't.'

'Why not?'

'Because it's late and I'm busy.'

'You're just lying on the floor talking to yourself. No wonder Daddy and Jade think you're mad.'

'Jack! Please go back to bed. I can tell that you're tired.'

'I'm not.'

'You are.'

'I'm not.'

'Jack, please go to bed.'

'No.'

'JACK! GO TO BED!'

'WHY ARE YOU SHOUTING?' he screams. 'Is this why Daddy went away? I hate you. I wish you weren't my mummy. I wish you were dead.'

'JACK!'

He turns and runs into his room, screaming, 'I HATE YOU,' before slamming his bedroom door.

'JACK!' I shout and then I realise. That's what Charlotte would have said, wouldn't she? If she was lying on the ground, knowing she was about to die and thinking about her son – she'd have said his name. Why didn't she say his name?

The Little Miss Sunshine cup is lying on its side. Cheap, scratchy wine is sinking into cheap, scratchy carpet. I pick it up and leave the room. Quiet sobs from behind Jack's door. I imagine him curled up in bed. That poor boy.

'I'm sorry,' I say through the door. 'I'll go and have a look for your goalkeeping gloves.' He doesn't respond.

I head downstairs. The house is a mess. I didn't finish clearing away all the toys. I'll tidy up the house, find the gloves and get to bed. That's the plan. It's a good plan. I go to the fridge. Tidy the house, find the gloves, go to bed, reach for the wine. There are bottles of it, queued up waiting for a weekend of no distraction. No children, no noise, no judgement. Just me, the dog, my project. I smile. Little Miss Sunshine. Filled to the brim.

Fourteen Months Ago

I place the phone down on the kitchen table. Count to twenty. Pick it up again. Redial.

'Rowan, it's me. This is the third message I've left, why don't you ever answer your bloody phone? How much longer are you going to be? Hope's been really unsettled all day and I've finally got her to take a bottle but it's doing my head in, being with the kids every day on my own. I know you're working hard but please let me know when you'll be back.'

I place the phone down on the kitchen table and count to twenty. Then pick it up again and call Jade.

'Jade, can you give me a call when you get this? I'm . . . I'm really struggling today. Oh God, listen to me, I'm such a mess. I don't even know why I'm crying. I stopped breastfeeding this week, so maybe that's it. I'm probably just tired and hormonal but I keep feeling so anxious. Anyway, I'm sorry to go on, give me a call when you can.'

I place the phone down on the kitchen table and count to twenty again. Pick it up. Another twenty. She's probably busy with her own kids but I need to talk to someone.

'Hi, Beth.'

'Oh Charlotte, thank God—'

'What's happened? What's wrong?'

'Nothing, but I can't stop crying. I feel like I'm losing my mind.'

'Take a deep breath. And another. That's it, now, tell me. What's going on?'

'I'm not sure. It's just a collection of things, you know? I think everything's getting too much for me. It's probably my hormones. I stopped breastfeeding Hope this week.'

'Well, that's a massive adjustment, really emotional.'

'And I'm feeling so tired.'

'Of course you are! You've got a four-month-old baby and two young sons, and the summer holidays have only just started so you've got them all day, every day. You must be exhausted.'

'I am.'

'Where's Rowan?'

'Well, that's the other thing. He's always working late and most of the time he doesn't answer my calls, so I never know when he's coming home. I think that's why I'm feeling so anxious because . . .'

'What?'

'I'm worried that he doesn't want to come home.'

'But this is Rowan we're talking about. The ultimate family man. He's devoted to you.'

'I know, but . . .'

'He's probably just working long hours because he wants to take care of you all. It's always tough when there's a new baby.'

I think back to when Jack and Freddie were babies. I don't remember it being this bad. Maybe I've just forgotten.

'Also, he's probably just trying to skive off nappies. Talk to him when he gets back, tell him to pull his weight a bit more.'

I laugh, then feel a sob in my throat. 'I need to stop looking at Instagram. Those mums make it look so easy.'

'Oh, don't pay any attention to them! Anyone who makes it look easy is either lying, or they've got nannies or they're all off their heads on drugs! Oh love, I wish I could come over there and give you a hug but Bill's playing badminton tonight and I can't leave the children on their own.'

'It's OK, you've already cheered me up. I'm feeling a lot better.'

'That's good. Where are the children now?'

'In bed. Hope shouldn't be due a feed for another couple of hours.'

'So do something nice. Just for you.'

'Like what?'

'I don't know. Light a candle and have a bath? Got any bath salts?'

'That sounds good. I think I might have won some on the tombola at the summer fair.'

'Yeah, I think you did! You won a shedload of stuff, didn't you?'

'I know! I came home with a whole bag of other people's discarded tat! Which I promptly dumped in the cupboard under the stairs.'

'Well, go find the bath salts and enjoy some pampering. And remember, I'm always here at the end of the phone, whenever you need me.'

'Thanks, Charlotte. I love you.'

'I love you too.'

I find the bag in the cupboard under the stairs and root through it. There's a bottle of bath salts, a bottle of wine, jigsaw puzzles, handkerchiefs, an air fryer cookbook and a pack of cards. I take the bottles through to the kitchen and sit down at the table. I haven't drunk wine for years, thanks to the constant round of pregnancies and breastfeeding. Not since I was young and reckless and couldn't handle it. But I'm middle-aged now, and responsible – probably too responsible. It might be good for me to unwind a little. I pick up the bath salts. I should turn the bathroom into a little spa. I could lie back, close my eyes, drift away . . . Why hasn't he called me back? I pick up the phone.

'Rowan, it's me. Again. Are you getting these messages? Are you listening to them? When are you coming home?'

I place the phone back down on the table, in between the two bottles. It's white wine. Always my favourite. Hasn't been chilled, but . . .

I pick up the phone again.

'Jade, it's Beth. I really need to speak to you. I'm wearing that pendant you gave me, you know, the one that's good for anxiety. But I've been wearing it for months and I'm still anxious. Please give me a call.'

Phone back on the table and I pick up a bottle. Charlotte's right. This is my time to do something nice. Something for me. I glance at the poster on the wall. Turn that frown upside down. Yeah, I think I will. I open the bottle and pour out a large glass of wine.

13

Hungover walks are the best kind of walks, managing as they do to loosen the chokehold of shame. Maybe it's because anxiety has somewhere to go when we walk. It can disappear into the ground, fly up into the trees – never forever but at least for a while. At least until the walking stops and the drinking starts. And it's more than that, more than just a buffer zone carving up slices of time into separate servings of stupor, hungover walks give me the chance to pretend. To be someone else. To pretend to belong. I'm just another dog walker out here in the fields. The trees don't care that I drank two bottles of wine on my own yesterday, or judge me for passing out on my bathroom floor.

'Excuse me!'

The shock makes my bubbling anxiety exit my body via a small scream. Where did *she* come from?

'I'm sorry,' says the woman. 'I didn't mean to make you

jump.' She's wearing a long, padded jacket zipped up to her chin, and looks very angry. 'It's just your dog. Can you call him off?'

'Wilfred!' I call, and he bounds towards me. Happiness encased in forty kilos of tail-wagging joy. 'I'm sorry,' I say, 'was he doing something wrong?'

'Yes, you could say that,' she replies. 'He was over there,' she says, pointing back down the path, 'eating fox poo.'

'Ah, that's his favourite,' I say with a smile. 'He's a Labrador, he'll eat anything.'

'But he was encouraging my dog to do the same,' she says, now pointing at the small dog by her side. It looks like one of those cross-breeds you see everywhere. A Cavapoo, maybe? Or a Cockapoo. A Peekaboo? Didgeridoo, Deliveroo – one of those.

'I was calling out to you,' she's saying, now pointing at me, 'but you were completely oblivious. You really should pay more attention to what your dog is doing.'

'OK,' I say, turning away.

'No, it's not OK, actually,' she says, catching up with me and pointing that finger again. 'I've seen you here before, and you never seem to pay any attention to what's going on. I even cleaned up after your dog once and you didn't even notice. I seriously contemplated presenting you with the bag of mess.'

'Well, why didn't you?' I ask, turning back, her eyes inches from mine. 'You're obviously well-practised at giving people shit.'

'There's no need to be rude,' she says, flinching. Did I brush my teeth before I left the house?

'No, *you're* being rude!' I say, feeling hot, my face reddening.

'I'm just asking you to pay more attention to your dog, that's all. Especially as he's such a . . .'

'Such a what?' I ask, moving my face closer; who cares about the stench of my breath? 'That dog,' I add, turning towards Wilfred, who looks like he's smiling, 'he's . . .' Why do I sound like I'm crying? 'He's the best bloody dog in the world.'

'Look, I didn't mean to upset you.'

'You haven't upset me,' I say, wiping the sleeve of my coat across my face.

'I just think you should keep a closer eye on him, especially as he . . .'

'What?'

'Seems to be a bad influence.'

'What do you mean?'

'Well, my dog never ate fox poo until he saw your dog do it.'

'You think my dog told your dog to eat it?'

'Obviously not, but if your dog is running wild, unsupervised—'

'He's not running wild,' I say, walking towards Wilfred. 'He's just a dog. Being a dog.' What's wrong with this lead? Why can't I attach it to his collar? 'That's what dogs do. They eat fox poo. Get over it.' I think it's my hands, they're shaking too much. 'Come on, Wilfred,' I say, giving up on the lead. 'Let's go.' I leave the path behind, take a shortcut across the field when I hear her voice again.

'Alkie.'

'What did you say?' She's still on the path, looking back towards the trees. I don't even think she heard me.

'Albie,' she calls out to her dog, who appears and hurries towards her side. 'Good boy, Albie. Good boy.' She pats the top of Albie's head and they head along the path in the opposite direction.

I'm halfway across the field when I identify a strange sound. It takes me a while to retrieve my ringing phone from my pocket. Takes me even longer to decipher the name on the display.

'Hello,' I say, placing the phone to my ear. Shaky voice. Shaky hands. Shaky mind.

'Hi Beth.'

'Hi Emily.'

'Just thought I'd give you a call as I haven't heard.'

'About what?'

'Seraphina's party. She's invited the whole class and you haven't RSVPed yet. I need to know whether Freddie's coming.'

'Oh, right,' I say. 'I don't remember seeing the invitation.'

'Seraphina took them into school with her on Friday. She said she gave one to every child in the class.'

'Yesterday? And you're already chasing up replies?'

'Most people reply straightaway, Beth. As soon as they see the invite.'

'But I haven't seen the invite, Rowan picked up the boys from school yesterday. They're all staying with him this weekend.'

'Oh, I didn't realise,' she says. 'I'm sorry.'

'When is it?'

'What?'

'The party?'

'Two weeks' time, last Saturday of the month,' she says. 'Three o'clock.'

'I'm sure that will be fine,' I say, 'but I'll have to check the calendar when I get home. I'm out with Wilfred at the moment.'

'Who?'

'My dog.'

'Of course,' she says and now we both become silent, and I don't think it's just my hangover. I think this conversation is genuinely weird. 'Right,' I say, 'so, I'll check the calendar when I get home . . .'

'That would be great, thanks, Beth,' she says. 'I'd like to get an idea of numbers today so I can confirm the entertainer. Mr Combustible's had a last-minute cancellation, you see, so I can get him at short notice. Normally he's booked up for almost a year. But I'm not going to pay his prices unless I've got the whole class coming. Otherwise I'll book Mr Swirly, the magical balloon animal man.' Silence again and this time I know it's not just my hangover. Sometimes there are simply no words. 'I guess he's good company,' she says eventually.

'Who? Mr Swirly?'

'No,' she says. 'Your dog. I guess it's nice having him around when, you know, the children aren't with you.'

'Yeah,' I say, smiling at Wilfred. 'He's the best.' Silence extends into awkwardness. I'm not sure whether she's still there.

'It must be so tough for you.' Her voice, when it arrives,

is quiet. 'Knowing your children are with Jade. I can't imagine what that's like.'

'It's fine,' I say.

'If you ever want to talk about it . . .'

'It's fine,' I say again. 'I'm fine.'

'But you and Jade used to be such good friends—'

'All that matters is the kids.' Wilfred has stopped and is sniffing something in the long grass. 'It's important they spend time with their dad. And I don't mind being on my own.'

'Of course, but if you ever feel like . . . I don't know . . . you can't be bothered to cook a meal for one, you're welcome round ours for something to eat. You know me, the more the merrier.'

'That's very kind of you,' I say. 'And ditto.'

'Sorry?'

'If you're ever having a difficult moment and the magical orchard doesn't appeal, you can always come to my house.'

'Right, but if you ever feel like you're not coping . . .'

'I *am* coping, Emily. In fact, I've been meaning to invite you all over to my place for a while.'

'Really?'

'Yeah,' I say, 'it's been ages since I had everyone over for a playdate. How about next Friday after school?'

'Are you sure it won't be too much trouble?'

'Not at all. I'll mention it to the others on Monday at Tea and Tots.'

'Oh, I heard you were only going there on Tuesdays. '

'Listen, Emily,' I say, balancing the phone under my chin as I grab hold of Wilfred's collar and attach the lead.

'I'm not going to invite her to my house, and we'll never be friends again, but I can't hide from Jade forever. Our kids go to the same school. Besides, it's good for Hope to socialise with children her own age.'

And I'd quite like another opportunity to talk to the women who used to be my friends. They were all at Emily's Halloween party, only five minutes down the road from where Charlotte was killed. Maybe they know something without knowing they know something.

'Of course it is,' she says, 'I completely agree. Thanks for the invitation.' There's a pause. 'I hope this doesn't sound preachy but, like you say, you haven't hosted a playdate for a long time, so may not be up to date with everyone's dietary requirements. I wouldn't serve any snacks containing gluten, dairy or nuts, just in case. Oh, I'm so sorry – I've got another call coming through, it might be an RSVP. I'll see you on Monday, have a good weekend.'

I place the phone in my pocket and file the conversation away. Shove it into one of the cluttered piles of information at the back of my mind, to be hunted for and retrieved at some other date. When I'm cleaning my house before Friday, perhaps. Or searching the supermarket for nut-free, gluten-free, dairy-free snacks. But for now, I can embrace the nothingness surrounding the clutter. The emptiness waiting for me at home, and enough wine to fill the hours.

'Come on, Wilfred,' I say, breaking into a jog. 'Let's go home.'

14

Almost blue, nearly green – his eyes and the waves of the ocean. 'Don't be frightened, Beth,' he says. 'There's nothing to worry about. I'm here. Trust me, Beth. You do trust me, don't you? Beth? Beth?'

'Sorry, what?'

'Are you OK?' Rowan asks. He's standing on my doorstep, staring.

'Yes,' I reply. 'You know me, Rowan – not great at Monday mornings. I'm just a bit tired, that's all. I never seem to sleep very well when the children aren't here.'

'Well, this little one is back now,' he says, passing Hope to me, 'and the boys will be home from school before you know it.' I kiss the top of my daughter's head and give her a cuddle as she babbles at me delightedly. She's wearing her Peppa Pig leggings with an orange unicorn top I don't recognise. I'd never pair Peppa with an orange unicorn and why is she wearing that stupid ribbon in her hair? Who got her dressed this morning? She looks ridiculous.

'She was great this weekend,' he says. 'They all were. Jack's a brilliant goalkeeper, I think he's got real talent, and how funny is Freddie? The sweetest kid – always making us smile.' He tickles our daughter under her chin. 'And this one was pushing a walker around nonstop. Can you believe it? Oh, and we were doing penalty shoot-outs in the garden on Saturday afternoon, and it was getting really tense, and all of a sudden, this cheeky monkey pulls down her nappy and does a poo right on the penalty spot! It was so funny!'

He's wearing those trousers I found for him online. The ones with all the pockets that I told him would be good for work. I did a lot of research about plumbers' trousers and those ones got the best reviews. Hard-wearing, with lots of space for tools and all the other things he might need.

'I wasn't sure whether you still had that toddler walker the boys used,' he's saying now, still smiling widely, 'so I brought ours.' *Ours?* 'Hope liked using it so much, and Jade thought it would help to be able to use it during the week.' Why is he mentioning Jade? And why did he use the word, 'ours'? Is this his way of letting me know they're getting even more serious? Leaving me even further behind.

'Right.' If they get married, will my boys be their page boys? And what about Hope, will she be a bridesmaid? Wearing another ridiculous ribbon in her hair?

'So, you're OK with me leaving the walker here, you got the space?' he asks.

'Of course.'

'Great.' He smiles. Almost blue, nearly green – suffocating

in its sudden intensity before disappearing, in a literal blink of the eye. He goes to the car and returns carrying rucksacks and a walker emblazoned with an orange unicorn.

'Here's all their weekend stuff,' he says, placing everything at my feet. 'All their clothes have been washed.'

'What's with the orange unicorns?' I say, and he looks confused. I shouldn't have said it out loud.

'What?'

'The obsession with orange unicorns,' I say, attempting a smile that I know has no chance of reaching my eyes. 'What's that about?'

'I don't understand what you mean.'

'The walker,' I say, tapping it with my foot. 'And this top Hope's wearing. Did Jade buy it?'

'I'm not sure, I guess so,' he says. 'Goodbye beautiful,' he adds, leaning towards Hope and kissing her forehead. 'Daddy will see you again soon.'

'Seriously, why is Jade obsessed with orange unicorns?' I ask, following him to his car. 'Why does she like them so much? Is it because they're not real? A bit like her.'

Quiet and calm, Beth. You should be quiet and calm.

'Because she isn't real, you know – your precious girlfriend. She isn't a real person. Not like me. I may not be perfect, but at least I'm real.' He's at the car, tapping at all those useful pockets, looking for his car keys. 'What you see is what you get with me.'

'Beth, listen—'

'No, you listen. Who found you those trousers? Was it her?' He's staring at me. 'No, it was me, wasn't it? I'm the one who went online and did all the research and found you those trousers, because I'm real. I live in the real world. Everything I do is real.'

'What the hell are you talking about? Why are you talking about my trousers?'

'This isn't about your trousers, Rowan! It's about Jade and her yoga and crystals and positive affirmations on Instagram, and me telling you that it's all bollocks. All of it. She may pretend to be kind and caring, but she isn't. She wasn't a good friend to me, and she isn't a good person, Rowan. Never has been, never will be. And I'm not sure she's the kind of person I want around my children.'

'And what about the kind of person you are?' he snarls.

'What do you mean?'

'What did you do this weekend, Beth?'

'It's none of your business what I do. I can do whatever I like.'

'In your own time, yes. But when you're looking after our children, you better not be . . .'

'What?'

'Are you drinking again, Beth?'

'What?'

'You don't seem right, and . . .'

'What?'

'It's just something that Jack said. Made me think. You know you shouldn't be drinking.'

'What did Jack say?'

He marches back towards the house. Towards the wheelie bins. He opens them up and starts rummaging inside.

'What are you looking for?' As if I'm going to be stupid enough to put empty bottles in there. 'What did Jack say?'

'Don't you dare drag him into this!' he snaps, making Hope jump. And as he walks towards us, she starts to cry. 'I'm sorry, Hope,' he says, reaching out towards her. 'Daddy shouldn't have raised his voice, I'm sorry, my darling little girl. Look, Beth,' he says, flicking his eyes towards mine. 'Please don't say anything to Jack about this. He's already going through so much, what with us splitting up and everything. We don't want to do anything to make him feel even worse.'

'I never do anything to make him feel worse,' I say, my eyes filling with tears. 'This situation is because of you and Jade, Rowan. Nothing to do with me.' He turns and moves towards his car again, almost jogging. 'And you don't need to tell me Jack's a great goalkeeper,' I say, trying to keep up with him, 'and Freddie's the sweetest kid alive and Hope is amazing, because I already know.' We've arrived at the car and tears are spilling down my face. 'Don't waste your time worrying about how I am with the children, Rowan,' I sniff, as he fumbles with the keys. 'Worry about your weird girlfriend. Her phoniness and freaky obsession with unicorns.'

'She isn't phoney, or obsessed with unicorns!' he hisses, shutting the car door behind him. Then he accelerates fast and disappears down the road.

An hour later, I'm sitting in Tea and Tots looking at Jade. Her mouth is smiling but her eyes are cold. And she's dressed as a unicorn.

15

'You may recall that last week we were all dressed as fairies.' Phoney smile. Phoney voice. 'This week, we're mythical creatures.'

I thought fairies *were* mythical creatures but what do I know?

'I must say, Jade, I think it's so commendable, how you make toddler group such an immersive experience for the children,' says Fara, smiling. She's sitting up against a beanbag, draped in a purple pashmina, and with such impeccable posture, she looks serene. All hail Fara, the Queen of Multitasking. Breastfeeding a baby, French plaiting a small child's hair, littering the conversation with words of the day while effortlessly blowing smoke up Jade's arse.

'I mean, look at them,' she says, surveying the kingdom of tiny humans. The shrieking turf wars at the painting table and violent rages in the ball pit. 'They all look so ebullient, don't they?' Yes. If ebullient is another word for deranged hooliganism.

'Thanks, Fara,' says Jade, looking pleased. 'I always think there's a lot we can learn from young children. When you think about it, they're very good at being in the moment and staying in the moment, aren't they? Whereas we're always rehashing the past,' she says, hand moving towards that amethyst bracelet. 'Or projecting our minds into the future.'

'I've never thought about it like that before,' says Danielle, her forehead scrunched in confusion. She's sitting on the floor next to Fara against a beanbag she seems reluctant to lean into. 'And it's so true, isn't it?' she says, hovering somewhere between sitting bolt upright and relaxing back – even her posture looks confused. 'All my kids ever seem to care about is what they're doing right now. They never seem to spend any time thinking about tomorrow, or yesterday, for that matter. Probably explains why they can never remember what they've just done or where they've put anything. I seem to spend half my life asking, "Where's your book bag? Where's your lunchbox? Where did you put it? When was the last time you saw it?"'

'Me too,' smiles Jade. 'But I don't think they do it on purpose, I think children genuinely find it difficult remembering the last time they did anything because, like you say, they're so busy living in the moment. Whereas we spend so little time there, in the present moment I mean, maybe that's why we're much better at remembering the last time.'

'I don't know about that,' says Fara with a smile. 'I don't

think I can remember the last time I had a full night's sleep!'

'Fair enough,' laughs Jade, loudly. Too loudly and for too long. Fara isn't funny enough to warrant a laugh of that volume or length. I look around the group in Story Time Corner. Fara, Jade, Emily and Danielle. It occurs to me that Emily and Danielle don't have kids young enough to come to Tea and Tots any more, and yet they're here every week. Are they that desperate for adult company? But then I remember how much I used to enjoy these mornings, before Jade took Rowan and my friends seemed to drift away. They didn't officially choose her over me, but then they didn't push her out either. So, I pushed myself out, and without Charlotte there was no one to pull me back in.

Ana is sitting on the floor opposite me, wearing blue jeans and a black jumper, and she looks miserable and bored, which is good. Shows she's real. Just like me.

'I have to say, Fara,' Jade adds, smiling. 'If you are sleep deprived, you're doing a very good job of hiding it.' The sycophancy between these two is becoming nauseating. 'You always look so elegant. I don't know how you do it.'

'You're very kind,' says Fara, returning the smile, 'but believe me, the sleep deprivation is playing havoc with my memory, leaving me in an almost constant state of befuddlement. I found myself standing in the fishmonger's yesterday and for the life of me I couldn't remember what I'd walked in for.'

Fish?

'Oh, Fara,' says Jade, phoney concern obliterating even

the memory of that phoney laugh. 'You've just given birth, you're not sleeping, and you've got six children. Six!' she exclaims, counting out the number on her fingers. How befuddled does she think Fara is?

'I know a memory game,' I say, suddenly grateful for Jade's phoniness and Fara's sleep deprivation. 'Do you want to try it?' I ask Fara.

'Sure,' she smiles.

'It's quite simple,' I say. 'We just go around and each answer the same question about something that happened in the past. Don't think too much about it, just allow your brain to answer for you. Ana, shall I start with you? When was . . . oh, I don't know. When was the last time you went to the dentist?'

'Er,' says Ana, twirling one of her beautiful long curls around her finger and staring up at the ceiling. 'I know it was springtime. May? I think it was May.'

'Me too!' smiles Jade. 'How funny.'

'You're not going to believe this, guys,' says Emily, 'but same here!'

'Do you know something?' says Fara, 'maybe my memory isn't as deficient as I feared because I can clearly remember the last time I went to the dentist and guess what? It was in May!'

Jade claps her hands. 'That's brilliant, what a coincidence. How about you, Danielle?'

'Well, it depends,' she says, borrowing a bit of Fara's befuddlement. 'Does it have to be the last time I saw the dentist, or does the hygienist count?'

'Either or,' I reply. 'You decide.'

'In that case, the last time I went to the dentist was . . . May!' Such a weird, confused-looking smile. Now they're all staring at me.

'Yeah, me too!' Thinking about it, I'm pretty sure we all go to the same dentist. I remember Charlotte sending round a WhatsApp saying that it was taking NHS patients and had a shorter waiting list, so we all signed up. Ever-efficient Charlotte. That's probably why we all have our yearly check-ups at around the same time.

I'm about to point this out when the woman who was pretending to be a fairy last week appears dressed as a mermaid. She shoots me a dirty look as she shuffles towards Jade. The skirt she's wearing is so long and tight she can hardly move. I don't care how immersive the experience is for children, I don't think a mermaid's tail can ever be considered appropriate work attire.

She leans over and starts talking quietly to Jade, gesturing towards a disturbance in the ball pit. There are raised voices and it looks like a couple of tantrums – a few of the children are looking slightly peeved too. It's a tinderbox, that ball pit, teeming with terrible twos, tattered nerves and rising tension. Thank God there's a unicorn to sort it all out.

'I'd better go smooth things over,' Jade says, standing up. 'But carry on without me.' She places her hand on Fara's shoulder. 'I'm sure you'll soon realise that you've got absolutely nothing to worry about.'

'Ooh, can I go next?' asks Emily as Jade leaves, followed by a lumbering mermaid. 'I've got a great memory question, just a bit of fun but I'd better ask it quietly,' she whispers, leaning in towards us, before glancing around the room at the tiny children playing nearby. 'Don't want our words ending up inside the wrong little ears. So,' she smiles, 'can you remember,' still whispering, 'the last time . . .' she's giggling now, 'you had sex? I'll go first, just to break the ice. The last time I had sex was this morning.' More giggling. 'Nigel woke up in a very adventurous mood!'

If the vomit I taste becomes projectile, there may be something far worse than words ending up inside those wrong little ears.

'Ana?' says Emily, still giggling. 'How about you?'

Ana thinks about it for a moment. 'A couple of days ago,' she replies.

'Nice,' says Emily. Bit creepy. 'Fara, how about you?'

'Oh, well it must have been when this one was overdue,' she says, gently patting her baby's back. 'We were at it like rabbits then. Anything to avoid the dreaded induction!'

'Of course,' smiles Emily. 'Danielle?'

'Well, it depends,' she says, looking confused. 'Do you mean oral or full intercourse? Oh no, don't worry,' she adds before Emily has a chance to answer. 'I've just realised the answer's the same. Last Saturday.'

'Good for you, Danielle,' laughs Emily. 'Beth? How about you?' She looks suddenly mortified, and her eyes flick to the ball pit where Jade is pacifying an irate parent. 'Sorry, I didn't think—'

'Don't worry. A long time ago. Right, moving on to the next question, when was the last time—'

'Beth, you can't ask another one,' says Emily.

'Why not?'

'Because you asked about the dentist.'

'My game, my rules,' I say with a smile. 'And this is a great question. Fara, do you want to answer first? When was the last time you saw Charlotte alive?'

16

'Oh, come on, Beth,' Emily says, tapping her manicured nails against the side of her mug. 'You can't ask that.'

'Why not?'

'Because it's morbid. Plus Ana didn't know Charlotte so she can't answer.'

'I don't mind,' says Ana, looking bored.

'Great!' I say, turning back to Fara.

She stares at me for a moment, moving her sleeping baby from her shoulder, before cradling him gently in her arms. 'It was that morning,' she says, her words delivered neatly, 'on the day she died. Halloween was a Saturday last year, wasn't it? And I'd taken the children to carve pumpkins in the community centre. You were there too, weren't you, Danielle?'

'Yes,' she replies, nibbling at her fingernail. 'And it was absolute chaos. All those children and pumpkins, why didn't they have a proper queuing system? I couldn't believe how disorganised it was. Far too crowded and that's why we didn't notice at first, did we?'

'What?' I ask.

Danielle glances towards Fara and that confusion on her face flickers. Like she knows how to answer my question, but she's not sure whether she should.

'You didn't notice what?' I ask again.

'Tayo,' says Fara, smiling down at her sleeping baby. 'It was so busy in there we didn't see what he was up to,' she adds, raising her eyes to meet mine, 'and you know what he can be like.'

Yes, we do. We all know what Tayo can be like. Out of Fara's many children, he's the annoying one. The one she never shouts at because Fara never shouts. Even when she probably should.

'Who's Tayo?'

'Oh, sorry, Ana,' smiles Fara. 'You won't have met Tayo yet, will you? He's my eight-year-old son. He's rather . . .'

Annoying? Disruptive? Attention-seeking? Rowdy?

'Sorry,' Fara says again, closing her eyes. 'It's difficult to think of the most felicitous word. Tayo can be . . .'

Boisterous? Uncontrollable? Wild? Demanding?

'Intransigent,' she says, opening her eyes. 'Tayo can be rather intransigent at times.'

'I'm sorry,' says Ana. 'I haven't heard this English word before. Intransigent, what does it mean?'

'Tenacious,' Fara says, after a moment of consideration. Mrs Word of the Day, scaling new heights. 'Wilful. He's a bit of a character, my Tayo. Indefatigable in his endeavours, but not very patient,' she adds with a smile.

'Well, to be fair to him, I think everyone was impatient that day,' says Danielle. 'I mean, they only wanted to carve pumpkins, didn't they? But with no proper queuing system it was taking ages and with the pushing in and children crying, it was—'

'Pandemonium,' agrees Fara. 'And I'm not making excuses but that's why I didn't notice at first that . . .'

'What?'

'That Tayo was missing,' she says, lowering her head. 'It still makes me nauseous,' she adds. 'When I think about what could have happened. One minute he was standing beside me, the next moment, he was gone. Once I realised he wasn't in the community centre any more, I left the others with Danielle and ran outside. You know how busy that road can be, I kept thinking he could be hit by a car. Or abducted.' She has her hand on her chest, the tips of her fingers pressing down hard. 'I knew he'd probably head for the park – you know, the one with the big, curly slide – so I started sprinting in that direction and that's when I saw Charlotte. She was running towards me and had Tayo with her, they were holding hands.' Fara's fingers curl inwards as her face relaxes into a smile. 'Charlotte said she'd seen him, on his own, racing towards the park, and I was so happy he was safe that I grabbed her and kissed her!'

'What a relief!' says Ana. 'And how was Tayo? Was he OK?'

'Absolutely fine,' says Fara, her smile reaching her eyes. 'Totally oblivious to all the worry he'd caused, all he cared about was getting to the park! I remember Charlotte laughing, saying she wished she had half his energy. How she was in the middle of a ten-mile run and still had four miles to go. It was just a brief chat and then she ran off in the other direction.' Fara lowers her face towards her baby and gently brushes her lips against his forehead, closing her eyes. 'I never saw her again.'

'How is Tayo?' asks Emily, after a moment of silence.

'Great,' smiles Fara, looking back up. 'He's so happy. He absolutely loves it there.'

'Where?' I ask.

'St Dunstan's.'

'What's that?'

'Tayo's new school,' Fara replies. 'Out towards Reading.'

'Reading? How long does it take you to drive there and back each day?'

'Oh, he boards during the week.'

'He's at boarding school?' I say, biting my lip. Don't ask the next question. I shouldn't ask the next question. 'Are any of your other children there?' I ask the question.

'No,' she says. 'Just Tayo, and honestly he couldn't be happier. It's such a great place with beautiful grounds, so much space for him to run. And there's a woodland with the most magnificent trees, plenty of nooks and crannies for him to explore. And obviously it's all gated,' she adds, 'so completely secure.' She's smiling, but the silence feels awkward. I don't care how many words of the day she throws at this conversation; we all know she's talking about her son like he's a spaniel. I wonder how Tayo feels about it. Carted off to boarding school while his siblings stay at home. His baby brother covered in gentle kisses as Tayo runs through those beautiful grounds.

'Is it my turn?' asks Danielle, peering at me through glasses designed entirely out of a furrowed brow. 'Do you want to know the last time I saw Charlotte?'

'Yeah, go on,' I reply.

'Well, it wasn't the day Fara's talking about, because I was inside the community centre, keeping an eye on the other children. It was so chaotic; I'll never understand why they had so many pumpkins but no proper queuing system. It could have been—'

'So, when *was* the last time you saw her?' I ask.

'I think it was the day before,' she says, uncertainly. 'In the playground, collecting the children from school. They all tend to blend into one another, don't they? The school runs, I mean, but I can remember that afternoon because it was a Friday, the day before Halloween, and all the children were in costume. They'd had a Halloween party that afternoon, so they were even more excited than usual. That's probably why the playground was so busy, with everyone hanging around so the children could run off some energy before going home. Anyway, I remember seeing Charlotte over by the climbing wall. A child had just fallen, I think, right from the top, and no doubt she'd rushed over there to save the day. I'm going to be honest,' she adds, looking a little embarrassed, which doesn't surprise me. What's with all the snide comments about Charlotte? 'We weren't very friendly. I know she—'

'Saved your life?'

'Well, yes, but what I was going to say is that I know you two were close, Beth, and all of us,' she says, glancing at the others, 'we were all in the same friendship group but . . .'

Friendship group? How old is she? '... Personally, I always found Charlotte rather stand-offish. Especially after what happened at the hospital when she—'

'Saved your life?'

'I *know* she saved my life,' says Danielle. 'And I was really grateful, of course I was. I'm not joking, I must have thanked her a thousand times. I thought it might bring us closer. Make us better friends. But, if anything, Charlotte seemed irritated with me after it happened. Almost as though I'd done something wrong, which hardly seemed fair. I mean, it wasn't my fault I went into anaphylactic shock while she was on duty. It's not like I planned it.'

'Exactly,' says Emily. 'And I never understood why you felt the need to keep thanking her anyway, Danielle. Charlotte was only doing her job, wasn't she? Hardly makes her a superhero.'

'When was the last time *you* saw her?' I ask, turning towards Emily.

'I can't remember exactly,' she says. 'I thought she'd be at my Halloween party, but she didn't turn up. Bill and the girls were there, I remember him making some excuse about why Charlotte couldn't make it ...'

'Bill?' Romanian accent.

'Charlotte's husband,' Emily says, turning to Ana. 'The guy you bought your house from. Did you never meet him?' Ana shakes her head. 'Right, well I suppose that makes sense,' says Emily, running a manicured hand down the length of her ponytail – casual yet freakishly sleek. 'You probably only dealt with the agents, didn't you? The house was empty and on the market for a few months before you bought it.'

'Such a beautiful house,' smiles Fara.

'Yes, a perfect family home,' says Emily. 'I'm sure you'll be very happy there,' she says to Ana. 'I know Charlotte and Bill were.'

Were they? They always *seemed* happy.

'They loved that house but after she died, I think it all got too much for Bill. Too many memories, I guess. And all he cared about was doing what was best for the children. Such a caring man.'

How can we ever know how happy people truly are?

'He felt they all needed a fresh start, so, they moved out towards Oxford. I think Bill wanted to be closer to his parents, they help a lot with the children. Anyway,' Emily says, 'Nigel and I are still in touch with Bill, he's a lovely guy and a great dad. Noah is still good friends with Bill's daughter Poppy, and Bill's going to bring her to Seraphina's birthday party in a couple of weeks, so you'll meet him then.'

When a woman dies in suspicious circumstances, it's almost always the husband, isn't it?

'Which reminds me,' Emily's staring at me, 'Beth, you're the only person who hasn't RSVPed yet. Can Freddie make it or not? If I'm going to book Mr Combustible, the deadline is today.'

'Yeah, Freddie will be there,' I say, as she retrieves a notebook from her handbag and adds my son's name to the bottom of a remarkably long list. 'Can you remember what he said?'

'Who?' Emily asks, returning the notebook to her bag. 'Mr Combustible?'

'No,' I reply. 'Bill. You said Bill made some excuse for why Charlotte wasn't at your party. Can you remember what?'

'Not really,' she replies, those eyes moving unblinking towards the ceiling. 'Something about her being busy, I think, but it was obviously just an excuse. And I don't like to speak ill of the dead,' her eyes flick back to mine, 'but I thought it incredibly rude. Even Bill seemed embarrassed.'

'Was he at the party the whole night?' I ask.

'Oh yes,' Emily replies. 'Such a hands-on dad, he threw himself into all of the Halloween games, even organised the Skeleton Scavenger Hunt. I think he felt bad about Charlotte not being there, especially when he saw all the effort I'd gone to. It took me days to decorate the house and front garden. Do you remember the life-sized horror figures I hired to stand along the driveway?' she asks, looking from Danielle to Fara. 'I got those from a company that supplies film sets.'

'They were brilliant, but it was a shame about the werewolf, wasn't it?' says Danielle. 'It kept toppling over.'

'Yes, I got money back for that,' says Emily, 'but the others stood up fine. There was a zombie, a devil, a skeleton and a witch, plus all those cauldrons filled with dry ice – they looked absolutely spectacular, didn't they? Everyone said so. And it wasn't just the money, I put so much time into that party and all people had to do was put on a costume and turn up, but Charlotte? She couldn't even be bothered to do that.'

'She didn't like Halloween,' Fara, Danielle and I say at the same time and now there's a moment of silence as we look at each other.

'Bit strange, isn't it?' I say. 'How we all know that, but does anyone know the reason why? I've racked my brain thinking about this and I can't remember Charlotte ever telling me. I just knew she didn't like Halloween and never celebrated it.'

'Yes, to be honest, it's not my favourite day of the year,' says Danielle with a shiver. 'Always reminds me of my near-death experience. You see, it was Halloween,' she adds, turning to Ana, 'that's when I had my anaphylactic shock and nearly died.'

'But that was years ago, Danielle,' I say, not hiding my irritation.

'It may have been six years ago, but I nearly died!' she says again. 'Something like that tends to stay with you.' She turns to Ana. 'That Halloween was a complete disaster. My son tripped over a pumpkin and I thought he'd broken his wrist. I took him to A&E and that's when it happened. My throat started closing up and I couldn't speak, couldn't breathe and then I collapsed, although I can't remember that part. If I hadn't been in the hospital I dread to think—'

'OK,' I say, 'so, you're not keen on Halloween, but you still carve pumpkins with your kids and take them to parties. Charlotte didn't celebrate it at all.'

'So what?' says Emily, looking bored. 'I bet loads of people don't bother with it.'

'But this is Charlotte we're talking about,' I say, leaning forward. 'The woman who celebrated everything. Don't you remember her dressing up as the Easter bunny every year to hide eggs around the school field? And what about the firework displays she put on every November? Then there were the summer barbecues, Valentine's Day dances and what about her Christmas cards? Charlotte and her children made them from scratch, with paint and glitter and pipe cleaners and glue guns! She let her children loose with glue guns, for God's sake. This was a woman who never shied away from any celebration, yet she hated Halloween. Really hated it. And then . . .'

'What?' asks Danielle, looking confused.

'She died. On Halloween. The one day she hated more than any other. Doesn't that strike you as odd?'

'Not really,' says Emily. 'I mean it was very sad, obviously, but . . .'

'Maybe she had a premonition,' I interrupt. 'Maybe she always knew she was going to die on Halloween. Maybe that's why she hated it so much.'

'Oh, come on, Beth,' says Emily. 'I know Charlotte was very accomplished, but she wasn't a fortune teller. How could she have possibly known?'

'I don't know. I just wish I knew why she hated Halloween so much. There must have been a reason. Are you sure she didn't mention it to anyone?'

'She never said anything to me,' says Fara, moving her waking baby towards her breast. 'It was more the impression she gave, that day outside the community centre. Tayo was shouting, wriggling to get away from me, so desperate to go to the park. And I remember trying to reason with him, telling him we were going to go back into the community centre and carve a pumpkin. I told Charlotte there was a plethora of pumpkins and offered to drop a couple round to her house later. I wanted to thank her for finding Tayo. But she wrinkled her nose a little at my suggestion, saying Bill and the girls would be going out later but she wouldn't be doing anything special.'

'See, I knew she never had any intention of coming to my party,' says Emily, manicured nails tapping at the side of the mug she's holding.

'I don't know anything about that,' says Fara. 'I just know she didn't want pumpkins.' Her baby starts crying and she rocks him gently, lavishing him with soothing little kisses before settling him back at her breast. 'She said she didn't want trick or treaters coming to the door.'

'Ah, yes. The unwritten rule of Halloween,' says Danielle. 'No pumpkins on the doorstep, no treats. No wonder she sounded angry.'

'Who?'

'Charlotte.'

'When?'

'When she spoke to the trick or treaters.'

'What trick or treaters?'

'The ones that came to her door.'

'How do you know trick or treaters came to her door?'

'Because I heard them, when I was on the phone to her,' she says, brow furrowed.

'Danielle, what are you talking about?' I ask, leaning even further towards her. 'Why were you on the phone to Charlotte? I thought you weren't friendly.'

'We weren't. But when I got to Emily's that evening and

saw all the work she'd put into the party, I understood why she was so angry at Charlotte for not turning up. I mean, you'd worked for weeks, hadn't you, Emily? And all Charlotte had to do was put on a costume . . .'

'I wasn't angry,' says Emily.

'Well, you had every right to be,' says Danielle. 'I mean, all that effort you went to. The dry ice, the figures, the food – and what about that bar! Honestly,' she says, turning to Ana, 'you should have seen the Shocktails bar Emily had in her kitchen. Plus plenty of wine,' she adds, glancing towards me. 'I think it was probably the best party I've ever been to, I'm not surprised Emily was upset at Charlotte—'

'I wasn't upset.'

'Well,' says Danielle, looking confused. 'Jade was. She was extremely upset.'

'Jade?' my voice is sharp. Fara's baby starts to cry again. 'What's she got to do with anything?'

'Like I said, she was upset,' says Danielle, staring at me. 'You probably didn't notice because you were on the Shocktails for most of the night, and no judgement,' she adds quickly, 'I was just concerned about you, that's all. I think we all were,' she says, glancing from Emily to Fara and back again. 'Do you remember when you nearly fell into the cauldron?' How can I? Memories from that night aren't mine, it's all a fog, thanks to the Shocktails.

'What were you saying about Jade?' I ask, finding my voice.

'Just that she was really upset,' she replies. 'I was outside trying to make the werewolf stand up – someone had just arrived and said it had fallen over – and saw Jade pacing up and down the driveway. I'd never seen her like that before and when I asked her what was wrong, she said she was nervous about seeing Charlotte. They'd had a disagreement, and Jade wanted to clear the air. That's why she was waiting outside, for Charlotte to arrive, and when I told her she wasn't coming, Jade looked really shaken up. I think she'd been geeing herself up to speak to Charlotte and was desperate to sort whatever it was out.'

'Yes, she was in such a state,' agrees Fara, gently running her hand over the back of her baby's head. 'I saw her in your driveway that night too,' she says, turning towards Emily, 'when I had to leave to take Tayo home. It was such a great party,' she adds, 'I think he just got a little overwhelmed. Anyway, Jade was a nervous wreck, pacing up and down; she was so anxious. The cloak thing she was wearing, do you remember? A physical manifestation of the solar plexus chakra – that's what she was dressed as. She told me she was hoping it would give her confidence.'

'I'm sorry,' Ana says. 'A physical manifestation of the . . .? What does that mean?'

'Nobody knows what that means, Ana,' I say. 'Literally nobody.'

'I do,' says Danielle. 'Jade explained it to me. Something to do with courage and the colour yellow, how she hoped that wearing it would give her the strength to speak her truth. And like I said, when she found out Charlotte wasn't coming, that's when she got really upset. I comforted her for a little while but she wouldn't say what she wanted to talk to Charlotte about, and I had to go back inside to tell you about the werewolf.' She turns to

Emily. 'You said you'd try to keep it upright by wedging rocks under its feet, but I told you I'd do it. I mean, you had so many other things to do that night. What with checking everyone was parking properly and organising all the Halloween games, you were rushed off your feet. So, once it all calmed down a little by the Shocktails,' why is she looking at me? 'I went back outside and tried to fix the werewolf again, but it didn't matter how many rocks I used, he just wouldn't stand up. I'm glad you got money back—'

'Danielle,' I interrupt. 'You were telling us why you phoned Charlotte.'

'Yes,' she says, annoyance winning the grapple with confusion. 'I'd given up on the werewolf and I started to feel angry. I mean, why couldn't Charlotte pop into the party for an hour? She only lived five minutes down the lane. I thought maybe if she knew how much effort Emily had gone to and how nervous Jade had been waiting for her to arrive, maybe she'd reconsider and put in an appearance. So I gave her a call.'

'And?'

'And, what?'

'What did Charlotte say to you, on the phone?'

'Not much,' Danielle says, leaning back slightly towards the beanbag before deciding against it and sitting up straight. 'She listened to what I had to say and was, as usual, fairly dismissive. She said she had no intention of coming to the party—'

'I knew it,' says Emily, nodding sadly. 'I knew it was an excuse.'

'Go on,' I say, remaining focused on Danielle. 'What else did she say? What were her exact words?'

'Just that she had no intention of coming to the party,' she says again, with a nervous glance towards Emily. 'And that she didn't want to talk to Jade today, she'd talk to her another time.'

'Anything else?'

'Er.' Danielle scrunches her forehead and closes her eyes. She certainly looks like she's trying to remember. 'Not much, honestly. Just that she didn't want to talk to Jade and wasn't coming to the party because she'd just poured herself a large glass of wine and Leo was already in bed. That's when I heard the trick or treaters knocking at her door. She ignored them at first but when they kept knocking, she said, "I'm sorry, Danielle, I'm going to have to go." That's when I heard her open the door and, to be honest, I thought she was quite rude to them at the time, but I suppose if she didn't have any pumpkins on her doorstep—'

'But how did you know it was trick or treaters?' I ask. 'Did Charlotte tell you? Did you hear them say "Trick or treat"?'

'No. But who else is going to be knocking on the door at Halloween?'

'I don't know,' I say. 'Maybe the person who made her run into the road and leave her kid? Maybe the person who killed her?'

150

17

'Nobody killed Charlotte, Beth,' says Emily. Her alien eyes are icy, unblinking. I shiver. 'She ran out without looking. It was an accident. She was training for a marathon.'

'In the dark? After she'd run ten miles earlier that same day? Fara saw her. And she was drinking wine, Danielle just said so. Her toddler was in the house. Why would she suddenly leave him and go out for a run? It doesn't make sense,' I say, staring at each of them in turn. 'I can't be the only person to think that.'

'No,' mumbles Danielle, looking down at her hands. 'It *was* trick or treaters, I'm sure of it.'

'How?'

'Because Charlotte didn't have any pumpkins on her doorstep.'

'So?'

'So, when she opened the door she asked them, "Why

have you come here?" I heard her clearly before the line went dead. Everyone knows you don't trick or treat a house that isn't decorated.'

'But if they *did* knock on the door, Danielle,' I say, staring at her, 'why would Charlotte ask them why they were there?'

'Because she hadn't put out any pumpkins.'

'But regardless of whether or not there are pumpkins on a doorstep at Halloween, isn't it obvious why trick or treaters come to your door?' I ask. 'Who, in their right mind,' I say, flicking my eyes to Fara and then Emily, 'would see people dressed up in Halloween costumes and ask them why they're there? You either give them a treat, or you don't. That's the deal, isn't it?'

'I'm not sure,' says Fara. 'It's not something I've often contemplated.'

'Me neither,' says Emily. 'But I'm very aware that poor Ana is being completely excluded from this conversation. Tell me, how is Halloween celebrated in Romania?'

They start talking but I zone out. There's no way Charlotte – probably the most intelligent person I've ever known – would ask trick or treaters, 'Why have you come here?' at Halloween. I close my eyes and picture the scene. She hears the knock on the door and opens it. *Why have you come here?* Who would she say that to?

I open my eyes and I have my answer. Over by the ball pit but walking towards us, fiddling with that amethyst bracelet. *Why have you come here?* Charlotte would say that to someone she knew, wouldn't she? Someone she didn't want to speak to.

'Hello again,' Jade says. 'How's the memory game going?' She's looking at each of us, mouth smiling, eyes cold. 'Has anyone remembered anything good?'

A Year Ago

I knock at her door. She doesn't know I'm coming but I'm sure it's OK. I don't need a formal invitation to see Charlotte.

'Beth.' *Her husband, Bill, is staring at me, checking his watch.* 'I didn't know you were coming over.'

'Is Charlotte in?' *I ask, peering past him.* 'I need to speak to her.'

'Yeah, although I think she's a bit busy with the kids.'

I stumble a little as I walk through the front door and glance towards the kitchen doorway where there's music and laughter. Charlotte is holding a laundry basket of washing and dancing with her three children. The music is loud.

'Beth!' *she says, looking in my direction.* 'Did we arrange something?' *She puts the laundry basket on the floor and turns down the radio.*

'I just wondered if I could talk to you?' *They're all looking at me.*

'Of course,' she says. 'It's bedtime anyway, guys,' she smiles at her children.

'One more song, Mummy!' they shout. 'Pleeeease! One more song.'

'In the morning.' She's still smiling. 'Bill, can you get these three into bed, please? I'll be up in a little while to tuck you all in.'

Bill herds the children out of the room. 'Is everything OK?' she asks, turning towards me.

'I don't mind if you turn it back up,' I say, pointing towards the radio. 'I'm in the mood for a dance.'

'You said you wanted to talk?' she says, pulling out a chair at the kitchen table and sitting down.

'Yes, if that's OK? I brought wine,' I say, pulling the bottle from my bag.

'Lovely.' She smiles and gets a corkscrew from a drawer.

'Oh, it's already open,' I say, 'I had a glass already. When I was waiting for the cab.'

'OK.' She places two glasses on the table and fills them. 'Is Rowan at home with the kids?' she asks, walking over to the fridge and placing the bottle of wine inside.

'Of course not,' I laugh, picking up my glass and clinking it against hers. 'Cheers!' I take a gulp. 'He's never at home with the kids.'

'So, who's looking after them?' she asks.

'One of the teenagers that live on our road.' My glass is already half empty. 'They're always available for a bit of babysitting. Grateful for the money, I suppose.'

'And where's Rowan?'

'At work, apparently.'

'You don't believe that?'

'No,' I say, draining my glass. 'I don't. I think he's up to something.'

'Like what?'

'I think he's having an affair.'

'Rowan? But he's crazy about you and the kids—'

'Please, Charlotte, don't be like her.'

'Who?'

'Jade. I tried to talk to her about it earlier. Phoned her up and told her I was worried because he's always working late. She said that it's all in my mind. That I'm looking for problems that don't exist. Where's the wine gone?'

'I put it in the fridge.'

'Why?'

'Because white wine should be served chilled.'

'Well, I need a top-up.'

'OK,' she says, standing up and walking to the fridge.

'I just want someone to be on my side, you know?' I say, as she refills my glass. 'I need someone to believe me. Because things haven't been right between me and Rowan for a long time, but everyone thinks he's the perfect family man.'

'Nobody's perfect, Beth,' she says, sitting back down.

'You are.'

'No, I'm not.'

'Yes, you are. You make Christmas cards from scratch, and you dress up as the Easter bunny and you have firework displays in your garden. You're the perfect mum. I can't compete with that.'

'It's not a competition. Are you OK, Beth? You don't seem yourself.'

'There *is* something wrong.'

'What?'

'I need another glass of wine.'

'The bottle's empty.'

'Are you telling me in your perfect life with your perfect husband—'

'I'm not perfect—'

'. . . in your perfect house, you don't have a single bottle of wine?'

'I think maybe you've had enough.'

'I haven't!'

'Don't shout. You'll wake the children.'

'They won't be asleep already. Oh God, they probably are, aren't they? Your perfect children probably fall asleep at the perfect time on their perfect pillows in your perfect life . . .'

'You have no idea what you're talking about.' She looks angry. 'I'm not perfect, Beth. Far from it.'

'Great,' I say, raising my glass towards her. 'In that case, you'll have no problem in joining me for another glass of wine.'

18

I think it was Danielle who said all the school runs blend into one after a while, and she's right. But it's not just school runs; when I think back over the last four days, I can't isolate any of them in my mind. I know the daylight hours were filled roughly the same way – CBeebies and fish fingers and arguments about brushing teeth – with the evenings filled with wine. Turning that frown upside down and scribbled notes, trying to work out what happened to Charlotte.

It's Friday, four days since Danielle told us someone knocked at Charlotte's door on the night that she died. Four days trying to figure out how I can prove it was Jade. Because if she *did* go to Charlotte's house but didn't tell the police, that's suspicious, isn't it?

I decide I need to talk it through with someone who doesn't have anything to hide.

I arrange to go round to Ana's house at one. It's almost two o'clock when I arrive and as soon as she opens the door, I realise how desperately the words in my mouth need to escape.

'See,' I say, staring at her. 'I knew something was wrong. As soon as I found out her son was in the house with her on the night that she died, I knew something wasn't right. Who leaves a toddler alone to go out for a jog in the dark? Not Charlotte, that's for sure. She loved her children, they made Christmas cards from scratch, have I told you that? And do you know *why* everyone thought she'd gone out for a run? Because she was wearing her running kit. But Charlotte always wore those kinds of clothes, that was her style. And not like Emily and the rest of the clickety-clique Sweaty Betty brigade, standing in the playground with their thigh gaps and yoga mats – have you seen them? Why do they bring their yoga mats to the playground anyway, haven't they got enough to carry? I think if you're the kind of person that takes a yoga mat to the playground just to let the rest of us know you're doing yoga, chances are – you're probably not doing a lot of yoga. But Charlotte, she wasn't like that. She didn't wear sporty clothes just to look the part, she was genuinely into fitness. Yes, she was competitive and wanted to run the marathon as fast as she could to raise money for charity but that doesn't mean she would go jogging in the dark, especially after already running ten miles earlier that day. Doesn't make any sense, does it?'

I can see Ana going a bit glassy-eyed, but I can't stop.

'And there's something else. The couple of weeks before her death, there was a weird atmosphere. We were all friends back then – me, Charlotte, Emily, Danielle, Fara and Jade. But something was off. A sense of foreboding, like something awful was going to happen and then something awful *did* happen. Charlotte died. We know someone was at her door that night, but whoever it was never told the police. Why? And it's not just that. Tobias was with Charlotte when she died and he thought someone else was there, hiding in the darkness, watching. He felt it.'

'Beth, do you want to come in? Take off your coat?' Ana pats Hope's cheek. My daughter has been in my arms the whole time, staring at me. Probably wondering whether I'm ever going to stop talking. 'Hiya darling girl, how are you?'

'Hiya,' Hope answers, looking past Ana, presumably for the far more interesting Willow.

I step inside her house. Charlotte's house. I haven't been here since the morning after it happened, when everyone turned up with casseroles and fresh bread. Everyone except me. There were dishes and dishes of the stuff lined up in the kitchen and I never understood why. Why so many people thought her family would want to eat casserole nonstop in the days after her death.

'Beth, are you OK?'

Ana is wearing black leggings and a black jumper covered in images of the moon, and the words – *it's just a phase.* The phases of the moon. I've always found it quite fascinating. Sometimes it's full, sometimes it's crescent, sometimes it's not there at all.

'Beth? Are you OK?' Ana says again.

'Sorry. This is the first time I've been back here since the day after she died.'

'It must be weird.'

'It is.' I shiver and glance over towards the kitchen doorway. I expect to see her appear, weighed down by a laundry basket of washing and a heavy smile.

'Shall we go into the kitchen?' I nod and follow Ana through the doorway. She stands at the sink, filling the kettle, while I stare at the empty space on the windowsill where Charlotte's radio once sat. I have a memory of her turning the dial until she found a song she liked. When I close my eyes I can see her dancing. With the laundry basket, with her children. With me.

Hope is wriggling in my arms and as soon as I put her on the floor she crawls towards Willow. As they start shrieking with delight, another memory arrives. Clinking glasses with Charlotte; we're sharing a bottle of wine, sitting at the kitchen table. I reach into the bag on my shoulder and blink the memory away.

'I brought something to show you. Can I lay it out on the kitchen table?'

'Sure,' Ana replies, pouring boiling water into mugs. I spread the poster out and stare at it. The answer to all of this is in here somewhere. I'm certain of it. Somewhere hidden within my scrawled handwriting is the clue that will start to unravel this whole thing.

'I keep thinking about Fara's little boy.'

Her voice is coming from behind the fridge door, the same fridge Charlotte used to stand at. Is it the same fridge? Looks the same. Should I ask? Would that be weird?

'I can't believe Fara sends him to boarding school,' she's saying now. She sounds angry. 'Why have a child if you're just going to send him away? And how must he feel? Knowing all his brothers and sisters are still at home. That poor boy.'

'Yeah,' I say, smoothing out the curled-up edges of the poster. *That poor boy* – three of Charlotte's last words, scrawled by my hand across the paper. 'Although, to be fair to Fara, Tayo is quite annoying.'

'Even so, bloody hell,' she exclaims, looking down at my project laid out across her kitchen table. 'What the hell is all this?' She points at the photos of Jade, Emily, Danielle and Fara that I've Sellotaped around the edges.

'I know it's a bit of a mess,' I say, taking a step back to look at it through her eyes. 'Just something I've been working on for the last week or so, in my spare time. I've never shown it to anyone before,' I add, glancing up at her. 'Jack caught sight of it once but you're the first to look at it properly.'

'Is this her?' she asks, pointing at the photograph in the centre. 'Is this Charlotte?'

'Yes.'

'What's all this writing?' she asks. 'I can't make out half the words. Is it written in code? And what's PSP?' She leans closer. 'You've written that a lot. What does it stand for?'

'I'm not sure.'

She stands up straight and stares at me. Looks confused. 'I don't understand. I thought you said this was all your work. That no one else has even looked at it.'

'They haven't,' I say, glancing down at the kitchen table before raising my eyes to meet hers. Maybe it's the kindness I see there, or maybe it's because I'm finally back here.

Standing inside Charlotte's kitchen. Maybe that's why I feel safe. 'Can I be honest with you, Ana?'

'Of course.'

'Sometimes I have a few glasses of wine in the evening. Once the children are in bed. It relaxes me. I think of it as my reward for getting through another day.'

'Yes?'

'Because it's a struggle sometimes, looking after the children on my own. I love them so much, of course I do, but it's relentless, isn't it? It's nice to relax with a glass of wine when they're finally in bed.'

'So, you like to have a drink,' she says, staring at me. 'Is that what you want to be honest about?'

'Partly,' I reply. 'You see, the evening is the only chance I get to work on this.' I tap the crumpled poster. 'And the thing is, everything I've seen during the day, everything I've heard – it all seems to get cluttered up inside my mind somehow and there's so much clutter in here,' now I tap my head, 'sometimes I can't seem to locate the one piece of information I need. But when I drink, something magical happens because it's there, without me even trying to find it. But the problem is, I don't always remember it. The next day, I mean. So, I try to write it down when I'm . . .'

'Drinking?'

'Yes. But my handwriting is never very good after a couple of glasses of wine, and I can't always read what I've written . . . I mean, some of it I *can* read. This bit, this is what I can remember about what Tobias told us, and here's what Danielle said at Tea and Tots, but a lot of this other stuff I must have written late at night and I'm afraid I don't tend to remember much if I've had a bit to drink. Rowan always used to tease me about it when we were younger . . .'

'Oh, Beth,' she says, passing me a cup of tea. 'This doesn't sound very healthy to me. It sounds like this is becoming a bit of an obsession.'

'Is that such a bad thing?' I ask. 'Charlotte was a good person, a brilliant friend to me; don't you think I owe it to her to work out what really happened? Because after she died, we all accepted the story we were told, and I hate myself for not questioning it at the time.' I sigh. 'But the truth is, in the weeks and months after Charlotte died, what with all the other clutter building up – in here,' I add, tapping at my head again, 'I wasn't able to think about anything very clearly. I knew something was going on with Rowan, that's my ex, but he kept telling me I was imagining it and when I confided in Jade, she made me doubt myself too. Then I found out they'd been seeing each other for ages. When he told me they were in love, it was . . .' I catch my breath.

'That must have been devastating,' Ana says, putting her arm around my shoulder.

'It was. I lost all three of them – Charlotte, Rowan, Jade – all at the same time, and maybe even worse than that, I lost myself. Because that's what it feels like, when you can't even trust your own mind. I think that's why I didn't question Charlotte's death at the time,' I say. 'Why I never thought about it properly, about what really happened to her.'

I brush the tips of my fingers gently across the photograph of her smiling face. Laid out on the table, in the middle of the kitchen where she used to dance.

'But ever since I found out her son was in the house, I can't stop thinking about it. And now we know something else for certain, don't we? On that night someone came to her front door. Someone who never told the police that they'd seen her just before she died.'

We both turn and stare at the front door. 'And I think I know who it was,' I say, and at that moment, it suddenly begins to open. A man I've never seen before walks through the door and starts coming towards me and there is no other sound but my scream.

'It's OK, Beth,' says Ana, positioning herself directly in front of me until all I can see is her face. Her concern. 'It's just Harry,' she's saying. 'Beth? It's OK, it's my husband, Harry.'

'I live here,' the man says, placing a briefcase on the floor and looking at me, confused. 'Are you all right?'

'Yeah, yeah, I'm fine,' I say, tripping over the words. 'I just got a bit spooked, that's all. I wasn't expecting anyone to walk through the door at that precise moment.'

'Am I that scary?' he asks.

'No, no, no! You're not scary at all,' I say, because he isn't. He's gorgeous. 'It's just that when you walked in, we were talking about the woman who used to live here. Weren't we?' I say, glancing towards Ana who's looking at her husband, the male model of a man, dressed in an expensive-looking suit, accessorised by confusion. 'She was a good friend of mine,' I'm saying now. 'On the night she died, she answered the door to someone. Your door. That door. But we don't know which someone. Well, not for sure. And we were talking about it, then you walked in, and it gave me a fright—'

'It's OK, Beth, calm down,' says Ana, before turning back to her husband. 'Harry, this is Beth. A mum at the school.'

'This is Beth?' he says, reaching his hand out towards me. 'The one you said seemed the most normal?'

I shake his hand and when he starts to smile, so do I. 'Well, you know what they say,' I laugh, 'everyone's normal until you get to know them.'

'So true.' He smiles. 'Nice to meet you, Beth. Wow, you two look like you're having fun,' he's saying now, walking over towards Willow and Hope, his daughter squealing with delight as he scoops her up into his arms.

'I've just made some tea,' says Ana. 'Do you want some?'

'Yes please,' he shouts, over the giggles of the two little girls.

'How come you're home so early?' asks Ana.

'The jury sent a note,' he replies. 'Doesn't look they're going to reach a decision today.'

'Is that a good sign?' she asks.

'Hope so,' he replies.

'Harry's a barrister,' Ana says, turning back to me.

'Oh wow, that's amazing. My husband, well – he's my ex, he's just a plumber.'

'What's wrong with being a plumber?' asks Harry, putting Willow down.

'Nothing,' I reply. 'It's just, you know . . . not the same as being a barrister, is it?'

'Well, no,' Harry says. 'They're different careers but I wouldn't say one is better than the other.'

'Wouldn't you?' I ask. 'Most people would. Especially those living here.'

'What do you mean, here?'

'Oh right, it's probably because you're new to the area so you haven't realised it yet, but once you've lived here for a while—' why do I keep tripping over my words? 'you'll realise there's a bit of a divide between the big houses on Herrywell Lane and the other houses, where people like me live. Don't get me wrong, my house is perfectly fine – I'm not poor or anything.' Is that manic laugh coming from me? 'I'm just not wealthy, like the people who live on the lane. Some of the lane people look down their noses at tradespeople. They probably don't mean to; it's just the way some people are, making assumptions about a person. Do you know what I mean?'

'I think I have a vague idea,' he replies. 'How many black barristers do you think there are in my chambers?'

'I'm not sure,' I reply. 'Not enough?'

'I'm the only one. Believe me, I know all about people and their assumptions.'

'I'm sorry,' I say, 'I didn't mean to . . .'

'You're fine,' he says, smiling. 'What's this on the table?'

'Oh, it's just some notes I've been making. About the woman who used to live here.'

'Is this her? In the photo in the middle, with you?'

'Yes,' I reply. 'That's her. That's Charlotte.'

'Right. And who are these people in the other photos?' he asks.

'Well, I think they might be involved somehow.'

'In what?'

'Her death.'

'You think one of them killed her?' he asks, staring up at me.

'Yes,' I say, realising I've never said this out loud before. 'Yes, I do. I had a feeling in the weeks before she died. Almost as though I knew something awful was going to happen.'

'You can't rely on feelings,' he says, reaching out to take a mug of tea from Ana. 'Thank you, darling,' he smiles at her before turning back to me. 'You need to deal in facts. Evidence. Start with motive. Who benefitted from her death?'

'Er, I'm still trying to work it all out. First of all, I thought it might have been Bill, Charlotte's husband—'

'Because?'

'It's always the husband, isn't it?'

'Not always,' he says, taking a sip of his tea. 'But often.'

'Right. Well, now I don't think it's him because Bill was at a Halloween party at Emily's house with his children on the evening that she died.' I point at the photograph of Emily. 'This is her.'

'But so were *all* these people,' Ana says. 'Emily, Fara, Danielle and Jade,' she says, touching each photo in turn. 'I thought you were all at the party that night.'

'We were,' I say, swallowing a mouthful of tea. 'But Bill never left the party. All these people did, or at least were alone outside at one point or another. Fara walked her son home early, Emily kept going out to check everyone was parking correctly, and it sounds like Danielle spent ages dealing with the broken werewolf.' Confusion scuttles across Harry's face but only for a moment before he appears to decide it's pointless to ask for details. 'And as for Jade, she spent most of the night pacing up and down Emily's driveway. Emily's house is only a five-minute walk from here. Any of them could have come over that night. They all had the time.'

'But what about motive?' Harry asks again.

'Look, it's more of a gut feeling at this stage, but I know there was something wrong about the way she died. It doesn't make any sense. Charlotte would never run out into the road without checking it was safe.'

'Is that what happened?' he asks, taking a sip of tea. 'Road traffic accident?'

'Yes,' I reply. 'She was hit by a car. Didn't you hear about it, when you were buying the house?'

'Not that I can recall. Did you hear anything?' he asks, turning to face his wife.

'Yes,' she replies. 'Yes, I did.'

'Ah, so that's why I never heard about it,' smiles Harry. 'You see, my wife assumed full responsibility for house-hunting, and you set your heart on this place, didn't you?' He walks towards her and encircles her in his arms. 'I could tell from the moment you came back from the first viewing; you loved this place straightaway, didn't you? Nothing would have changed your mind.'

'Well, look at it.' Ana grins at him. 'It's perfect. Right in the middle of catchment for the good schools, beautiful big back garden, long driveway, open-plan – it's everything we wanted. The estate agent may have said something about the previous owner getting hit by a car by the bend in the lane, but . . .'

'She got killed in the lane?' he says, stepping away from her. 'Right outside the house?'

'Yes,' she replies.

'Bloody hell, Ana,' he says. 'I keep telling you about that bend, it's treacherous. We need to make sure the girls never play out the front—'

'They won't,' she says, taking a step towards him. 'They've got the back garden to play in. We'll make sure they never run out there.'

'If it makes you feel any better,' I say, finishing the last of my tea, 'I don't think Charlotte ran out into the lane. Not voluntarily, anyway. She would never leave her toddler on his own.'

'So, what do you think happened?' asks Ana, turning to face me. 'You think someone chased her out there? Forced her in front of the car?'

'Maybe,' I say.

'But who would do that?' asks Harry, walking back over to the kitchen table. He stares at the photographs surrounding Charlotte's. 'And how?'

'What do you mean?' I ask.

'If one of these people wanted her dead,' he says, staring down at the poster, 'how could they possibly have known that a car was going to drive around the bend at that exact moment? Unless they colluded with the driver, I suppose,' his eyes back on mine. 'Do you think that's what happened?'

'Well, no,' I say, my hand shaking slightly as I place my mug on the kitchen table. 'I don't think the driver had anything to do with it.'

'Why not?'

'Because the police investigated him at the time and couldn't find any fault. He was just a young lad driving

Emily's son Tobias home from chess club. I don't see how he could have known Charlotte, none of her kids were in secondary school. Plus I talked to Tobias. He said it happened so fast that James – that's the driver – couldn't have done anything to avoid hitting her.'

'And you're convinced?'

I think about the question for a moment before answering. 'I think the car was there at the wrong time,' I say, staring down at the photograph of Charlotte's smiling face. 'I think *that* part of it was an accident.' She looks so happy. If I close my eyes, I can almost hear her laugh. 'But what I don't understand,' my eyes back on his, 'is why she was out there in the first place. Danielle said trick or treaters knocked at her door that night, but the way she described it sounds like it was someone Charlotte knew, but who never came forward after the accident. At the very least, I think it's worth looking into.'

'But *what* are you investigating?' Harry asks. 'Because I'm not sure it sounds like murder. Manslaughter, potentially. At a push.'

'Maybe literally,' I say.

'You think someone pushed her in front of the car?' asks Ana.

'Look, I know it's a bit of a muddle,' I say. 'And I haven't got it all worked out properly yet, but I can't shake the feeling that someone else was involved. Like I said, someone she knew.'

'So we're back to motive,' Harry says. 'Which one of them wanted her dead?'

'Well,' I say, tapping the photo of Jade – her long,

flowing hair and nose ring, the mini dreamcatchers hanging from each over-pierced ear. Boho bitch. 'This is my prime suspect – Jade. She had some kind of disagreement with Charlotte shortly before her death and wanted to talk to her that night. And this is Fara,' I say, moving my finger to the next photograph. 'She spoke to Charlotte that morning, hours before she died, but we only have Fara's version of that conversation and why is someone as accomplished as Fara hanging out with us lot anyway? I've never understood why she's so utterly beholden to Emily especially. Makes me wonder whether Emily knows something about her, bringing us nicely on to this one,' I say, pointing at the next photo. 'Emily, the local Queen Bee, angry at Charlotte for not turning up at her party that night,' I say, glancing up at Ana and then Harry. 'And here's the thing about Emily. She wasn't always Queen Bee, and never would have been – not while Charlotte was still alive. And then there's Danielle,' I say, tapping at the last photograph. 'Who never seems to have a good word to say about Charlotte who once saved her life when she had an allergic reaction to trail mix, which you have to admit, is very odd.'

'Right,' says Harry, walking over to the kitchen sink and rinsing his mug. 'Sounds like a lot of supposition. You need to dig deeper. Find evidence. Get some proof.'

'Would you like another cup of tea, Beth?' asks Ana, as I pass her my empty mug.

'That would be great,' I reply, checking my watch. 'Oh no, is that the time? I still need to get to the supermarket before collecting the boys from school. Need to get snacks for the playdate. You are coming, aren't you?' I ask her. 'Four-thirty.'

'Of course,' she nods. 'Do you need me to bring anything?'

'No, just you and the girls,' I smile.

'What's this?' Harry asks.

'Some mums and kids are coming over to mine later,' I say. 'And there must be snacks, but no dairy, nuts or gluten allowed.'

'Sounds like hard work.'

'It is. I've been cleaning the house all day, that's why I was late getting round here,' I say, looking at Ana. 'It took me two hours to sort out the kitchen cupboards and hide all our food.'

'Why did you need to do that?' Ana asks, looking confused.

'Because everything we eat contains dairy, nuts and gluten.'

'How many mums have you got coming over?' Harry asks.

'Ana and this lot,' I reply, pointing to the photos on my project. 'Well, all of them except Jade,' I say. 'There's no way I'd let her into my house. She shagged my ex,' I explain, looking up at Harry. 'That's why he's my ex. She's still shagging him, as a matter of fact.'

'I see.'

'You're very welcome to come along too,' I say, still holding his stare. 'If you've got no other plans.'

'To the dairy-free playdate with a bunch of maybe murder but more likely manslaughter suspects? Thanks,' he says with a smile, 'but I might give it a miss.'

'Fair enough. Right, I'd better get going,' I say, rolling up the poster before walking with Ana towards the front door. 'Harry's great,' I whisper into her ear as she passes me my coat.

'Yes,' she says, looking back towards the kitchen. 'He is.'

'And he's so right. I do need to get focused and think about motive. I owe it to Charlotte to do this properly. Organisation and focus, that's what I need.'

'And hope. Don't you need hope?'

'I have hope,' I say with a smile. 'Believe me, Ana, I'm going to do this. I'm going to work it all out for Charlotte. Nothing is ever going to stop me getting justice for her.'

'No, I mean don't you need Hope? Your daughter.'

'Oh yes, of course,' I say, running back into the kitchen and scooping up Hope from the floor. She starts crying as I run with her out to the car, start the engine and accelerate down the long driveway, away from Charlotte's home.

My brakes screech as I speed around the treacherous bend. It's fitting somehow, a perfect soundtrack for my mind. Mangled with murder and motive.

19

I'm late getting to the supermarket and Hope's still angry. I don't think she likes being separated from Willow and, as her screams reverberate off every shelf in aisle seven, I'm finding it difficult to decide. Should I get gluten-free biscuits or muffins? Or biscuits *and* muffins? In the end, I chuck a load of both into the trolley, break open a packet of chocolate wafers, pass one to Hope and the screaming disappears, sucked out of aisle seven into the same void as gluten and dairy.

I grab a couple of bottles of wine and speed through the checkout but by the time I get to the school, Caretaker Carl is already locking the gate to the playground.

'You're late,' he mutters, as I approach. 'This gate is now locked and will not be opened again until Monday morning.'

'Great,' I smile, turning to leave. 'I'll come back and

collect my children then. Really good of you to keep them for the weekend, much appreciated.'

'Follow me,' he snarls, hobbling down the path towards the front of the school. Such a grumpy little man and why's he hobbling? He presses the intercom and we both stand in silence.

'Have you hurt your leg?' I ask. He doesn't reply. What a misery.

'Sweary Mum's here to collect her children,' he says, as the intercom starts to crackle.

'No worries,' says an Australian voice through the intercom.

'Sweary Mum?' I say, as Hope jumps a little in my arms. My voice sounding loud and high-pitched. 'Is that what you call me?'

'Yes.'

'Why don't you call me by my name?'

'I don't know your name.'

'You could ask.'

'And then I'd have to ask every other parent their name,' he says, looking up at me, his little face sharpened into a point of perpetual displeasure. 'How would that work? There are hundreds of parents. How am I supposed to know all their names?'

'I don't know! I just know you're not supposed to be rude. Sweary Mum,' I mutter, 'what a cheek. I'm not the only mum who swears in the playground.'

'Yes, there's a few of you, unfortunately,' he says, nodding his head. 'You're Sweary Mum who lets her children play unsupervised on the climbing wall. That's how I tell you apart from the others.'

'You've got a bloody nerve,' I say.

'Have I?'

'Everyone lets their children play unsupervised on that climbing wall.'

'No,' he says simply. 'They don't.' And with that a buzzer sounds and he pushes the door open for me. Stepping inside the school, I turn and watch him shuffle back down the path. Nasty little hobbling goblin.

'G'day!' says Kylie, the Australian mum who works in the school office.

'Good day,' I say, which is a greeting I don't think I've ever used before and one that makes me sound as though I've just stepped out of a Jane Austen novel. 'Sorry I'm late,' I add, glancing around the reception area. Kylie's son Finn, the kid with the eyepatch, is sitting behind the desk next to his mum, drawing something with a red pencil. 'Do you know where my kids are?' I ask. 'Jack and Freddie.'

'Yeah, we had to book them into after-school club,' Kylie says, staring at her computer screen. 'You'll be charged.'

'Really? Couldn't they just have waited out here with you?'

'I'm working,' she says, glancing up at me.

'But he's here,' I say, nodding towards Finn with the eyepatch.

'He's my son,' she says, staring back at the computer screen.

'Right. Well, can I have my children, please?'

'Yeah, in a minute,' she says, picking up the phone on her desk. 'I think Miss Lane wants a word with you first.'

'The headmistress?' Hope flinches in my arms and Finn with the eyepatch drops his pencil. My voice is loud and high-pitched once again. 'Why?'

'Oh geez, I dunno,' Kylie says, glancing up towards the clock on the wall. 'Maybe because school finished twenty minutes ago, and you've only just turned up to collect your kids.'

'I haven't only just turned up. I arrived ten minutes ago. It's not my fault Caretaker Carl moves so slowly.'

'He's got arthritis.'

'Again, not my fault.'

'Well, lucky for you, Miss Lane's not answering,' she says, replacing the phone. 'I'll just WhatsApp Martin, he's running the after-school club today. He'll bring your kids out shortly.'

'Thank you,' I say, glancing up at the clock. 'Do you think it will take long? I'm in a bit of a hurry.' She's tapping at her keyboard again and doesn't reply. I'm irritated by the silence. 'Don't you think he's a bit out of order?' I say to the top of her head.

'Who?' Kylie asks, looking up at me.

'Caretaker Carl,' I reply. 'Calling me Sweary Mum – don't you think that's rude?'

'Sticks and stones,' she shrugs.

'I'm thinking about making an official complaint.'

'About what?'

'Caretaker Carl.'

'You'll have to fill in a very long form,' she says. 'Do you want me to get you one? You can work on it over the weekend, although to be honest, I'm not sure you'll have time.'

'What do you mean?'

'The eco house project.'

'The what?'

'The project all the kids have to do this weekend.' I'm staring at her blankly. 'They have to build a model of an eco house,' she says slowly. 'As part of their "Save the Planet" topic. Didn't you know? They're giving out prizes for the best designs in each year group.'

'I haven't heard anything about it.'

'Well, you will. Plus all the other projects. It's Miss Lane's new homework policy. From now on, the kids have to do a project every other weekend.'

'Why?'

'To help them learn, I guess,' she says, with another shrug.

'So, next weekend they *won't* have to do a project?'

'That's right.'

'And the weekend after that, they will?'

'Yes, that's the concept of every other weekend. That's how it works.'

'Not for me.'

'I'm sorry?'

'Doesn't work for me.'

'I don't understand.'

'Well, what you're telling me is that on the weekends my ex has the children, he gets to run around in the garden with them, saving penalties and being Super Dad. Whereas, when it's my turn, I have to sit indoors making them do homework and save the bloody planet.'

'Hey! It's not my fault,' she says, reaching for the phone

again. 'Do you want to discuss it with Miss Lane? Add it to your official complaint?'

'No, that won't be necessary,' I say, as she replaces the phone. 'I just think it's bloody ridiculous. I mean, what's the point of all the kids doing these projects? We all know who's going to win.'

'Who?'

'Whichever kid has the most intelligent and creative parent with time on their hands,' I say, rearranging Hope in my arms. 'These projects, they're not fair, are they? There are probably parents at this school with multiple degrees who actually build eco houses for a living. At the very least some kid is going to have an architect for a mum or a dad with his own bandsaw and a pile of MDF handy. How am I supposed to compete with that?'

'It isn't a competition for parents.'

'Of course it is!' Is that manic laugh coming from me? 'That's exactly what it is.'

'No, it isn't,' she says again. 'Don't forget, the children have been learning about eco houses in class, haven't you, Finn?' she says to her son, who raises his eye and nods. 'And in assembly today, they had a big discussion about insulation and water conservation. They know what they have to do.'

'Really? I bet most of the kids don't even remember they were *in* assembly this morning.'

'I think you're underestimating—'

'I don't think I am. Have you met my sons? Freddie is a five-year-old whose idea of water conservation is peeing in the bath. If I thought for one moment that any of my children might be capable of designing and building a winning model of an eco house all on their own, do you honestly think I'd be wasting their time sending them here? They'd be working for NASA. Or Tesla. Or Coca-Cola.'

I'm trying to think of another big corporation ending in the letter A, when I spy the clock on the wall. Bloody hell, is that the time?

'Seriously, where are my kids?' I ask Kylie. 'I need to get going. I've got quite a lot to do today before, you know, I start on this weekend's *Grand Designs*.'

Suddenly the door buzzes and Freddie appears, clutching his book bag. Closely followed by Jack, angrily swinging his bag, looking absolutely furious.

'Why are you so late?' he shouts. 'I've had to sit in there for ages and ages. Why didn't you get here on time? Why can't you do anything right?'

'I'm sorry, Jack,' I say. 'I'm sorry, Freddie. Let's go home.'

We step out of the school and start walking towards the car as Carl the Snarl approaches, carrying a rake.

'I'm thinking about making an official complaint about you,' I say, as he steps off the path, giving us room to walk past.

'Okey doke,' he says.

'I shouldn't imagine Miss Lane will be very happy about it,' I say. 'When she hears about you having rude nicknames for parents,' I add. 'I shouldn't imagine she'll be very happy at all.'

'Oh well,' he says, continuing along the path. 'Have a good weekend, Sweary Mum.'

'Fuck off Carl,' I silently snarl.

20

I'm late getting home and haven't even taken my coat off, when there's a knock at the door.

'Bloody hell!' I yell, glancing at my watch. 'Is that them, already? Why can't they be late, like normal people? Stop eating everything, Jack!'

'Mummy, Mummy . . .'

'I know, Freddie, I know someone's knocking at the door, but before I let them in, I need to get all the snacks onto platters.'

'Platters? What's that?' asks Jack.

'Long plates,' I reply.

'I didn't know we had long plates.'

'Well, now you do.'

'Why do you have to put the snacks on platters? Why can't you put them on normal plates?'

'Because it looks better,' I reply. 'Posher. Freddie? Can

you help me?' I ask, desperately unpacking the shopping. 'Can you get the platters out of the cupboard over there?'

'Yes, Mummy,' he says, opening the cupboard I'm pointing at. 'What are platters?'

'Long plates,' Jack replies.

'I didn't know we had long plates!' shouts Freddie, jumping up and down. 'Mummy, can I eat my dinner on platters from now on?'

'Yes,' I reply, ripping open a packet of muffins as another knock lands on the door. 'But for now, can you bring the platters over here and start putting biscuits on them?'

'OK, Mummy,' he says. 'Why is all this food in here?' he asks, rummaging in the cupboard, packets of cookies and crisps spilling onto the floor. 'Look, here's my Rice Krispies! Mummy, my Rice Krispies are in here.'

I stuff everything back into its hiding place. 'I know, just ignore all that food, Freddie, and get out the platters. That's it, bring them over here and now we have to arrange all these biscuits nicely. I really hope I've bought enough. That's it! Well done, Freddie, you're such a good boy. OK!' I yell, turning towards the knocking at the front door. I trip and fall hard to the kitchen floor. Which I should have mopped because from down here, I can see all the dirt. 'Ow!' I shout, grabbing my ankle. 'Great place to leave your book bags, guys! I could have broken my neck.'

'Sorry, Mummy.'

'It's OK, Freddie,' I say, getting to my feet. I haul Hope out of her highchair, where I'd put her out of reach of a king's ransom in gluten-free muffins, and place her on my hip. 'Jack, can you please put the bags away? That's it,

Freddie!' I say, turning to him. 'Good boy, take the biscuits out of the packets, put them on the platters and then put the packets in the bin. That's it, Freddie – packets to platters, packets to platters, packets to platters, packets to bin, packets to bin, packets to bin.' Why am I repeating these words over and over, as I limp towards the front door? Am I chanting? Is that what I do now? And why am I clapping? Have I finally lost my mind?

'Hello, hello!' I say, opening the door. They're all standing there, staring at me. Fara, Danielle, an alarming number of children – all of whom appear to be boys – and Emily at the front, looking worried.

'Hi Beth,' she says. 'This is a lovely street,' she adds, glancing towards the gang of teenage boys standing in a group on the corner, vaping and chatting. 'Very vibrant.'

'Thank you,' I say, closing the door behind everyone as they all pile in, before leading them into the living room.

'Well, isn't this lovely and cosy,' smiles Emily, but she's still looking worried. She removes her coat and places it on the seat of an armchair before perching her skinny arse down.

'Right,' I say, putting Hope on the floor and turning towards the kitchen, 'make yourselves comfortable. I'll go get some snacks.'

'And what about the children?' asks Emily, squeezing sanitising gel onto her hands.

'The snacks are for them too. There should be enough—'

'No, I mean, what can the children do? Where can they play? Have you got any activities planned?'

'Activities?'

'She won't have got anything planned,' says Jack. 'There's never anything to do here, it's so boring. That's why I want to live with my dad—'

'Don't be silly, Jack,' I say, manic laugh gate-crashing its way into my words once again. 'I have lots of fun activities planned. There's Lego and over there, look, children! There's a television and . . .'

'My dad's got a PlayStation 5 at his house,' Jack's saying to the other boys. 'And he says he's going to give me his old PSP soon, so I have something to play with when I'm here.'

'Sorry, what?'

'I wasn't talking to you,' he says, glaring at me.

'I know, but what did you just say? Daddy's going to give you what?'

'It's none of your business!' he shouts. 'He's my dad and he can do what he wants. If he wants to give me his old PSP, you can't stop him.'

'I don't want to stop him. I just want to know what PSP is. What does it stand for?'

'PlayStation Portable,' says Fara, carefully removing her baby from his car seat. 'My nephews used to have one,' she adds, settling into my sofa, baby cradled in her arms. 'I remember them playing on it for hours, completely beguiled. A forerunner of the Nintendo Switch,' she's saying now, 'PSP is a classic, may even be prototypical, but obviously,' she smiles, 'I'm no expert.'

Look at her. Sitting there with her baby, draped in a silver pashmina, making my old sofa look elegant, though she's not being very helpful. I've still got no idea what PSP is and even less of a clue why I've written it all over my project. What has a PlayStation Portable got to do with Charlotte's death?

'Let's go in the garden,' shouts Jack and the living room suddenly empties, leaving behind only adults and toddlers.

There's another knock at the front door. It's Ana, with Willow in her arms and a little girl at her side.

'Hello Beth,' the girl says, shaking my hand. 'I'm Summer. Me and Freddie, we're in the same class.'

'Hi Summer,' I say, smiling at one of the cutest children I think I've ever seen. A beautiful blend of her parents, with her long hair plaited and tied with red ribbons.

There's a loud whistle, closely followed by another. Ana and Summer turn, and I peer out the door to see the teenage boys on the corner, all of whom seem to be staring this way and whistling. Except the kind one. He's telling the others to shut up.

'I'm sorry!' he shouts to me. 'They're not whistling at you. No offence,' he adds quickly.

'It may not be an offence,' says Summer, stepping inside. 'But it is harassment.'

'Sorry, what?' I ask, closing the door behind us.

'Whistling at a lady can be harassment. My daddy told me.' What is this tiny child talking about? And why is she speaking so slowly? Is that for my benefit? 'They were whistling at you, Mummy,' Summer says, turning to Ana. 'Shall we call the police?'

'No, Summer,' says Ana, lowering Willow and her bag to the ground. 'Let's try to enjoy the afternoon without involving the police. I'm sorry,' Ana says, whispering into my ear, 'she and Harry are always discussing criminal law.'

'Freddie!' Summer yells, smiling up at my son as he hurls himself down the stairs. She looks him up and down. 'Freddie, you've done it again.'

'Done what?'

'Put your shoes on the wrong feet! He's always doing it,' she adds, grinning at me.

'They're not on the wrong feet,' Freddie says, glancing down. 'Like I keep telling you, I don't have any other feet.'

'Kids,' Summer says, shaking her head as Freddie bolts through the house towards the garden. How the hell are those two in the same class?

I lead Ana and Willow into the living room which, in my absence, seems to have adopted a rather scholarly tone. Fara's sitting on my sofa, feeding her baby, with a large book of fairy tales balanced on her lap. There are other books scattered by her feet as well as Hope and two of Fara's other children, all quietly listening.

'Summer,' Fara says with a smile, looking up as we enter the room, 'would you like to listen to the story?'

'No, thank you,' replies Summer. 'I prefer to write my own. Do you have my journal, Mummy?' she asks, taking a notebook and pencil from Ana. 'This story will be called, "The Playdate at Beth's House",' she adds, sitting down cross-legged on the floor and opening the notebook.

'What a lovely idea,' smiles Emily, perched awkwardly on the edge of my armchair. What's wrong with her, today? She looks more anxious than Danielle. 'Beth,' she says, staring up at me, 'could I have some tea? Just a splash of milk and no sugar,' she adds.

'Of course,' I say, going into the kitchen, wondering

about the average length of a playdate. The time it takes to drink one cup of tea, maybe? Two? Can't be longer than that, surely.

I'm sitting at the kitchen table, waiting for the kettle to boil, when Ana appears. She's carrying Hope under one arm, a screaming Willow under the other with Summer following close behind. I wonder what that little girl is writing in her journal. I wonder whether she's written anything about me. And what the hell is Willow screaming about? Must be something important because she sounds very determined, repeating the same words over and over again. Ory? Bory? Dory?

'I don't think the girls enjoyed story time with Fara,' Ana says with a smile. Of course! 'Boring story', that's what Willow's trying to say. 'I think they'd rather be outside,' Ana continues, looking out the window at the boys playing in the garden. She flinches as Willow screams straight into her ear. 'Summer, I think Willow and Hope want to play in the garden with the big children. Could you do me a favour and keep an eye on them? Maybe write your story outside?'

'Yes, I can do that, Mummy,' Summer replies. 'But if any of the boys annoy me, even just for a moment, I will kill them. In my story, I mean. I will make sure they all die.'

'That sounds fair,' says Ana. She takes the girls out into the garden before returning a moment later, alone. 'I'm sorry about that,' she says, smiling. 'I'm sure she won't really kill anyone in her story. It's just her imagination. It's . . . what's the word in English? Overactive, that's it! She's always had an overactive imagination. Are you OK,

Beth?' she's asking now, looking at me with concern. 'You haven't even taken your coat off yet. Do you need any help?'

'Yes please,' I say, removing my coat and throwing it onto the back of a kitchen chair. 'Can you start taking some of these snacks through to the living room?'

'Of course,' she replies, looking at the kitchen table covered in platters of biscuits and muffins. 'Did you buy all of this today? Just for the playdate?'

'Yes,' I say. 'I wanted there to be a selection.' She leaves the room but within a moment she's back.

'Does any of this contain nuts?' she asks. 'Danielle wanted me to check with you.'

'No, no nuts,' I reply. 'You can tell her it's all perfectly safe.' As I pick up the kettle, Ana disappears into the living room again, only to be replaced by Danielle.

'Beth, I'm not sure if you know,' she says, her hair sticking out at weird angles. 'But I'm allergic to nuts.'

'Are you, Danielle?' I start pouring boiling water into mugs. 'Why have you never mentioned it?'

'I don't like to make a fuss,' she says, looking confused. 'But it's a very serious allergy. I can't go anywhere without my EpiPen.'

'Well, don't worry,' I smile. 'Everything is completely nut free.'

'Right,' she says, still looking confused. 'Thank you.'

'Danielle?' I say, before she turns and walks away.

'Yes?'

'Did you tell the police?'

'About what?'

'Your phone call with Charlotte on the night that she

died,' I say, putting the kettle down. 'Hearing someone knock at her door. Did you tell them?'

'Of course,' she says, and I think she's going to walk back into the living room, but instead she pulls out a chair at the table and sits down. 'Beth,' she says, her voice gentle. 'I know you and Charlotte were close and it's obvious you still miss her very much, but the police did a thorough investigation.'

'Did they?'

'Yes! They knew I spoke to Charlotte that night because they checked the call history on her phone. And I didn't hide anything from them, why would I? I told them Emily was angry at her for not showing up at the party, and that Jade and Charlotte had had a row. The police spoke to everyone. They decided it was an accident.'

'But what did you actually say to them, Danielle? Did you tell them it was trick or treaters at her door? Because you don't know that for certain, do you?'

Danielle looks tired as she gets up from the chair. 'I've already told you what I think about this. I don't want to talk about it any more.'

'Why not?' I ask.

Danielle glances towards the living room. 'Because I don't think it's appropriate,' she says, lowering her voice. 'And besides, Emily doesn't like it.'

'What's it got to do with her?'

'It makes her uncomfortable. Us talking about Charlotte.'

'Why?'

'It isn't my place to say and anyway, this isn't the right time.' Another anxious glance. 'Maybe later.' She's chewing at the corner of her thumbnail. 'But not where Emily can overhear. She's got enough on her mind as it is,' she adds. 'I think that's why she could really do with a cup of tea.'

'Of course,' I say as Danielle disappears into the living room, and I start removing tea bags from mugs. Can't keep Queen Bee waiting for her tea.

A child runs in from the garden, followed by Wilfred the best dog in the world. I stare into his eyes. He has that look. That look he has just before he's about to do something terrible.

Out of nowhere and almost in slow motion, he jumps up towards the edge of the kitchen table with the grace and agility of a ninja, mouth open, aiming for a pile of dairy-free biscuits. I manage to block him, knocking him off course, so he regroups and snaffles a used tea bag off the work surface, the glee of success in his eyes. At the exact moment he remembers he's not a cat, gravity gets involved and the glee is replaced with panic as he lands clumsily on the floor. He chews the tea bag as if nothing just happened. Extraordinary. There is literally nothing that dog won't eat.

'You're such a funny boy, aren't you, Wilfred,' I say, stroking his head. 'Best dog in the world, such a lovely boy.'

'It's boring in the garden,' shouts Jack, charging in through the back door, followed by a gang of boys all sporting the same look – sweaty clothes, scuffed face. Jack pushes past me to get to the kitchen sink and starts drinking water straight from the tap. 'How do we get into the shed?' he asks between gulps. 'I can't open the door.'

'You know you're not allowed to play in there,' I say.

'Why not?'

'Because I said so. And why would you want to anyway? There's nothing in there.'

'Then why do we have it? What's the point of having an empty shed?'

'Oh, I forgot,' I say, walking to the fridge and removing a carton of milk. 'There is something inside.'

'What?'

'Spiders. Huge, enormous, hairy spiders.'

'Yeah!' shouts one of the boys, astonishingly loudly, almost making me drop the milk. 'I like spiders. Can I see the spiders?'

'No,' I say. 'You can't.'

'Why not?' he shouts. Why is he so loud? 'I really like spiders!'

'Well, they don't like you,' I say. 'In fact, they eat shouting children for breakfast.'

'That's OK,' he yells. 'It isn't breakfast time.'

'It is for them,' I say, placing the milk carton onto a tray. 'They're only just waking up.'

'I want to see the spiders waking up!' he screams. 'Let me see the spiders.'

'Can he see the spiders?' asks Danielle, an apparition of anxious confusion reappearing at the kitchen door.

'No, Danielle, he can't,' I reply. 'And why does he want to?'

'He really likes spiders.'

'That's so weird,' I say, placing the mugs onto the tray.

'Did you just call my son weird?'

'No, I didn't. OK, yes, I did,' I say, turning to face her. 'But I wasn't being rude. It's just that I'm terrified of spiders, so I find it strange when someone likes them. I tell you what, kids,' I say, turning my attention to the group of boys flicking water at each other from the kitchen sink. 'Who likes Haribo?'

'Me! Me! Me!' they all scream.

'Great! Because I've got a big bowl of them somewhere. Where did I put that bowl?'

'How much longer are you going to be, Beth?' asks Danielle. 'I think Emily could do with a cup of tea.'

'All right, Danielle,' I say as more children spill into the kitchen. 'Just give me a minute to sort this lot out.'

There are so many children in here now. Too many to count, with a huge list of demands and as many complaints. Someone's toe has been trodden on, someone isn't playing nicely and someone else is ruining another person's life. Freddie's shouting at a little girl over by the fridge. My big brother is going to beat you up. No, my big brother is going to beat you up! Another fight, maybe between the big brothers, is breaking out in the corner of the kitchen and as I walk over to break it up, someone spills juice all over the floor. Somebody slips, somebody laughs, someone else cries. Snacks are dropped to the ground, the dog moves at the speed of light, the snacks disappear, laughter and crying intensify and fighting resumes. The child that spilled the juice asks why my kitchen is messy but doesn't wait for a reply, presumably too busy returning to the important business of ruining lives. I open the cupboard next to the fridge and there it is! The answer to all my problems. A salad bowl of Haribo.

'I've found the sweets!' I shout. 'Who wants a sweet?' I hold the salad bowl up high and carry it out into the garden.

The pied piper of gelatine, with a line of children following behind. Leaving the sweets outside for them to fight over, I return to the kitchen, pick up the tray of mugs and head into the living room where Ana is passing around a platter of biscuits.

'Are you sure none of these contain nuts?' asks Danielle, peering at the platter with suspicion.

'Yes, Danielle,' I say, lowering the tray towards the coffee table. 'I told you, they're all perfectly safe.'

'I know, it's just that I have such a serious nut allergy, I can't go anywhere without my EpiPen and—'

'You talk about that a lot,' says Summer, who is standing beside me. She must have followed me in from the garden, pen and journal still clutched in her hands. 'If you're that worried,' she says, staring up at Danielle, 'maybe you shouldn't eat anything.'

'Summer!' says Ana, glaring at her daughter, who turns and scampers from the room. 'Don't be so rude.'

'It's fine,' says Danielle, with a nervous smile. 'I'm fine,' she adds, glancing towards me, before reaching towards the platter and taking a muffin. We all stare as she cautiously nibbles the edge and I hold my breath as she takes a bigger bite and starts chewing. She looks anxious but still alive, so I pass everyone a cup of tea.

'Emily,' I say, once I'm settled into the sofa next to Fara. 'Can I ask you something?'

'Of course,' she says, leaning forward in my armchair and blowing gently onto her tea.

'There's something I don't understand,' I say. 'Why don't you like us talking about Charlotte?'

21

'I know you enjoy raking over things in the past, Beth.' Emily's eyes are unblinking. 'But personally, I prefer to focus on the future.' Why does she keep shifting like that? Is she doing it on purpose, trying to make my armchair look uncomfortable? 'Like Seraphina's party next Saturday, which is snowballing into a huge event.'

'Did you decide to combine it with a leaving do for Georgina then?' asks Fara.

'Yes,' replies Emily. 'Can you believe she's off to Oxford University the following week? So, now I've got loads of her friends turning up next Saturday, along with the whole of Year One and all their parents. As soon as everyone heard Mr Combustible had confirmed, I don't think anyone wanted to miss out! It's going to be a great day, but there's a lot to organise.'

'I don't know how you manage everything,' says Danielle. 'What can I do to help?'

'A couple of new signs for orchard parking would be great,' Emily replies. 'If you don't mind?'

'Of course.'

I take a sip of my tea. How have we got off the subject of Charlotte and on to this?

'Is Seraphina looking forward to her birthday?' Fara asks, moving her baby onto her shoulder.

'Yes,' Emily replies, alien eyes dropping towards the floor.

'Where *is* Seraphina?' Fara asks, her forehead crinkling slightly, with just the right level of confusion and concern. 'She's not here, is she?'

'She didn't want to come,' says Emily, cradling her mug with both hands.

'That's a shame,' says Fara.

'Yes,' says Emily, still staring down at her feet. 'It is a shame.' The room falls silent. 'If I'm honest,' she says, slowly looking up at each of us in turn, 'I'm really worried about her. You see, I hate to say it, but there's a problem with Seraphina.'

'Oh no,' everyone says, as Danielle rushes to Emily's side.

'I hope it's nothing serious,' Fara says.

'No, nothing serious,' Emily says with a brave smile, as I take another sip of my tea and wonder about the problem with Seraphina. Name too long to be embroidered into socks? 'It's ridiculous really,' Emily's talking again, 'and completely irrational, of course. But she's absolutely terrified of dogs.'

'Dogs?' I say, unimpressed.

'Yes,' Emily says. 'And it might sound trivial but it's beginning to have a hugely negative effect on her daily life. She doesn't like going to the park any more, and she even gets nervous walking into school when there's a dog tied up outside. That's why she isn't here today, because she knows you have a dog, Beth. It's becoming such a worry.'

'I'm sure she'll grow out of it,' I say.

'I hope so,' Emily says, raising the mug to her mouth. 'Because you know what they say about fear?'

'No,' I say, once the silence became awkward and I realise the question isn't rhetorical.

'It's a sign of weakness,' Emily says.

'And do you know what else they say about fear?' We all turn to look at Fara. 'The best way to overcome it is by exposure,' she adds. Even with a baby on her shoulder, her posture is impeccable. 'One should immerse oneself in the source of what one finds fearful.'

Suddenly I feel fearful. All that overuse of the third person makes Fara sound rather sinister. I glance at Danielle, perched on the floor next to Emily. I hope she hasn't mentioned my fear of spiders. The school run can be treacherous enough without one of these women showing up with a basket of tarantulas.

'I certainly don't want to be presumptuous but perhaps we find ourselves presented with a fortuitous opportunity here today,' Fara says. I'm trying to decide on the word of the day but it's difficult when she keeps throwing new contenders into the ring. 'Beth, your dog seems very affable.'

'Er, yeah,' I say.

'So, maybe Seraphina could come over and meet him.'

'Oh, I don't know about that,' I say over Emily, who I think is saying words to the same effect.

'Think about it,' Fara says. 'We're all here to support her, so surely this is the most auspicious opportunity for Seraphina to conquer her fear.'

'I don't know,' Emily says. 'I'll have to run it past her and Nigel. See what they both think.'

'Of course,' Fara smiles. 'And how about you, Beth?' she asks, turning to me. 'If Seraphina agrees?'

'OK, I guess,' I shrug.

'And how about your dog?' Emily asks.

'Sorry?'

'Do you think he'll be nervous? Is he likely to pick up on Seraphina's fear? Has he ever been near anyone frightened of dogs before? Do you think it will unsettle him?'

'I don't think he thinks that deeply about anything,' I reply. 'He just ate a tea bag.'

Emily phones Nigel and after an intense conversation that only narrowly avoids becoming fraught, they agree that he will drive Seraphina over to meet Wilfred. As we wait for their arrival, the other women speak about people I don't know, events I haven't been invited to, eco house designs I have no interest in, and stratospheric reading levels I'm not even sure *I've* ever achieved. As soon as I hear a knock, I'm out of my seat and running to open the front door.

Nigel is on the step, holding Seraphina's hand. His daughter looks terrified.

'Hello Beth,' he says. 'It's very good of you and your dog to do this. We're extremely grateful to you both.'

'I just hope it helps,' I say, smiling. 'I think you're very brave,' I say to Seraphina.

'I don't feel brave,' she whispers, clutching her father's hand and peering past me into the house. 'I feel scared.'

'Don't worry,' I say, 'my dog's in the back garden. I won't bring him to meet you until you feel completely ready.'

'OK,' she nods.

'And if you decide you don't want to meet him, that's completely fine,' says Nigel. 'Just do what feels right.'

'I want to try, Daddy,' Seraphina whispers.

'You're so brave,' I say again.

'Well, it's irrational, isn't it,' she says, staring up at me. 'And beginning to have a negative effect on my life.'

'Right.' Why are other people's kids so smart? 'Would you like to come in?'

Seraphina follows me to the living room, where she is immediately swept up into Emily's arms.

'Good luck, Seraphina,' Nigel says, turning to leave. 'I've got to get back for a Zoom call with New York, but I can't wait to hear how you get on. I'm so proud of you.'

Seraphina is shaking with fear but nods with determination when I ask whether she's ready to meet Wilfred. I coax him into the living room, telling him to be good, which is probably about as effectual as telling a tiger to be vegetarian, but I say it anyway because I don't think it matters. Wilfred doesn't have to be good; he just has to be friendly, funny and lovable. Not a problem for the best dog in the world. What could possibly go wrong?

When Seraphina sees him, she freezes and so do I, as all the clutter inside my mind starts drifting into a torrent of possibility, heading into the murky depths of everything that could possibly go wrong. Yes, my dog has never shown any aggression before, but he's an animal and animals can be unpredictable. What if he *does* pick up on Seraphina's fear? What if it *does* unsettle him? Those teeth, have they always been that pointy and so visibly displayed? He looks like he's smiling but I can't possibly know for sure. He might be getting ready to attack. And what's with all the unnecessary wagging? What if he whips her with that fast-moving tail?

Suddenly, I'm not so sure about this exposure therapy. It seems like a lot of responsibility and I'm not convinced Wilfred and I are the right duo for the job. Surely the gravitas of the occasion requires professionals. A guide dog and a vet, perhaps. Or a sniffer dog and handler. At the very least there should be a St Bernard and a dog groomer.

My brain is spiralling and I'm just about to expose the risks of exposure before committing to the exposure when Wilfred plods over to Seraphina, sits at her feet and nuzzles his big yellow head into her tummy. Slowly, she raises her hand to his head and strokes his soft, velvety ears. He closes his eyes and nuzzles even closer towards her as Seraphina strokes his face, his neck, his back. Now he's lying on the ground with Seraphina sitting beside him, giggling with delight as he places his head in her lap and swings his paws up into the air. Rubbing his tummy, she moves her face closer to his and he licks her. A big, excited Labrador lick. I move towards them to tell him to stop licking, but Emily holds me back.

'Wait, Beth,' she says. 'Seraphina needs to immerse herself completely.'

I watch in silence as Seraphina's confidence grows. With every lick of her face, her arms and her hands, she marvels at the dog's whiskers, laughs at the crazy tail-wagging, declaring him a 'good dog', and even lies down beside him on the ground. Danielle, Fara and Ana seem utterly spellbound. Danielle has even relaxed enough to eat another biscuit. Emily's face has softened into the most beautiful smile and suddenly I feel enormous warmth towards her, this woman who does everything so much better than me, but really, are we so different? Don't we just want the best for our children? Isn't that what we all want?

My heart soars. Is this it? Have I finally found my purpose? Maybe this is it. Maybe my purpose is using Wilfred to cure people's dogphobia, transforming fear into smiles and joy. Bit of a random, unexpected purpose but my imagination runs with it anyway. Wilfred and I are at Buckingham Palace just about to receive our OBEs when it happens. The living room door bursts open and Freddie is standing inside a super-charged whirlwind of excitable energy.

'Mummy! Mummy!' he shouts, scanning the sea of mummies until his eyes lock onto the one he recognises.

'Yes?' I say, as Summer and Willow follow him into the room, Hope close behind, pushing the horrible orange unicorn walker.

'Mummy, Mummy!' he's still shouting. 'I forgot to tell you about two funny things that happened before. Hope did a poo in the garden, Mummy! A big ginormous, stinky poo.'

'OK, Freddie,' I say, scooping Hope up into my arms. 'Thanks for letting me know. I'll change her nappy.'

'No, Mummy! You don't need to change her,' Freddie says, jumping up and down on the spot. Shoes still on the wrong feet. 'She did the poo on the grass, Mummy! Hope took her nappy off and did a poo on the grass!'

'Oh right,' I say. I turn to the other women. 'Rowan said she did that last weekend too. Must be her new thing,' I smile. 'OK, Freddie, I'll go out and clear it up.'

'You don't have to,' he says, still jumping up and down.

'What do you mean?' I ask.

'That's the other funny thing,' he says, laughing. 'You don't *have* to clean the poo up.'

'Why not?'

'Because Wilfred already ate it.'

All eyes turn to Wilfred licking Seraphina's wide-eyed face.

There's a moment of complete silence before the screaming begins. Danielle is the first on her feet, emptying the contents of her bag over the floor, throwing tissues and hand cream towards Emily. Why is she throwing hand cream? Fara is more methodical, placing her baby into his car seat before rummaging through her bag and passing Emily a packet of wipes.

'Hot water!' Danielle screams. 'And towels!' she adds, running from the room, heading towards the kitchen. 'Hot water and towels! We need hot water and towels!' Why? Is someone giving birth? In a movie?

Hope is still in my arms, wriggling to get down, pointing at Willow. She's clutching a pen and scribbling on the wall, though mercifully doesn't seem to be doing any damage, the cap isn't even off. I need to stop her before she figures this out – can't kids choke on pen caps? I'm sure they were on Jade's light-hearted list of everyday dangers – but I'm distracted by Seraphina's sobbing.

'The dog licked the inside of my mouth!' she cries, each word a staccato, interspersed with breathless, choking gags. Is she hyperventilating? 'And the outside of my mouth,' she sobs. 'He licked everywhere! I'm going to be sick. Mummy!' More gagging. 'I'm going to be sick!'

'My poor baby!' says Emily. Is she crying too? She's holding her sanitising gel and her hands are shaking. 'Just be sick, my darling,' she's saying, between undeniable sobs. 'Mummy's here.' Tears in her huge alien eyes. Now they're both gagging. As playdates go, I don't think this is a very good one.

Fara puts a hand on Emily's shoulder. 'I'm going to make you a fresh cup of tea,' she says gently, turning towards the kitchen. 'That's what you need.'

Yes. Good plan, Fara. A nice cup of tea should calm everything down. Damage limitation. That's what matters now. Just need to make sure this situation doesn't get any worse.

I lower Hope to the ground, and she immediately shuffles towards Willow, who is still trying to draw on the wall. I glance at Ana. She catches my eye. Is she completely repulsed? Or trying not to laugh? Sometimes her face is so difficult to read. 'I'll go and help Fara with the tea,' she says, biting her lip, before leaving the room.

Wilfred has been sitting quietly by my side but now he plods over to Seraphina to comfort her because that's what dogs do. They're compassionate, much kinder than humans. Certainly, a lot kinder than the one screaming into his confused Labrador face.

'Get away from us!' Emily cries, hugging Seraphina tight. 'Stupid, disgusting dog. Why would he eat human excrement? What's wrong with him? Revolting animal!'

Wilfred plods back towards me. Happy Labrador looking so sad.

Emily turns to Hope. 'And why did she go to the toilet on the ground?' she asks before staring with disgust at Willow still scribbling on the wall. Lucky that pen doesn't work. 'I knew this was a mistake,' she sobs. 'I'm sorry I made you come here, my darling,' she says, dabbing at Seraphina's face with an antibacterial wipe. 'We never should have come.'

I take a deep breath. Damage limitation. Quiet and calm, Beth. Stay quiet and calm. I stroke Wilfred's head. Thanks to my wonderful dog, this playdate is petering out earlier than expected. It will all be over soon.

'Stupid, disgusting dog!'

Emily's shouting. No need to say that again.

'Revolting animal!'

Or that. Quiet and calm, Beth. Stay quiet and calm.

'And why the hell did she poo on the grass?'

I focus on Willow and Hope, such gorgeous little girls.

'And that disgusting animal better not take one step towards us.'

I look at Wilfred. Best dog in the world.

'Revolting animal!'

My eyes flick back towards Willow and Hope, skim over their heads, towards the mirror on the wall. And that's when I wonder whether what they say is right. That dogs and their owners end up looking alike. Because as I stare at my reflection, I recognise the look in my eyes. It's the same look I see in Wilfred's eyes. Just before he's about to do something terrible.

'We never should have come here, Seraphina—'

'So, why the fuck did you?' I scream. Seraphina starts to wail, burying her face into her mother's shoulder, covering her Sweaty Betty vest top in antibacterial gel. 'How dare you come to my house and be so bloody rude?'

'Rude? Me?' she shouts. 'You're the one swearing!'

'Too fucking right!' I yell. 'I'll swear at anyone who has the cheek to call my dog revolting! How dare you?'

'He is revolting!' she screams.

'No, he isn't.' I'm bellowing now. 'You're the revolting one, Emily! Sitting there with your ponytail and your manicure and your judgement and your yoga mat—'

'I don't have my yoga mat!'

'Doesn't matter. You're still revolting. YOU ARE REVOLTING!'

'No, I'm not!' she screams, covering Seraphina's ears.

Fara runs back into the room. Where's the tea?

'And why don't you like us talking about Charlotte?' I'm shouting again. 'You cleverly swerved that question, didn't you?'

'Where's Danielle's bag?' Fara's scrabbling on the floor. What's she looking for?

'Why don't you want me raking over the past, Emily?' I shout. 'What have you got to hide?'

'Where's Danielle's bloody bag?' Why is *Fara* shouting now?

'I don't know,' I say, turning towards her. 'I think she emptied it over here. Why?'

'I need her bag.' Why is she looking panicked? 'I need her bloody bag!' And swearing? What's happening?

'Fara, what's wrong?'

'Danielle's collapsed,' she says, grabbing hold of Danielle's bag, her hands shaking. 'She's not breathing. I need to find her EpiPen.' She empties the remaining contents of Danielle's bag onto the floor. 'I think she's in anaphylactic shock.'

'Oh my God.' Emily rushes towards Fara and starts searching through the debris on the floor.

'No, that can't be right,' I say. 'There weren't any nuts. I made sure of it. How can she be?'

'I don't know, Beth!' shouts Fara. 'Just help us find the EpiPen. Where's the fucking EpiPen?'

There's a scream from the kitchen.

The kettle is still boiling. Hot water and towels. Her hair is sticking out at weird angles. Why didn't I mop the floor? Ana's cradling her head. She looks up at us.

'She's dead.'

And all I can think about is how sad it is for Danielle. To be lying there dead on my kitchen floor. Still looking so bloody confused.

22

'Beth, what the hell happened? Beth!'

'Yes?'

He's sitting on the sofa, staring at me. Everyone else has gone now, even Danielle. They took her body away and then he arrived.

'What did the police say?' Almost blue, nearly green eyes staring straight into me.

'They asked me questions.'

All those questions tumbling into more questions.

If you knew about Danielle's nut allergy, why did you give her food containing nuts?

I didn't.

You didn't know about her nut allergy?

No. I mean, yes.

Yes, or no?

Yes, I knew about her allergy but no, I didn't give her anything containing nuts.

How can you be sure?

Because I bought everything from aisle seven and there are no nuts in aisle seven. Or dairy or gluten. You can check.

Why didn't you check?

I did.

Did you?

Didn't I?

I'm perching on the seat of my armchair. I'm not sure I'll ever feel comfortable again.

'Did the police say what happens now?'

'They're making enquiries.'

'What kind of enquiries?'

'I don't know. They didn't say.' Too busy asking me questions.

When you invited Danielle over, why did you tell her everything was safe to eat?

Because it was.

What about this packaging we found in the bin?

What packaging?

This packaging.

It says 'not suitable for customers with an allergy to peanuts or nuts due to manufacturing methods'. She had a very severe allergy, didn't she? Even traces of nut were dangerous for her. But you served her these biscuits.

No.

No, you didn't serve biscuits?

No, I mean, yes.

Yes, or no?

'Beth,' Rowan says, leaning towards me. 'Why are the police making enquiries? Are you in trouble? Do they suspect you of—?'

'Of what?'

'I don't know. I just don't understand why the police are making enquiries.'

'Me neither.' I answered all their questions. Question after question after question.

Why did you empty biscuits onto platters rather than leaving them in their packets so Danielle could see what they were?

Because I wanted it to look nice. Posher.

And you told Danielle everything on the platters was safe to eat.

Yes, because it was.

But some of the biscuits contained traces of nut.

Someone else must have brought them.

Who?

I don't know.

We've asked everyone. No one else brought any food into your house. You told Danielle everything was safe to eat.

No, I didn't!

You didn't tell her everything was safe to eat?

No, I mean yes.

Yes, or no?

Yes, I told her everything was safe to eat but no, I didn't buy those biscuits. Someone else did.

Who?

Someone who wanted her dead.

'Beth.' Almost blue, nearly green minus the anger. 'Let's think about this logically,' he's saying. 'The police questioned you but now they've gone, and that's got to be a good sign, don't you think? Must mean they're not treating the house as a . . .'

'As a what?'

'As a crime scene.'

'I never should have invited them over,' I say, searching Rowan's eyes for the compassion I used to find there. 'I'm out of practice when it comes to playdates. I'd forgotten how much work is involved and I tried my best, but it could have gone better.'

'Could have gone better? Beth, a woman died.'

'I know, but that wasn't my fault. You have to believe me, I was so careful. I checked all the snacks, nothing had nuts. And even Summer told her.'

'Summer?'

'She's very clever. She has a journal. Even she told Danielle that if she was so worried about her nut allergy, she probably shouldn't eat anything at all. It wasn't my fault, Rowan. I can't be blamed for it. Not that part anyway.'

'What do you mean?'

'Her allergic reaction, that wasn't my fault. I can't take responsibility for that, but I will admit I didn't have enough activities for the kids. That's what I did wrong.'

'What are you talking about?'

'If I'd sorted better entertainment for the kids, maybe Willow wouldn't have started drawing on the wall with Danielle's EpiPen. Fara would have found it in time, she might have saved her . . . That was my mistake – focusing on the snacks when I should have been thinking about the children.'

Those poor children. Running in from the garden. The loud one, the one who likes spiders, seeing his mum lying dead on the floor. The screaming . . .

'Beth, why don't I take the children for a week, and Wilfred too? You've had a terrible time. I think you need a break.'

I don't argue. He's not wrong. I do need a break, so I pack their bags, load our children and dog into his car, wave them goodbye and then walk to my own. I open the boot and take out the wine I bought earlier in the supermarket. Back when anything mattered. The poster is in the car too. I remember placing it there hours ago, when Danielle was still alive.

The bag of wine is heavy as I carry it into the house, but not as heavy a burden as my project. I'm weighed down by the images of two dead women. I wonder whether they've met up with each other yet, Charlotte and Danielle. I wonder whether they'd want to. They weren't particularly friendly in life but maybe the afterlife is different. Maybe it's more like a foreign holiday, with everyone excited about meeting someone from their hometown. I sit down at the kitchen table. The bottles of wine are screw top. No need for a corkscrew. No need for a glass. Drinking in continuum allowing thoroughness of thought.

Who brought those biscuits into the house and put them on the platter? Because I know it wasn't me. I wish I could find the receipt from the supermarket, just to put my mind at rest, but hopefully it's already with the police. Together with the contents of my kitchen bin, helping with enquiries. I've got an enquiry, who wanted Danielle dead? Need more wine. Another bottle.

I think she knew something about Charlotte's death, and that's why she's dead. Maybe she remembered something from the phone conversation. Maybe she realised it wasn't trick or treaters at the door.

And what about Jade? I'm certain she's involved somehow but Jade wasn't here this afternoon. Was she? Maybe she was. Maybe it was Jade. Maybe she brought the biscuits into my house, just to get me into trouble. She'd love it if I got locked up, wouldn't she? Then she could cook her famous macaroni cheese for my children every bloody day. Maybe she was here the whole time, disguised as a kid. She's about the same size as one of those boys running around the garden, with their flushed faces, trying to get into the shed.

I'm not making sense any more. Need to drink more wine. Someone brought those biscuits into my house, someone that wasn't me. Someone that wanted Danielle dead and me blamed. Same someone who probably walked into the kitchen and emptied those biscuits onto one of the platters while I was at the front door, talking to Nigel and Seraphina. More wine needed. Important to keep drinking wine.

I left them all sitting in the living room. Emily, Danielle, Fara, Ana and Summer – she was there too, wasn't she? Clever little girl writing in her journal. Of course! She was writing everything down. I need to read the journal, that's important. Essential evidence. I need to remember to read the journal.

The wine is working, I'm starting to think clearly. I need to drink more. And quicker. Another bottle. Easy to open. Wants to be opened. Wants to be drunk. I'm starting to understand what happened but I'm not going to remember tomorrow, not going to be able to read what I write. I need to stop writing on the poster, lock it away, start typing my thoughts because the solution to every puzzle should be typed, not scrawled. That's the rules of puzzles. Rules of life. More wine needed.

Outside now looking for something. What am I looking for? The rock that isn't really a rock. The key. Unlocking the shed. Piles of boxes keep moving, impossible not to fall into them. Hello spiders. Friendly spiders. Are you awake? Why didn't I let that little boy look at the spiders? He lost his mum today; I should have let him look at the spiders. Goodbye project, you stay in here tonight. With the spiders. Goodbye spiders. Key in the lock then key in the rock and now goodbye rock that isn't really a rock. Maybe I'll never find you again.

Back in the kitchen. More wine. Laptop open. I'm typing the answers because I know the answers and typing can't be cluttered. Can't be misunderstood. Like those teenagers on the street corner. Nice kids really. Misunderstood. More wine. Drinking and typing. Drinking and typing. Where are you, Danielle? Where did you go and what did you know? You knew something, didn't you? And you were going to tell me later. But there is no later, is there, Danielle? Not for you.

Not any more.

Last Halloween

I have to hand it to Emily. She knows how to throw a good party. This Shocktails bar has got everything a person could ever need.

'Ah, Beth, there you are. The children are about to start a skeleton scavenger hunt in the living room. It looks brilliant.'

'So?'

'I thought you'd want to watch.'

'I'm always with the children, Rowan. Can't you parent for a while, and give me a bloody break?'

'Of course, I just thought you'd enjoy watching, that's all. They're having a great time.'

'Good.'

'Are you getting another one? Do you think that's a good idea? How many drinks have you had?'

'Chill out, it's a party.'

'Yeah, for children.'

'Then, why is there a bar? Ah, here she is – the hostess with the mostest. Emily, I was just telling Rowan how much I appreciate all the effort you've put into this Shocktails establishment. It's better stocked than most pubs.'

'Thank you, Beth.' Her huge eyes look even bigger with all that expertly applied makeup. I wonder if she got it professionally done. 'I'm glad you're having a good time, but please be careful,' smoky eyes flickering with phoney concern. 'I heard you nearly fell into the cauldron of dry ice in the living room earlier. And the thing is, Rowan,' her eyes flicking towards his, 'if anyone hurts themselves while they're here, Nigel and I – we won't be accepting any liability. Beth could have got badly burnt.'

'By ice?' I laugh. 'What are you talking about?'

'Dry ice is much colder than normal ice,' Rowan says. 'If you get any on your skin it can feel like a burn, but it can give you severe frostbite—'

'If you're going to mansplain the fun out of everything,' I say, reaching for another bottle of wine, 'I'm definitely going to need another drink. And can I just say,' I add, refilling my glass, spilling some onto the bar, 'severe frostbite sounds rather nice at the moment. Why's it so bloody hot in here?'

'Well, you are wearing a huge coat,' he says.

'It's my costume. I'm Big Bird.'

'Right.'

'At least I'm wearing a costume, Rowan,' I say, taking a gulp of wine. 'At least I'm trying to get into the party spirit. Look at all the effort Emily's gone to, and you turn up wearing your plumber trousers.'

'I've come straight from work,' he says, glancing at Emily.

'Have you?' I ask. 'Is that where you've been?'

'What?'

'You're always coming straight from work, aren't you? Or at least, that's what you say.'

'You know I've got a lot on at the moment.' Rowan's phone starts to ring. 'Talking of which,' he says, checking the display, 'I have to take this. It's about a job I did earlier.' He disappears from the kitchen to be magically replaced by Danielle. She's wearing a pointy green hat and a huge yellow high-vis jacket.

'What have you come as?' I ask. 'H-elf and Safety?' I laugh. 'Get it?'

'No.' Danielle looks confused. 'I'm a green witch. Oh, I forgot I was wearing this,' she says, staring down at the jacket. 'Thank you for lending it to me.'

'No problem,' Emily says, spraying antibacterial cleaner onto the spilled wine. 'While you're out the front, I'd prefer that you wear it. It's so dark and with people still turning up and parking, I don't want anyone getting run over.'

'Of course,' Danielle says. 'I told Jade to be careful of the cars. She's been out there for ages, the whole time I've been trying to get the werewolf to stand up. I think there's something wrong with its legs.'

'Thanks for trying,' Emily says, wiping invisible crumbs from the bar into her hand. 'I'll go out in a minute and wedge its feet with rocks. What's Jade doing outside? Isn't it freezing out there?'

'Is it?' I ask, refilling my glass. 'I might go outside then. It's boiling hot here.'

'Why don't you take off your coat?' Emily asks.

'It's my costume,' I reply. 'I'm Big Bird.'

'She's really upset,' Danielle says.

'Who?' I ask.

'Jade. I think she's had a row with Charlotte.'

'Where is Charlotte?' asks Fara. Where did she come from?

'At home, I believe.' Emily's still wiping invisible crumbs but with more force than before. 'Bill's here with the kids, but Charlotte's a no-show.'

'I can't believe she didn't even ring you to say she wasn't coming,' says Danielle.

'I know.' Emily stops cleaning and stands tall. 'I mean, look at all the trouble I've gone to.' She points the cloth towards a row of Shocktails and everyone turns. Which is unfortunate timing because I've just picked up another bottle of wine. 'All she had to do was put on a costume and walk up the road,' Emily says, 'and she couldn't even be bothered to do that.'

'You're quite right,' Danielle agrees. 'I think she's dreadfully rude. In fact, I think I might give her a piece of my mind.'

'Not too big a piece, Danielle!' I laugh, splashing wine into my glass. 'Oh, lighten up, everyone. It's a party.'

'Emily, I hope you don't mind but I'm going to vamoose.' What is Fara talking about? 'I think all the excitement has got to Tayo and I'm going to take him home.'

For the first time I notice she's holding a child by the hand. He's squirming away from her and reaching out for a beaker of Shocktails straws with his free hand, knocking them to the ground.

'Tayo!' Fara says, calmly. 'Stop it!'

'Yes, be careful,' Emily adds, dropping to the floor and collecting straws at remarkable speed. 'There are glass bottles up there,' she adds, glancing up at the little boy. 'I'm not worried about anything getting damaged, but I don't want you hurting yourself.'

'I'll get him settled at home and then come back,' says Fara. 'My mum is on her way over to babysit.' Tayo looks up at me. I stick out my tongue and he laughs before doing the same.

'If you're going out the front,' Emily says, back on her feet, 'let me give you one of these.' She opens a cupboard and passes Fara something bright yellow. 'It's so dark outside and people are still driving in and parking. I don't want anyone getting run over.'

'Thanks, Emily,' says Fara, momentarily releasing her hold on Tayo to slip the high-vis jacket over her head. It takes less than a moment for the beaker of straws to be scattered all over the floor again.

'Tayo!' says Fara, still sounding oddly calm as she takes his hand again and leads him from the kitchen.

'I'm going outside too,' I say. 'I need some fresh air and no,' I add as Emily approaches the cupboard. 'I'm not wearing a bloody high-vis.'

'OK,' she says, back on her knees on the floor, collecting straws. 'But please be careful. I don't want you hurting yourself.' Bloody hell, she's so condescending. Talking to me like I'm a child.

I head outside and now I'm here, I have to hand it to Emily. She knows how to throw a good party. Look at all the decorations. Life-size figures of a skeleton and a witch and what's that? A zombie? And over there . . . bloody hell! I trip over but somehow manage to hold onto my wine. What's this on the ground? Is it a werewolf?

'I'm not sleeping.' The voice is muffled. 'I haven't eaten properly for weeks.'

Who's that talking? I try to push myself up, but the werewolf isn't the only one finding it difficult to stand.

'I feel sick,' the voice says. Me too. And dizzy. Maybe I've overdone it a little at the Shocktails bar. 'Properly sick.' Might as well sit here in the darkness and finish my glass of wine.

'Why would Charlotte do this to her best friend?'

Hang on, aren't I Charlotte's best friend? Who's talking? Is that Jade?

'She's delicate at the moment.' Who? 'Anyone can see that. She's been delicate ever since Hope was born.' Me? Am I delicate? 'I know, but we didn't set out to deliberately hurt her, did we? Charlotte doesn't need to do this.' Do what?

'I know she'll find out eventually, but not now. Not yet. At least not until she's stronger.' Who's she talking to? I can't hear another voice.

'Charlotte's going to ruin everything.'

'Jade!' I shout into the darkness.

'Beth?' The light from the screen of her phone approaches, before joining everything else in the dark. 'What are you doing down there?' she asks. 'Are you hurt?'

'I fell over the werewolf,' I say, as she helps me to my feet. 'Who were you talking to, Jade? Why is Charlotte going to ruin everything?'

'Don't worry about it,' she says quickly. 'I think maybe you misheard. Let's go back inside. We're missing all the fun.'

'Have you been to the Shocktails bar?' I ask her. 'It's really good.'

'No,' she replies. 'Let's go there.'

'Yeah,' I say, walking with her towards the front door. 'Let's have a drink and then walk up the road and see Charlotte.'

'Why?' she asks, turning to face me.

'I want to find out what you don't want me to know.'

We push open the front door and step into the light. Why is she wearing that ugly yellow cloak?

'OK, Beth,' she says, placing her arm around my shoulder. 'But let's go and get a drink first.'

23

Daylight. Again. The relentless rising of the sun, whether we like it or not. The kitchen is flooded in it, and it hurts. But nobody cares. Maybe they'd care about me if I was lying on the floor, as dead as Danielle.

I wonder at what point they arrived and which one of them turned up first – the pain drilling into my head or the nausea. Did the pain cause the nausea, or nausea cause the pain? Chicken and egg. Don't think about chickens. Don't think about eggs. Kitchen chair knocked to the floor as I move towards the sink. Edges held tightly, gagging with no vomit but there is clutter. Even more clutter inside my head than this time yesterday. Was it only yesterday? When Jack and his friends stood here, drinking water straight from the tap. All those kids running in and out from the garden. So much life. Isn't it strange how it only takes one person to stop breathing, and the whole room becomes saturated in death.

I get a glass of water, inch back towards the kitchen table and settle into one of the chairs that hasn't been tipped over. My laptop is closed and as I reach for it, I notice my hand. It's shaking. I open the laptop. My vision blurs into focus at the four words staring back at me. Only four. All typed in capital letters. I never type in capital letters. It looks like I'm shouting. I *am* shouting. No, I'm screaming. At the four words staring at me from the screen.

WHY DON'T YOU DIE?

There's another noise, blending with my hoarse scream. It sounds like my name. There it is again. Is that banging at the front door real?

It's Ana. She looks concerned.

'Beth, I heard you screaming.' She peers round me into the house. 'Are you OK?'

'What are you doing here so early?'

'Early? It's two o'clock in the afternoon. I've been trying to call you for hours. What the hell happened last night?'

'What do you mean?'

'All the messages you left me. Don't you remember?'

'No.' She follows me into the kitchen and there it is – my phone on the floor. It hurts to bend down and retrieve it. Hurts even more when I look at the display. Ana's standing in the middle of my kitchen, counting. Four empty wine bottles, two fallen chairs. And last night – forty-eight missed calls from me.

'Sorry about the mess in here,' I say, picking up one of the chairs, then sitting down and closing the laptop. 'I would have cleaned up, but the police took my bin.' I laugh. She doesn't. Not even a smile. Why doesn't she smile? She was such fun when I first met her but lately she's become so serious. Maybe she should forget about perfecting the English language and work on rediscovering her sense of humour.

'Beth, I didn't hear my phone ringing last night,' she says, picking up the other fallen chair and sitting down. 'Because I leave it downstairs when I sleep. But all those missed calls. And the messages you left me. It's you, but not you. You sound different. Listen.'

'No,' I say, standing back up. 'I don't want to.'

'Beth.' She stands too. Holds her phone towards me. 'Listen.'

The voice in the message is sharp. Cold. Uncluttered. 'Why aren't you taking my calls?' it asks, keeps repeating the words. 'Too good for me? Is that it?'

'Delete it,' I say, turning away.

'Little Miss Perfect,' the voice says again. 'But is any of it real? Or are you just pretending? Like you pretend to be friends with me.'

'Please. Please press delete.'

'Just like Charlotte, that's what you are.' Different message, same voice. 'And look what happened to her.'

I'm walking over to the sink by the window. Because that's where the daylight is strongest. That's where it hurts the most.

'With your perfect house. Perfect husband,' the voice snarls. 'Why are you so fucking miserable?'

'Ana, please. We don't need to hear this . . .'

'And so fucking serious!' the voice shouts from her phone. 'You used to be fun. Why don't you forget about perfecting the English language and work on rediscovering your sense of humour?'

'I don't know why I said that,' I say. 'I don't even think that. You have to believe me—'

'Just like Charlotte.' Another new message. 'And look what happened . . .'

'ANA! GET OUT OF MY HOUSE!' I scream, turning to face her. 'I don't want to listen to any more of this and I don't want you here. I don't want *anyone* here. Just get out and leave me alone!'

Ana doesn't move.

'Ana, I mean it. You're not welcome here. It's safer for everyone when I'm on my own. Safer for me. Please, Ana, get out.'

She still doesn't move. 'Where are the children?' she asks instead, putting her phone in her pocket.

'They're with Rowan. They're staying with him for a week.' Rowan. My mind pounces on his name. 'Please don't tell him about any of this. About the wine,' I say, glancing at the empty bottles. 'Or the messages. Please don't tell Rowan. Or Jade. They'll try to take my children away from me. My drinking got bad before, you see, but then I got better and if he knows I'm drinking again, I'll lose the kids. I'll lose everything. Please . . .'

I'm crying now and her arms are around me. She's hugging and leading me to a chair, helping me sit down. I'm a person who needs help to sit down. Now she's passing me a glass of water and I take a sip. And a moment. Just a moment and then I decide. To tell her the truth.

'I'm frightened, Ana,' I say. 'So frightened of the person I become when I drink.'

'Oh, Beth.' Her arms are around me again.

'Because I don't think she likes me,' I say, staring down at my hands. 'The person I become when I drink. I don't remember what she does. But I think she wants to destroy me.'

'Why don't you pack a bag and come and stay with us?' she asks gently. 'Just for a few days. Just until the children come home.'

'But do you know what scares me even more, Ana?'

'What?'

'The thought of never drinking again. That's what frightens me most.'

'Beth,' she says, pulling up another chair. 'Everyone struggles sometimes. On the surface it might look like everything is perfect, but it isn't. Life isn't perfect for anyone; I don't think it's supposed to be.'

I flinch as she reaches into her pocket. Is she going to get out her phone and start playing those messages again? That awful voice.

'All we can do is show up every day and do what we have to do,' she says, passing me a tissue. 'And what you need to do today, is let me help you. Listen to me.' She puts her hand on mine. 'You need help, Beth. Please, let me help you.'

I stare at her. Her beautiful, serious face illuminated by concern, and just for a moment the daylight streaming in through the window doesn't hurt. Allowing me instead a glimpse of a different path. Leading me somewhere towards peace.

24

It's the seventh consecutive morning of waking up in Ana's spare bedroom. Sound is emanating from the kitchen below. Kettle boiling, plates clinking, saucepans shifting, another meal being prepared from scratch. She says it's the process of cooking she enjoys most; chopping vegetables, collecting herbs from the garden. Ana is a person who tastes her food as it simmers. Even breakfast. Even when she's only stirring porridge on the stove. And it all tastes good, even the porridge. Makes me feel good too. Providing my body with nutrients and vitamins; helping me sleep more deeply. Think more clearly.

I can hear Harry and the girls playing in the living room. Willow's laughter rising above the rhythm of conversation. I picture him chasing them around the house, catching up with them, swinging them through the air. Now Ana's calling them for breakfast, telling them to wash their hands.

I get out of bed and stare at my reflection in the mirror. It's brighter than it was yesterday – the light beginning to return to my eyes, cheekbones reappearing underneath a complexion that has started to improve. It's tiny now, the slightest red mark on my chin, marking the place where that spot used to be. I pull my hair into a ponytail and my dressing gown on, inside a sanctuary created entirely out of other people's spare space. I love this room. They haven't redecorated in here yet and the wholesome energy of Leo's Spider-Man wallpaper – hung by Charlotte with such care – is comforting. Infiltrating perhaps the darkest collections of thoughts piled up in my mind – the ones that aren't even mine.

My phone rings and Emily's name appears on the display. I glance at my reflection in the mirror, amber flecks in my eyes giving me the confidence I need. I go over to the cushioned window seat that I remember once being covered with Leo's stuffed toys and sit down, resting my head on the cool windowpane. I take the call.

'Hello,' I say.

'Beth, it's Emily.'

'I know.'

'Right. Look, Beth, I know we haven't spoken since—'

'Danielle died?'

'Since last Friday. And I know that things got a little heated between us, you know before . . .'

'Danielle died?'

'Yes, but I'm hoping that we can put our differences behind us because you know, what happened to Danielle, it puts everything into perspective, don't you think?'

'Yes.'

'And I keep thinking about her.'

'Of course.'

'About what she'd want me to do.'

'About what?'

'Today.'

'Today?'

'Seraphina's party. I've got the whole of Year One and their parents arriving this afternoon.'

'Right.'

'And I'm combining it with a leaving party for Georgina. She's off to Oxford University in a few days.'

'Yes, you said.'

'So, what with the whole of Year One, Georgina and her friends, Mr Combustible and his team, it's going to be quite a houseful.'

'Mr Combustible has a team?'

'Of course he does. How else do you think he assembles a working science lab at parties? The man sets himself on fire, Beth. Obviously in a safe, tidy, educational way.'

'Right.'

'And this week, as you can imagine, it's been unbelievably difficult for me. Practically impossible, in fact – trying to decide what to do for the best. Ever since, you know . . .'

'Danielle died?'

'Exactly. But I think she'd want me to go ahead with the party. For Seraphina and Georgina to have their special day.'

'Right.'

'And there's something else I think she'd want.'

'What?'

'For you not to be here.'

'What?'

'For you not to come to the party, Beth. I think that's what Danielle would have wanted.'

'Would she?'

'Yes, I think she would.'

'If you don't want me at your house today, Emily, you only have to say.'

'Oh no!' I can almost hear the unblinking of those huge, alien eyes. 'This has got nothing to do with me. I would never rescind an invitation, and I want you at the party, of course I do. It's just . . .'

'What?'

'Danielle and I, we were extremely close, almost like sisters, and that's why I'm very conscious of what *she* would have wanted. Surely the least we can all do, to honour her memory, is respect her wishes.'

'It's funny,' I say. 'Between you and Danielle, I always thought you were the bossy one. It's difficult imagining her calling the shots,' I add, staring out the window to the driveway below. 'Especially from beyond the grave.'

Sharp intake of breath. 'Please don't use that word, Beth.'

'What word?' Did I swear without noticing?

'Grave,' she says, and I can hear the grimace. 'I can't bear hearing any words associated with . . .'

'What?'

'You know, when someone isn't alive any more. Words associated with . . .'

'Death?'

'Yes.' Another deep breath. 'Makes me feel quite light-headed and queasy.'

'You're frightened of death words?' Unusual kryptonite. 'Isn't fear a sign of weakness?'

'That's why I don't like it when you keep asking questions about Charlotte.' Deflection? Or did she not hear my last question? 'It makes me uncomfortable, when you go on and on about it. Questioning how she . . .'

'Died?'

'And Beth, I'm not suggesting that Danielle is calling the shots, but the truth is – she knew me and understood I've got very little patience for drama. Especially when I'm putting on a big event. If she wasn't . . . not alive any more . . . she'd be here right now, helping me prepare for the party. Whereas now I'm having to do everything without her and the thing is, Beth, I've got neither the time nor the energy for any drama today. I think that's why Danielle wouldn't want you to come. She wouldn't want you turning up, getting emotional, cracking jokes, making things awkward with Jade—'

'Jade?'

'Yes. Obviously, she'll be at the party with Rowan, and I've told them they can bring all the children—'

'*My* children?'

'Together with Jade's children, and obviously there's still a lot of tension between you two.'

'Well, she did fuck my husband.'

'And that's the other thing. I don't want any swearing today. Not with so many little ones running around.'

'Right.'

'The more I think about it, the more I can see where she's coming from.'

'Who?'

'Danielle. Surely you must be able to see why she wouldn't want you coming . . .'

From the window seat of Charlotte's son's bedroom, I can see the driveway snaking out into that treacherous bend in Herrywell Lane. The place where she died. Dead. Deceased. Demised. In a coffin. Buried in a grave. Emily's still talking but I'm not listening. Funeral. Eulogy. Wake. Lilies. Perhaps overexposure will take away a little of my fear. Hearse. Wreath. Murder.

When I'm certain I can't think of any more death words – *Why don't you die?* – I silently end the call.

25

Porridge isn't on the Saturday breakfast menu in Ana's house but there is bacon, mushrooms, toast, scrambled eggs, boiled eggs and the offer of a poached egg if I'd prefer. I say thank you for everything, as I do at every mealtime, and take my seat at the kitchen table next to Willow who always looks at me quizzically, wondering where Hope is. Wondering what the point of me is, how I can exist without her best friend in my arms.

'How did you sleep?' asks Harry, pouring coffee into my cup from the cafetière.

'Great. I slept great. I always sleep great here. Thank you so much.'

'Beth, how long are you going to live in our house for?' asks Summer, holding an immaculately cut toast soldier in her tiny fingers, dipping it with finesse into the top of a boiled egg. 'And why are you allowed to live here, anyway?

Aren't you supposed to be looking after Freddie and your other children? And your dog. The one that eats everything. Even poo,' she says, popping the toast into her mouth.

'Come on, Summer,' says Harry, shaking his head. 'Not at the breakfast table.'

'It's OK,' I smile, 'and those are very good questions, Summer. Freddie and his brother and sister, they've been living with their daddy this week and that's why I've been able to stay here with you. I've had such a lovely time and you've all been so kind,' I add, 'but I'll be going home later today.'

'Didn't you want to stay in your house on your own, Beth?' Summer asks, nibbling another perfect rectangle of toast. 'Were you frightened that the lady who died in your kitchen might live there as a ghost now?'

'Another good question.' I take a sip of coffee. 'But no, I'm not frightened of ghosts.'

'Why not?' she asks. 'Don't you believe in them?'

'Oh, I believe in them,' I say, my eyes moving towards that empty space on the kitchen windowsill. Remembering the radio she used to keep there. 'I just don't find them very scary.'

'Why not?'

'Because I believe ghosts are our friends,' I say. 'They're just the friends we can't see.'

'Oh, this is getting ridiculous now,' says Ana, looking at her phone. 'Sixty-five unread messages on that bloody WhatsApp group!' She's staring at the screen. 'My phone hasn't stopped pinging all morning. Isn't it driving you crazy?' she says to me.

'What WhatsApp group?' I check my phone. No messages.

'The one Emily set up for Seraphina's party,' Ana replies. 'There's been hundreds of messages, haven't you seen them? Mostly about Mr Combustible,' she adds. 'All these terms, conditions and indemnities, I didn't know a child's party could become so legal. He's going to set himself on fire, apparently.'

'Who?' asks Harry.

'Mr Combustible,' Ana replies. 'And if any of our kids "attempt to replicate any of his act at home" Emily and her family will not be accepting liability. She's very clear about that,' Ana adds. 'Mentioned it at least thirty times so far and now she's going on about a second parking area. How everyone should follow signs to the orchard when they arrive.'

'Emily has an orchard?' asks Harry.

'Only in her mind,' I reply.

'Mummy, Daddy,' says Summer. 'We've finished, can Willow and I go outside and play?'

'Yes,' says Ana, placing her phone onto the table. 'It's still lovely and sunny out there. I'll let you know when you need to come inside and get ready for the party.'

As the two little girls disappear into the back garden, Harry refills my coffee cup before settling back in his chair.

'So, how are you, Beth?' he asks. 'How are you feeling about going home today?'

'Good,' I say, swallowing a mouthful of scrambled eggs. 'I'm feeling good.'

'And do you think you'll carry on with the . . .'

'AA meetings?' I say, raising my coffee cup to my mouth. 'Yes, I think I will. I know I was rather reluctant initially,' I add, 'well, I hated the idea, didn't I? But I have to admit, I'm finding the meetings really helpful, and I can't thank you enough for persuading me to go. Both of you,' I say, looking from Harry to Ana. 'I can't thank you enough for everything. For letting me stay in your home, cooking me all these amazing meals, driving me to and from the community centre every day, and all without any judgement. You're amazing. Taking in a loser like me – honestly, I don't deserve friends like—'

'You're not a loser, Beth,' says Harry. 'And you don't have to keep thanking us. There isn't a person alive who hasn't had a difficult time and needed a bit of help on occasion. I know I certainly have and so has this one,' he says, tapping his hand gently on Ana's. 'When we first met, it took months of my most sparkling wit to make her smile.'

'That was your most sparkling wit?' she asks.

'Charming!' He laughs. 'And yes, it was! Don't you remember all those effortlessly hilarious one-liners? I spent ages working on them.'

'Where did you meet?' I ask.

'In a little coffee shop round the corner from chambers,' he says. 'That's where Ana was working at the time and as soon as I walked in and saw her, that was it – I was in love. I started buying my lunch from there every day after that, just so I could try to talk to her.'

'You two are so cute,' I say, reaching for another slice of bacon and putting it between two slices of toast. 'Nauseating, obviously, but extremely cute. I don't think Rowan and I were ever so in love.'

'Really?' asks Harry.

'Well, maybe we were in the beginning,' I say. 'I remember our honeymoon being very romantic.'

'Where did you go?' asks Ana.

'Mexico,' I reply, 'and it was amazing, the best time of my life. Rowan signed us up for a scuba diving course and I was so nervous at first but strangely enough, swimming around in the ocean, holding his hand – I think it was the safest I've ever felt. Cocooned in love, I suppose. Happiness at the bottom of the ocean. Ironic that it all went downhill from there.'

'How long were you married?' asks Harry.

'Seven years,' I reply, biting into my bacon sandwich. 'We're such a cliché. Just another two victims of the seven-year itch. How long have you two been together?'

'It's been almost six years already,' Harry says, turning towards Ana. 'Since I started stalking you in that café . . .'

'With your sparkling stand-up routine,' she laughs.

'Well, I don't think you've got anything to worry about,' I say. 'I don't think the seven-year itch applies to lovebirds like you two. And besides, Rowan and I had a lot going on in our lives when our relationship ended. I'd just had Hope a few months earlier, the boys were really young and then when Charlotte died, I was devastated. A total mess. Though of course, the affair started before that.'

'And how are you feeling about it now?' asks Harry.

'About Charlotte's death?'

'Yes,' he replies. 'Well, more specifically, about your

investigation into her death. Do you think you'll keep working on it?' He glances towards his wife. 'Now that you're not . . .'

'What?'

'Now that you're not drinking any more.'

'I'm not sure,' I say. 'I haven't really thought about it.'

'We're not prying, Beth,' says Ana. Why is she looking so concerned? 'It's just that you already seem a little better after not drinking for a week and it would be such a shame . . .'

'What?'

'If anything were to make you start drinking again.'

'Right.'

'We're worried that your project might trigger your drinking,' says Harry.

'Right.'

'Because you only seemed to work on it when you were drinking, didn't you?' says Ana gently. 'And because they seemed to be so . . .' she's interlacing the fingers of both hands, '. . . I can't think of the word in English,' she's saying, looking from Harry to me. 'How do you say it, when two things are tightly linked to one another?'

'Interwoven?' says Harry.

'Knitted together?' I suggest.

'Yes, that's it,' says Ana. 'Because your drinking and project were so interknitted.' Today's word of the day. 'It would be horrible if your project led you to start drinking again.'

'Right,' I say for a third time, and when neither of them speaks, I realise I probably should. 'Well, like I said, I haven't thought much about it since I've been here.' I lower my eyes. 'It still doesn't make any sense to me – why Charlotte ran out into the lane in the dark, leaving Leo alone in the house. But maybe you're right,' I say, raising my eyes to meet theirs. 'Maybe my drinking and this little obsession started feeding into one another. Because the truth is, I'm never going to know for certain what happened to Charlotte, am I? So much time has passed, any evidence will have been destroyed long ago and as for motive, I can't think why anyone would want her dead. Yes, she was irritatingly perfect, but she was also kind and she cared about people. She was genuine, like you two. I don't know,' my eyes drop back down towards the table, 'maybe she went out for some air, or to scare a fox away from the bins, or a dozen other completely normal things. Maybe it *was* just a tragic accident. Maybe it's time for me to accept that and move on.'

Ana's phone beeps. 'Yet another message about the second parking area,' she says. 'But no mention whatsoever about dress code. What are you planning to wear this afternoon, Beth?' she asks. 'I was thinking smart-casual but now it seems like such a big event, I'm not sure whether I should get more dressed up.'

'You'll look beautiful in whatever you wear,' I say.

'Thank you,' she smiles. 'As will you.'

'I don't know about that,' I say, picking up my sandwich and taking another bite.

'So, what are you going to wear?' she asks again.

'Oh, I'm not going,' I say. 'I'm not invited.'

'What? I thought all the Year One parents were invited.'

'They are,' I say. 'Well, they were, but Emily phoned me this morning. She said it would be better if I didn't go.'

'Why?' says Ana, her voice raised. 'What are you talking about?'

'It's no big deal,' I say. 'She just can't handle any drama today.'

'What drama?'

'You know, any jokes or swearing,' I say. 'Plus, the occasional mean comment that may accidentally escape my mouth when I see Jade. She's going to be there with Rowan and the kids.'

'Your kids?'

'And hers.'

'But don't you want to be there today, to see your children?'

'Of course I do,' I say, picking at a piece of bacon. 'I'm desperate to see them, but I can wait until Rowan drops them home after the party. It works out quite well, actually. Gives me a chance to clean the house before they get back and, to be honest, I didn't fancy going to Emily's today anyway. I can just imagine it. Everyone gawping at me, blaming me for Danielle's death.'

'You're scared?' asks Harry, although I'm not completely certain it's a question.

'Yeah, I guess I am. I'd rather stay at home.'

'I understand,' he says, tapping the fingers of his right hand gently on the table. 'It's just . . .'

'What?' I ask.

'Nothing,' he says, pushing his chair back and standing up. 'None of my business. Do you want any more coffee?'

'No, thank you,' I say as he starts piling cutlery on plates. 'Harry, what were you going to say?'

'I guess it just makes me uncomfortable,' he says, the plates and cutlery clattering as he takes them over to the sink.

'What?'

'Someone letting other people tell them what they should do and where they should go. Do you know how many people have tried to tell me where *I* don't belong?'

'But it's different for you,' I say, looking up at him. 'You're a barrister, for goodness' sake! I'm not like you—'

'It doesn't matter who you are,' he says. 'It's the same rules for everyone, Beth. All of us – we all have to show up for life, no matter how difficult it is.'

'But surely there's a difference between showing up for life and gate-crashing a party?' I ask. 'After all, Emily uninvited me.'

'Did she really say that?' asks Ana.

'Well, not exactly. She said she would never rescind an invitation—'

'So, what's the problem?' she asks.

'Emily said *Danielle* wouldn't want me there.'

'Well, no disrespect to the dead woman,' Harry says, 'but I don't think she's going to be checking off names at the door. Look,' he leans towards me, 'it's up to you, Beth. What do you think they'd tell you to do at AA?'

'They don't really tell me what to do at AA,' I say. 'We just listen to each other . . .'

'But if they *did* tell you what to do?'

'I'm not sure really.' My eyes drop to the table.

'Do you know what I think they'd say?' I'm fairly certain he's about to tell me. 'I think they'd tell you to go to the party with your head held high.'

'Would they?'

'Yes, and if anyone starts gossiping about you, do you know what I think your friends at AA would say?'

'They're not really my friends—'

'I think they'd tell them to fuck off.'

'Would they?'

'Yes, and if they don't, I will. I mean it, if anyone talks shit about you today, Beth, I'll tell them to fuck off.'

'Are you going to the party as well?' asks Ana. 'I thought you had to work on that new case today.'

'I can work later,' Harry replies. 'If Beth is going to be brave enough to go, I think we should both be there too. In her corner. Plus,' he adds, 'I'm quite intrigued about the bloke setting himself on fire.'

They smile and that's when I feel her, because she's everywhere – almost more of a presence than when she was alive. Sitting at this table in the middle of the kitchen where she used to dance, I feel her arms around me together with the arms of the people who now occupy her home. And I realise I'm crying.

26

I follow the signs and park my car next to one of the apple trees in Emily's imaginary orchard. I told Harry and Ana that I'd meet them here. Told them I wanted to go home first and tidy up a bit. I thought about mopping the kitchen floor but washed my hair instead, then blow-dried it and put on makeup, which looks much better when it's accentuating features rather than concealing imperfections. I'm wearing black leggings and a long, flowing top that manages to skim over my hips while suggesting a much smaller waist than my own. A little deceptive and extremely flattering – qualities I can't help but admire. And I'm wearing heels too. My favourite black heeled boots that I found underneath a load of clutter at the bottom of my wardrobe. Hoping perhaps a little extra height can be filled with a little extra confidence, strengthening the connection between who I am now and the person I used to be.

I lock my car and pause to glance at my reflection in the window. If I saw this version of myself standing in the playground, I wonder what I would think. Someone with friends, that's what I look like. An array of long-term friendships that I've managed to nurture and maintain over the years, while juggling the demands of my job. Because I look like someone with a career; a person with ambition, who knows where she's going and takes the time to congratulate herself on how far she's come. And I imagine she still gets on with her parents and siblings – I bet she didn't get drunk and messy at her nephew's christening last year and behave so disgracefully that none of them speak to her any more. She probably even holidays with her extended family once a year. In the south of France perhaps, or maybe Spain – somewhere with a pool so the children can play water polo with their cousins, while I sit in the shade, listening to their laughter, sipping a cold glass of white wine. Because she can do that – this version of myself. She knows how to sip wine. She knows how to stop.

More cars are arriving in the second parking area. I stare up into the apple trees. Shouldering all that responsibility for being an orchard, they're magnificent in the sunshine – almost majestic, even when pretending to be something they're not. I wonder how they do it, those beautiful trees. Must have strong roots, I suppose, is that the secret? Is that how they can stand there with such effortless pride?

I don't recognise any of the people getting out of their cars, so walk up to the front door on my own, where I meet Nigel.

'Beth,' he says, as I approach. 'How lovely to see you.' His smile looks genuine. 'How is everything?'

'Good,' I say, returning the smile. 'Everything's good.'

'Great!' A brief glance over his shoulder. 'Does Emily know that you're here?'

'Not yet,' I reply. 'But I'm sure it won't be a problem,' I add. *'The more the merrier,* that's what she always says, isn't it?'

'Of course,' he says, standing aside. 'And has there been any news?'

'About?'

'Danielle. Any new developments?'

'I think she's still dead, Nigel.'

'Of course,' he says again, leaning towards me and lowering his voice. 'I just wondered whether you've heard anything from the police. About their enquiries.'

'Not yet,' I reply, stepping into the grand hallway and staring at the enormous collection of shoes and boots covering half of the floor.

'Everyone's leaving their footwear over there,' he says, his finger pointing towards the pile.

'Really? Is there any chance I could keep my boots on?' I ask, turning to face him. 'They're perfectly clean – look!'

'Everyone's leaving their footwear over there,' he says again, his finger still pointing.

'OK,' I say, kicking off my boots.

'And the presents for Seraphina and Georgina, please leave them over here.' Same finger, but pointing in a different direction, towards what I assume is a table, hidden completely by hundreds of gift bags. Not sure why he's telling me about it though. Clearly, I'm not carrying anything.

'Sorry,' I say, making my way back through the field of footwear, 'I haven't had time to buy any presents this week. I've been a bit busy.'

I head towards the living room and glance into the kitchen as I pass. A middle-aged man in a lab coat is holding a Bunsen burner and shouting. He looks pissed off and fiery. Mr Combustible, I presume.

The living room still looks enormous, despite being filled with people, all of whom appear to be standing in two separate camps. Across the ceiling on the left side of the room is a 'Happy Birthday Seraphina!' banner and on the right side is another banner, 'Good Luck Georgina!' Everyone entering the room is faced with an immediate dilemma – which banner to stand underneath? Some guests are certain of their decision. Many of the Year One parents, for example: they don't know Georgina, so they head straight for Seraphina's side of the room. But for other people, it's a trickier decision, requiring a little soul-searching and considerable thought. Like wedding guests who know both the bride and groom, which side will they choose? Emily is patrolling no man's land and attempting to clarify the situation, armed with words of encouragement and an unwavering smile.

'Please feel free to go wherever you like,' she's saying. 'Mingle with one another, there's no need to pick a side.'

Of all the idiotic things I've ever heard anyone say, that may possibly be the most stupid. We're human beings, Emily, governed by centuries of human behaviour. The one thing we're good at is picking a side. I spot a flicker of shock as those unblinking alien eyes meet mine, but she recovers quickly, approaching at speed and leaning in for a pretend kiss before issuing a whispered warning.

'Any drama today, Beth, and you will have to leave. Immediately. I mean it, I've got more than enough to contend with, as it is. Mr Combustible is turning out to be rather difficult, and there's a silent auction to organise. Oh, hello!' she says, spotting new arrivals in the living room, before turning and moving away. Her skyscraper heels leave a trail of tiny dents in the luxurious carpet. Why is *she* allowed to wear shoes?

'Hello Beth.'

I turn and stare into a face I haven't seen for a while. Still attractive but beginning to blur a little around the edges. Could be the deep wrinkles running from the edge of each eye, or his hairline speckled with grey.

'Hi,' I say to Bill, Charlotte's husband. 'Good to see you. It's been a long time.'

'Yeah, I wasn't sure whether I was going to come,' he says, raising a beer bottle towards his mouth. 'It's a bit weird being back here but Poppy is still friends with Noah,' he explains. 'They stay in touch, you know, online,' he adds, typing on an imaginary keyboard. 'She wanted to come and see him.'

'Right,' I say. 'And how are you, Bill? How's everything going?'

'OK,' he says, taking another swig.

'And how are Amber, Poppy and Leo?' I ask.

'Not too bad,' he replies, and I'm so pleased to see that

the kindness in his eyes is still there. It hasn't been completely eroded by grief.

'I'm sorry I haven't been in touch,' I say, looking down at my feet. Thank goodness I put on matching socks today. 'After Charlotte died I found it almost impossible to know what to say.'

'I understand,' he says.

'But I think about your children all the time.' I raise my eyes to meet his. 'And you too, of course. It must have been so awful for them, for all of you, but especially the children – losing their mum at such a young age. I can't begin to imagine what that was like.'

'There's been some tough moments,' he says, with a brave smile. 'But they're doing OK now. Poppy and Amber seem very settled in their new school. Made some good friends and they talk about their mum all the time. Lots of tears still, but more and more laughter these days too.'

'That's good. And how about Leo?'

'It hit him the hardest.' Another swig of beer. 'He hardly talked for months. He wasn't talking much even when she died, he was only two and a half, but the doctors reckon the stress of what happened caused a delay in his speech.'

'That's awful.'

'Yes.' He nods his head once, then again. 'It was the not knowing. Trying to guess what was going on inside his head. For ages it felt like I couldn't connect with him at all – he was like a different boy; didn't even want to play with his Spider-Man toys. He just seemed lost, you know?' Another swig of his beer. 'Alone with his thoughts, and his drawings.'

'Drawings?'

'Yes, that was the one blessing – at least he could express himself that way. I'm sorry,' Bill says, 'it's not all doom and gloom, honestly. Lately everything has started to get much better. His speech is improving, and he seems happier, drawing trees and rainbows and animals and other things that aren't . . .'

'What?'

'About that night.' Another swig of beer. 'After she died, that's all he drew, over and over again.'

'What exactly did he draw?'

'The accident. The lane, the car, Charlotte lying in the road.'

I feel suddenly sick. 'How did he know what happened to Charlotte? Wasn't he too little to understand the details?'

Bill looks as sick as I feel. 'I thought you knew – Leo saw it happen. He was in the house that night. His bedroom window looked out onto the road.'

I think back to earlier this morning, sitting in the window seat and looking down at Herrywell Lane, talking to Emily on the phone.

'But how do you know he was looking out of the window when it happened? Surely people were talking about it around him, perhaps he just picked up on what he heard?'

Bill shakes his head. 'No. I wish that *were* true. But the morning after Charlotte died – I hadn't even told the girls exactly what had happened at that stage – I came downstairs and found Leo at the kitchen table. He had drawn a picture of it, as close as a child that age could. I hadn't even told him his mummy was dead. But he already knew.'

'Oh, Bill, I'm so sorry.'

'Yeah. It's bloody awful. Leo had a window seat in his room, he was always climbing onto it to look out.' He smiles. 'Charlotte was so terrified he'd figure out how to open the window she made me put the window key in the safe.'

I smile too. Typical Charlotte, Super Mum.

'But that wasn't the worst of it.' Bill's smile disappears. 'He'd draw what he wished had happened instead.'

'Like what?'

'The lollipop lady in a big yellow coat, or a set of traffic lights in the lane. Anything that could have stopped what happened from happening. Anything that could have kept his mum safe.'

'That poor boy.'

'Yeah.' Another swig of beer. 'That's why I didn't bring him here today. Don't want to risk dredging up any bad memories.'

'And how about you?' I ask. 'How is it for you coming back?'

'Hasn't got any easier,' he says. 'I thought I'd be able to manage it by now, but I still can't bring myself to look at the old house. When I was driving here, I just focused on the road ahead, searching for the big white gates, and then followed signs for the second parking area.' He's smiling now, the kindness in his eyes making way for a twinkle of humour. 'And before I knew it, there I was – in the middle of an orchard!' I start to giggle. 'Why does she call it an orchard?' he laughs.

'I have no idea. And why does everyone go along with

it? It's like we're all stuck inside the same twisted fairy tale, but instead of the emperor having new clothes, Emily's got an orchard.'

He laughs again. 'She means well, though, doesn't she?' he says, taking another mouthful of beer.

'Who?'

'Emily,' he replies. 'She told me she's donating some of the proceeds from the silent auction to Charlotte's favourite charity. That's another reason I felt I should come today. So,' he says, locking those kind eyes onto mine, 'how are you, Beth? You look well.'

'Do I?'

'Yes,' he replies, with another swig of beer. 'You do, all things considered.'

'What do you mean?'

'Emily told me about what happened last week. That must have been one hell of a shock.'

'It was,' I agree. 'Very shocking,' I add. 'Poor Danielle.'

'How are her husband and children?'

'They're ... shocked, I should imagine. Probably still in shock.'

'You don't know?'

'No, I don't,' I say, running my hand through my hair, pleasantly surprised to find it feeling so silky and soft. 'To be honest with you, Bill, Danielle and I – we weren't very close. She was more of an acquaintance. Not a proper friend. Not like Charlotte.'

He finishes his drink. 'I might get another,' he says, indicating his beer bottle. 'There's a bar in the cinema room. Do you want me to get you one?'

'No thanks, I'm not drinking.'
'Really?'
'Yes, I don't drink any more.'
'Oh, right,' he says, stepping back and looking at me, as though with fresh eyes. 'Good for you.' He's still staring at me. 'You know . . .'
'What?'
'Nothing,' he says, his eyes flicking up towards something above my head. 'I don't want to speak out of turn, it's just . . .'
'What?'
'I think it would make Charlotte really happy,' he says, his eyes back on mine. 'Between you and me, she was starting to get a bit worried.'
'When?'
'The last few weeks before she died. No big deal,' he adds quickly. 'Just a bit concerned, that's all.'
'About?'
'Your drinking,' he replies. 'And I'm not saying this to make you feel bad,' he's speaking quickly again, 'she just noticed that you were drinking more and more, you know – once you started – and probably because of that you were becoming a bit messy, forgetting what you said and what you did, and—'
'Mummy, Mummy!'
Freddie is running towards me. I'm sure he's grown taller in the last week, but still my little boy. I scoop him up into my arms, hold him close and swing him around so much we encroach into Seraphina's side of the room. He's laughing and I'm giggling when I hear her voice.

'Freddie!' Yoga-toned arms on display in a sleeveless bohemian maxi dress, cinched in at her tiny waist. I stand taller, suck in my stomach. 'Freddie! Don't run off,' she's saying with a smile. 'I don't want to lose you. Oh, hello Beth,' hand moving to that amethyst bracelet as her eyes meet mine. 'I didn't know you were here.'

'Jade!' and now Fara is appearing, a vision of unflappable accomplishment and charm. Wearing an elegant white trouser suit, accessorised by simple gold jewellery and a sleeping baby. 'Have you found him?' she asks, catching up with Jade.

'Yes,' I say, hugging my son tighter. 'He's here, with me. His mother.'

'Hello Beth,' smiles Fara, 'I didn't know you were here. Quelle surprise!' Why is she speaking in French? Maybe that's what she does when she's caught on the hop and hasn't planned any sophisticated words of the day. Maybe she just says regular words in a different language. Two can play at that game.

'Oui,' I say, 'je suis ... here.' Awkward silence. Bill appears to be glaring at Jade.

'Right,' says Fara, 'well, I'd better get back to my progeny.' Seriously, what's with all the French? 'They're waiting for me in the drawing room. Nice to see you, Beth. You too, Bill,' she adds, before turning and walking away.

'Wait for me, Fara,' calls Jade before turning back towards us. 'I'll be in the drawing room too,' she says, her words aimed vaguely in our direction. 'If you need me.' Why would we need her? I wait for them both to move away before turning to Bill.

'The drawing room?' I say, smirking. 'Who the hell has a drawing room?'

'It's just a room I've set up for drawing,' says Emily, huge alien eyes appearing from . . . where did she come from? 'Nothing spectacular,' she's saying, 'just some basic activities, you know – a painting table, some colouring books and pencils, but it's proving to be very popular with the little ones. Your daughter's having the most wonderful time in there. Ladies and gentlemen,' she's saying now, clinking a spoon against the side of her glass. 'Can I have your attention, please?'

27

'Firstly,' Emily says, as the room falls silent, 'I'd like to thank you all for coming here today to celebrate both my beautiful daughters. Georgina, my eldest, will be leaving us for Oxford University in a few days, and while I will miss her so much,' her voice cracks a little as she retrieves a handkerchief from her pocket, 'I couldn't be prouder of the brilliant young woman she has become. The truth is, I couldn't be prouder of all my children.' She's dabbing at one of her unblinking eyes. 'Seraphina, my fearless little warrior, may be turning six today, but she has the reading age of a ten-year-old! And then there's Tobias. A chess wizard, on course to get the best A-level results his school has ever seen. And as for Noah, his eco house model just won first prize at school.' She laughs. 'Knowing him, it will probably be used as a blueprint for real eco houses in the future! To say I'm proud of my children is an understatement, and it means so much to me and my family that you're all here today, to help us celebrate, especially at such a sad time.

'As you may or may not know, I lost my dear friend Danielle last week.' The handkerchief moves to her other eye. 'And with her in mind, I'd urge you all to take a look at the silent auction I've set up in the conservatory. There are some wonderful prizes on offer and any money raised will be split between a meningitis charity, which was the preferred charity of my other dear friend Charlotte, and an anaphylaxis charity in memory of Danielle. As Danielle has only recently . . . only recently . . .'

What's the matter with her? Oh, of course! Emily's aversion to death words.

'As Danielle has only recently left us, I think it would be fitting to hold a minute's silence in her honour.' She turns her tear-filled alien eyes towards Bill. 'And I think we should also have a minute's silence for Charlotte.' At the same time? Or consecutively? 'So, let's have a two-minute silence.' She closes those alien eyes, tears are still streaming. Has the silence started already? Is anyone timing it?

'Mummy, Mummy!' Freddie says loudly. 'What's happening, Mummy? Is this the silent auction, Mummy? What's a silent auction?'

'Thank you, ladies and gentlemen.' Emily's eyes are open again. No way was that two minutes. 'And now, if you'd like to follow me – the laboratory has been set up in the kitchen, where Mr Combustible is so excited to meet you all, he's ready to burst . . . into flames!'

We're all traipsing out of the living room, shuffling towards the kitchen, when I see them, a few rows of people ahead. Rowan has Hope in his arms and Jack by his side, who is staring up at Jade, talking to her, looking excited. Freddie's hand is in mine. I squeeze tighter.

'Children should sit at the front to get the best view,' Mr Combustible's minions are saying as we enter the kitchen.

'You can stay with me, Freddie,' I say as we walk towards the back of the room. 'You can sit on my shoulders; I'll make sure you can see.'

'All the other children are sitting at the front, Mummy,' he says, wriggling his hand free. I squeeze tighter. 'Can I sit at the front, Mummy?' He's pulling away.

'Of course,' I say, with a smile that I don't think he sees, because he's already gone. Disappearing before I even decided to let go.

'That must be tough,' says Bill, as we squish into a space at the back of the kitchen. 'Having to see those two together.' He nods in the direction of Rowan and Jade. 'Playing happy families, with your children.'

'Yeah,' I say, attempting to recreate his brave smile. 'And it never seems to get any easier. Double the betrayal, double the pain, I guess.' Another attempt at that smile. 'It wasn't just my husband I lost, was it? Jade and I, we used to be such good friends.'

'I know. What a treacherous bitch she turned out to be.'

'Bill!' I laugh. 'I'm not going to disagree, but I'm surprised you feel so strongly.'

'Well, it's the truth, isn't it? She *is* a treacherous bitch. Charlotte couldn't stand her by the end.'

'Yeah, I heard they fell out,' I say, shuffling even closer

towards him as more people cram into the room. 'Although I never knew why.'

'It was about you.'

'Me?'

'Well, about your drinking.'

'What do you mean?'

'It's like I said before, Charlotte was getting worried about you. She said you felt like Rowan was pulling away, always working late, and she could see you were using alcohol to deal with it. She thought it might be getting a bit out of control and she wanted to talk to you about it, but . . .'

'What?'

'It's difficult, isn't it? Talking to someone about their behaviour. Especially someone you care about. Charlotte loved you so much, Beth,' he says. 'The last thing she wanted to do was upset you, especially when you already seemed so sad. She was scared of pushing you away, but it got to the point where she felt she had to do something because your drinking – it seemed to be getting worse and . . .'

'Bill, what did she do?'

'Well, I think long-term, her plan was for the group to—'

'The group?'

'Yes, Charlotte, Emily, Fara, Danielle, Jade,' he says, counting out the names on his fingers. 'Charlotte thought it would be a good idea for everyone to get together and support you. She thought you might be more receptive to what she had to say if you knew they all shared her concerns. But before talking about it to any of the others, she spoke about it with Jade. Charlotte knew the two of you were very close and she thought you might listen to Jade, what with her being so . . .'

'What?'

'I'm not sure of the word,' he says, the lines around his eyes reaching right out into his hairline. 'Spiritual? You know, what with her reiki and crystals and all that, but . . .'

'But, what?'

'Jade shrugged it off and didn't seem the slightest bit concerned about you. Even implied that Charlotte was just being nosy. It drove Charlotte mad. Well, at first she was angry, but after a while she grew suspicious. Started to wonder whether there was an ulterior motive for Jade not wanting to help, for not even wanting to talk about you.' His words are starting to hurt. 'And then after Charlotte's death, we found out why, didn't we? Jade and Rowan had been having an affair for ages. My wife's suspicions had been spot on. Jade didn't want to talk about you struggling because she and Rowan were the reason for it. She probably felt guilty.' Treacherous bitch. 'At least, I *hope* she felt guilty.'

'Bill?' I want to talk about something else. The memories of that time are making me itch for a glass of wine.

'Yes?'

'Didn't you ever think it was odd that Charlotte went out for a run that night, leaving Leo in the house on his own?'

'Well,' he says, 'I don't think she was planning on running very far.'

'Even so,' I say, surprised at his response. 'Surely she wouldn't . . .'

'I think she was just doing sprints in the driveway. You know, interval training. It was a normal part of her marathon prep.'

'But she'd already run ten miles that morning.'

'Wouldn't stop her going out to do short sprints later the same day. Ten miles wasn't that much for Charlotte.'

Maybe I've been thinking about this wrong. I've been coming at it from how *I'd* be after running ten miles – half dead. But Charlotte? She'd done marathons before, perhaps ten miles really wasn't a big deal. Still . . .

'But would she have done it so late? In the dark?'

'Well, the security lights would have been on,' Bill says. 'They came on every time anyone approached the house from the driveway.'

'And what about other security?' I ask. 'Did you have cameras?'

'No.' He shakes his head. 'We had an excellent alarm system, but no cameras.'

'Not even a doorbell one?'

'No,' he says again. 'Kept meaning to get one but never got round to it. I guess life kept getting in the way.'

'But if Charlotte *was* just doing sprints in the driveway,' I ask, 'why did she run out into the road?'

Bill shrugs. 'Maybe she was sprinting so fast, she didn't stop in time. Maybe she overran into the lane. I mean, it *was* very dark.'

'But you just said the security lights were on.'

'Well, yes,' he says, 'near the house. But towards the lane it would have been dark.'

'I don't know, Bill,' I say, shuffling a little further into the kitchen, as more people spill into the room. 'Charlotte was one of the most sensible people I've ever known. I'm struggling to accept that she ran straight out into the road.'

'But that's what the witnesses said, didn't they?' Bill says, shuffling alongside me. 'The kids in the car all said the same thing. That Charlotte just suddenly appeared.'

'But why? Why was she out there running at that time of night?'

'She often had to go out in the evenings to fit in all the training. Most runners do.'

'Do most of them go out running after drinking wine?'

'Look, Beth,' Bill says. 'I know Charlotte's death was devastating but all these questions, what's the point? The truth is, I'll never know what happened because I wasn't with her that night. I was here instead, at a stupid Halloween party, when I should have been at home with my wife.' He looks away from me, staring at something on the other side of the room. 'And that's something I'm going to have to live with for the rest of my life.'

'Why do you say that?'

'Because I never should have left her on her own that night,' he says.

'Why not?'

'Because it was Halloween.'

'So?'

'Beth,' he says, turning back to face me. 'Do you honestly not remember?'

28

Some of the children at the front are shouting. I think they're getting bored. Emily's facing the crowd and fiddling with a microphone that doesn't appear to be working.

'One two, one two,' she's saying into it, a smile fixed onto her lips, whereas the man standing next to her in the white lab coat, his face is frozen into a scowl.

'It was a few months after you'd given birth to Hope,' Bill says, his voice close to my head. Everyone's voice is close to my head. There's no personal space in here any more. 'You came round to our house one evening,' he adds, his breath on my face, 'sat at the kitchen table with Charlotte and drank wine together.'

'One two, one two,' Emily's still tapping at the microphone. A fragment of memory arrives. I'm staring into Charlotte's face. We're clinking glasses, sipping wine.

'Everything was fine to begin with,' he says. 'That's what

she told me afterwards. Do you remember that radio she used to have? The one she kept on the windowsill.' I nod. 'Well, apparently you wanted to turn the volume up and start dancing!' he smiles. 'She said you seemed happy, until . . .'

'What?'

'Until you weren't.' Is it getting hotter in here? 'And I'm not saying this to be unkind.'

I know he isn't. There's no escaping the kindness in his eyes.

'But Charlotte said it was like someone flicked a switch, changing you into a completely different person. You got really angry, started calling her irritatingly perfect and . . . Well, she'd had a couple of drinks too, hadn't she? And maybe that's why she started shouting back, telling you . . .'

'What?'

'That she wasn't perfect. Far from it. That she'd made this dreadful mistake . . .' The microphone screeches. I jump. Everyone puts their hands to their ears. 'Something she could never forgive herself for.'

'One two, one two,' Emily's voice is amplified into something distorted.

'What mistake?' I ask, flinching. Another screech of the microphone. Nails on a chalkboard. 'When?'

'It was something that happened years ago,' he's standing so close, 'when Charlotte was working in paediatric A&E.' I can smell his breath on my face. 'The hospital was busy that night and, at some point, she examined a two-year-old boy, presenting with a temperature. Charlotte thought it was a virus, nothing serious, and she sent the boy and his mother home.'

His breath smells of beer. It's comforting and familiar. Where did he say there was a fully stocked bar?

'But it *was* serious,' Bill says, closing his eyes. 'The little boy's condition worsened when they got home, and his mother had to rush him back to the hospital. Danielle was in the waiting room by then.'

'Danielle? What was she doing there?'

'It was Halloween and one of her children had tripped over while they were out trick or treating or something. As if it wasn't busy enough that night,' he's shaking his head, eyes still closed, 'Danielle had an allergic reaction and collapsed. Charlotte ran over and started working on her. She saved her life. But at the same time that little boy with the temperature . . . He died. In his mother's arms. Sitting there in the waiting area. That poor boy.'

That poor boy.

'Charlotte never forgave herself.' Bill opens his eyes. 'The child had meningitis, and she'd missed it. After that it didn't matter how many times I tried to remind her of all the lives she'd saved during her career, she never stopped blaming herself for his death. She stopped working soon after that. She said she wanted to focus on our kids for a bit. And when that wasn't enough, she started volunteering, ran the PTA, started raising money for meningitis charities. She raised thousands of pounds over the years, but never enough to stop thinking about that little boy.'

He's silent and I think about all the conversations I had with Charlotte. The cups of tea, her smile and laughter.

'Why didn't she ever tell me?'

'She did, Beth. She told you that night, but you obviously got too drunk to remember.' Another flinch.

'But why didn't she talk about it more? Something as devastating as that, why did she only mention it once?'

'You know what Charlotte was like,' he says. 'She didn't want to make it about her. Truth is, she hardly talked about it with anyone, even me. As the years went by, the only time it was mentioned was . . .'

'When?'

'When she'd wake up in the middle of the night, shouting. Saying she could hear the mother's screams, begging Charlotte to help her, to save her little boy. She'd wake up shouting, "I'm sorry. I'm so sorry." I don't think she ever stopped feeling sorry.'

That poor boy. I'm so sorry.

29

'Ladies, gentlemen and children,' Emily's voice cuts through the restless chatter of bored children. 'Apologies for the delay but it looks like I've finally got this microphone to work. So, who's ready for something explosive?'

The man wants to set himself on fire and everyone wants to watch the man set himself on fire. Why is she still talking?

'Before we start and while I've got everyone's attention,' Emily says with a smile, 'I'd like to make a quick announcement about an event I'm organising – as head of the PTA at St Michael's Primary – an early term tombola! And it will be happening in the playground this Tuesday after school, so please remember to bring some money when you collect your children. We've got some great prizes . . .'

Bill's mouth is moving but I can't hear what he's saying over Emily's monologue. He shakes the empty beer bottle in his hand and starts weaving his way through the crowd, so I assume he's heading to the bar. At the front of the kitchen, Mr Combustible is looking furious, rolling up the sleeve of his lab coat and glancing at his watch, but Emily's still talking. Her words ricocheting off every wall, almost distracting me from the sound of something falling into place.

I see them over by the door. They're late, only just walking into the kitchen. Harry's holding Willow and he's followed by Ana. I slowly start inching through the crowd towards them.

'Hi Beth,' Ana says, as I approach. 'You look nice.' She smiles. She seems pleased to see me. 'We haven't missed anything yet, have we?'

'No.'

'What's Emily talking about?'

'I'm not sure,' I reply. 'The tombola, I think.' Mr Combustible is trying to grab hold of the microphone. 'Ana, can I speak to you?' I ask, as Summer pulls Harry by the hand and he guides his daughters towards the front.

'Of course.'

Ana follows me back towards the kitchen door where there are slightly fewer people. Slightly more space, and a little more distance from Emily's amplified voice. Ana's wearing a long red skirt and matching top. It looks soft. Cashmere, perhaps. She's barefoot and her toenails are painted the exact same shade of red as her outfit. I wonder if she suspected she'd have to take off her shoes. 'Beth.' I raise my eyes to meet hers. 'Is everything OK?'

'I was just talking to Bill, Charlotte's husband.'

'Oh, right.'

'And now I think I know why someone wanted Charlotte dead.'

'What?'

'Motive.' I pause. 'That's what Harry said I needed to think about, didn't he? And that's what I couldn't understand before. Why anyone would want Charlotte dead, but now I think I do.'

'What are you talking about? I thought you were going to leave all this alone.'

'I was, but then I spoke to Bill and now I know why Charlotte hated Halloween.'

'Are you OK? You're not making much sense.' The concern in her eyes looks more like panic. 'You haven't been drinking, have you?'

'No! See, Danielle was always going on about it, wasn't she? That Halloween years ago when she collapsed in A&E and Charlotte saved her life.'

'Yes, I remember.'

'Well, there was someone else there that night, Bill just told me. A mother with her little boy.'

'And?'

'He died of meningitis, Ana, waiting for a doctor to see him. And Charlotte never forgave herself.'

'Why?'

'Because she was the doctor responsible for looking after him, but she made a mistake. She sent him home, didn't realise how ill he was and then when his mother rushed him back to hospital, Charlotte was busy saving Danielle's life and that's when the little boy died.'

'That's so sad,' Ana says. 'But I don't understand what any of it has got to do with Charlotte's death.'

'We know someone came to her house, your house, the night that she died, don't we? Maybe it was a trick or treater. Or maybe . . .'

'What?'

'Maybe it was a grieving mother who blamed Charlotte for the death of her son.' Ana's staring at me in silence. 'Motive enough for you?'

'But how can you possibly know that it was the child's mother at the door?'

'Because of Charlotte's last words. *That poor boy. I'm sorry.* It makes sense, don't you see?'

'Not really,' Ana says, staring down at her hands. Her fingernails are painted the same colour as her outfit. Same colour as her toenails. 'It might have been what Charlotte was thinking about at the end of her life,' she says, 'but that doesn't mean she was chased into the road by the boy's mother. And . . . wait a minute,' her eyes back on mine. 'What about that sinister feeling you had in the weeks before Charlotte died? Like you knew something terrible was going to happen. Didn't you think it was someone in your group of friends, that one of them killed Charlotte?'

'Yes,' I say. 'But I may have been wrong about what was causing that feeling.'

'So it wasn't that Charlotte was going to die?'

'No. Bill just told me that Charlotte was planning a . . . well, I suppose you could call it an intervention. She was worried about my drinking, apparently.'

'She's not the only one.'

'I'm not drunk, Ana. I promise you. But I will admit that maybe I got it wrong. Maybe it wasn't one of our friends, maybe it was someone else. Someone who had a motive for killing Charlotte, a proper one. Someone who bided their time and made her pay for her mistake. A life for a life. It's biblical, isn't it?'

'I suppose . . .'

'I never believed she ran out into the road. I've never believed that for a moment. And finally, I've stumbled across an explanation that makes sense.'

'Have you?'

'Yes! Think about it, Ana. It's the anniversary of her son's death, and this woman tracks Charlotte down and bangs on her door.'

'And then what?'

'Well, if Charlotte thought she was in any danger, her instinct would have been to draw the woman *outside*, wouldn't it? Away from the house where Leo was sleeping upstairs. Maybe the woman was intending to kill Charlotte last Halloween. Or maybe just vent her anger. But then the car did the job for her.'

'But even if there was a woman who blamed Charlotte for the death of her child, how are you ever going to find her? Or even know who you're looking for? Like you said earlier, it's been almost a year since Charlotte died. Any evidence will be long gone. And how many years ago did that little boy die?'

'Six.'

'Six! How are you going to find out the identity of a woman who was in A&E six years ago?'

'I don't know, Ana, this is all new information. I haven't had time to think about it properly yet. But when I get home, I'll write everything down and go through it methodically and . . .'

'Beth.' Her hand is on my arm. 'Do you think that's a good idea? Despite everything you've just found out, don't you think for your own sake, for your own health, it might be best to leave all this alone?'

There are raised voices at the other end of the kitchen and we both turn our heads. Mr Combustible has finally wrestled the microphone away from Emily.

'While we're making announcements,' Mr Combustible's speech is clipped, 'I'd like to let everyone know about a huge science demonstration I'll be hosting this half term. It's going to be spectacular. Far too large to stage within the confines of a normal home,' a glance around the kitchen, his facial expression morphing into a sneer, 'so we'll be constructing a super-sized laboratory in the playground at a local school – Pond Street Primary. Everyone is welcome, you don't have to attend the school to come along. It's going to be busy so probably best to book tickets online beforehand. All the details are on the leaflets we'll be handing out after today's experiments—'

'And don't forget the tombola this Tuesday at St Michael's.' Emily's voice is raised and she's contorting her neck to get her face near the microphone when I realise my hand is at my mouth.

'Oh my God.'

'What?' Ana's hand still on my arm. 'What is it, Beth?'

'PSP. I couldn't read half my writing but that's what

I wrote all over my project. That's what I was trying to remind myself about.'

'What do you mean?'

'Pond Street Primary. That's what I needed to remember because that's what she said.'

'Who?'

'This crazy woman I met at A&E when Freddie fell off the climbing wall. She had her accident-prone son with her, always falling from a height, she said. He'd fallen out of a tree that day and she started telling me about all the times she'd been to A&E and that's when she said it! She actually said it, why am I so stupid?'

'What? What did she say?'

'Never go to A&E at Halloween. She said she was there one year when her son was a toddler, and . . . why am I only remembering this now? I can't believe she actually said it!'

'What?'

'That the waiting area was crazy. There was a woman collapsing in one corner and a kid dying in the other. What if she was talking about Danielle going into anaphylaxis and the little boy dying of meningitis?'

'Well, you don't know that. You can't *possibly* know that.'

'But she said it happened at Halloween and you have to admit it's a bit of a coincidence, isn't it? Maybe I don't know for certain but it's a lead.'

'A lead?'

'Yes. Because if she *was* there that night, the night Danielle collapsed and the little boy died, she would have seen the child's mother, wouldn't she? She'd be able to give me a description.'

'From six years ago? You think she'd remember?'

'She seemed to remember all sorts of things from her trips to A&E.'

'I don't know, Beth. It's a bit of a . . . what do you say in English? A bit of a long . . .?'

'Shot?'

'Yes, because even if she was there that night, even if she could remember the boy's mother, how are you going to find this woman? Are you going to start hanging around outside A&E, hoping her son falls out of another tree?'

'No, I don't have to.'

'Why?'

'Because I know where he goes to school, she told me. Pond Street Primary. All I have to do is go there when school ends on Monday and I'll find her.'

'But don't you have to pick your own children up from school on Monday?'

'Yes, but I can ask Jade or Rowan to do it. They won't mind.'

'But haven't they looked after the children for the last week?'

'Yes. So?'

'I just thought you were going to let all this go and move on.' Her hand on my arm, the grip softens. 'I thought you were going to focus on your family. And your health.'

'I will, Ana. I promise. But I have to find that woman, ask her what she knows. Either she was there that night and remembers the mother of the dead boy or she doesn't. I've got nothing to lose by asking her, have I? And I owe it to Charlotte. Actually,' I say, glancing at my watch, 'she might be in the park right now.'

'How could you possibly know that?'

'They're always in the park apparently, she said it's her son's favourite place in the world. If I go there now, I might be able to find them.'

'Beth, you're sounding a bit crazy.'

'Why? Because I want to go to the park on a sunny Saturday afternoon, rather than stand in a crowded kitchen watching a man set himself on fire? I bet loads of people are in the park. They can't all be crazy. If I leave now, I might be able to get answers today.'

'But Beth, your children are here. Why would you leave and—'

'No one's going to miss me if I slip out. Everyone's too busy watching Mr Combustible,' I glance towards the front of the room, 'and look, he's still faffing around with test tubes, hasn't even got the Bunsen burners out yet. He'll probably go on for ages and then there's the silent auction afterwards. If I leave now, I'll be back before anyone realises I've gone.'

'Beth, I'm worried about you. Promise me you haven't been drinking.'

'I swear on my children's lives. I'll be back in less than an hour.'

I make my way into the entrance hall and locate my boots in the huge pile of discarded footwear, then head out through the front door towards the orchard that isn't really an orchard. Rummaging in my bag for my keys, I'm almost at the car when I realise I'm standing in between the two apple trees. Leaves are rustling somewhere above me, but I'm focused solely on the strong roots under my feet. Such impenetrable pride. I close my eyes, no longer sure what's real and what's imaginary but resolutely certain of one thing. *I'm getting close, Charlotte; I can feel it. I'm going to find out what happened to you.*

30

It's two days later – Monday, I think – and I'm collecting my children from school. Someone has set up a remembrance table in a corner of the playground. It's covered with a pastel-blue tablecloth and photographs of Danielle at various events over the last couple of years. In one she's about to run in the mums' race at Sports Day, in another she's helping her son up the climbing wall. I wonder whose idea it was, and who chose the pictures. She looks anxious and confused in most of them, but maybe they were the best of the bunch. And what is the purpose of the remembrance table, anyway? Other than serving as a cumbersome visual reminder that no one knows what to do after a sudden, unexpected death.

Fara is standing behind the table, staring down at a silver photo frame in her hand. She's clutching a handkerchief in the other and her baby is strapped to her chest.

'People keep picking up this photograph,' she says, without raising her head. 'They keep leaving smudgy fingerprints all over the frame.' She starts polishing it with the handkerchief.

She places it back down in the centre of the table. Unlike the other photos, this one is of Danielle as a younger woman. She's smiling and looks less troubled than usual, almost carefree.

'I think it's only just started to sink in,' Fara says, picking up other photographs and rearranging them slightly, even though there's no need. 'That she's gone. It's the shock, I suspect. Makes everything unfathomable for a while. I can't believe I'll never see her again.'

I wonder whether I'll ever see *her* again. A&E lady. She wasn't at the park on Saturday, or yesterday either. I waited for hours on both days before hurrying home to work on my project – once the children were in bed, of course.

'I feel so awful for her family,' Fara says. 'I think that's why we're all so desperate to do whatever we can to help.' I open my water bottle and take a sip. 'Did you hear about the silent auction?' she asks, but I don't think it's a proper question because she doesn't appear to be waiting for my reply. 'Emily did such a great job, raising so much money for the anaphylaxis charity which I'm sure Danielle's family will appreciate, but I can't begin to imagine what they're going through,' she adds, picking up the silver frame once again, covering it in fresh smudges for her to wipe clean. 'I just wish there was more I could do to help. I feel so powerless, so useless.'

Is that what's driving this incessant need to speak?

'I miss her so much.' Her voice cracks. 'Hopefully this will bring them a little comfort.' She taps her fingers lightly on a book with the words 'In Remembrance' embossed in gold foil on the cover. 'I want Danielle's husband and children to know that everyone's thinking about them and the book's almost full,' she adds, flicking through the pages. 'All the teachers, parents and pupils, everyone's written messages, and some are so poignant.' Another turn of the page. 'Have you signed it yet?'

I glance at my watch. When are the children coming out of school? I don't like this playground at the best of times. Even without a shrine.

'Have you signed it yet?' she asks again, despite already knowing the answer. Why else is she passing me a pen?

'I don't know what to write.' Another sip from my water bottle. 'I don't know what to say.'

'Nobody knows what to say, Beth.' Fara's eyes are on mine. She looks haunted.

My mouth is dry. I take another sip.

'But if it provides Danielle's family with even a modicum of support,' she adds, 'knowing that people are thinking about them, then I think it's worth making the effort, don't you?'

I take the pen. My hand is shaking. Another sip.

'This is hard for me,' I say, looking up from the book. 'I mean, she died in my house. Her family probably blame me, even though it wasn't my fault. Honestly, it's so . . .'

'Emily!' Fara says loudly over my shoulder. I put the pen on the table and move the water bottle to my lips again. I take a mouthful and then another before turning around.

Emily is standing behind me and looks like she's been crying. Her huge alien eyes are red, as red as A&E lady's hair. I need to find her.

Fara hurries to the other side of the table and throws her arms around Emily. I take another sip.

'I'm so sorry,' Fara whispers to Emily. She sounds like she's crying too. 'Now the party's out of the way, it's starting to sink in, isn't it? You did such a great job with the silent auction; Danielle would have been so proud.' Emily's shoulders start to shudder. 'I'm so sorry,' Fara says again, holding her tighter. There's a baby somewhere inside that embrace. 'I wish I had the words to make you feel better.'

If *she* doesn't have the words, what hope is there for the rest of us?

'So many people have written the most beautiful messages about Danielle,' she says, pointing to the book. 'Beth was just about to add her message, weren't you, Beth?'

Their eyes are on me. Emily's are narrowed and filled with tears.

'I'm still thinking about what to write,' I say, raising the water bottle to my mouth. 'I don't know what to say.'

'Well, that's honest, I suppose,' Emily sniffs, staring down at the book then turning a page.

'It's very difficult, isn't it?' I say to the top of her head. She's turning another page. Reading other people's memories, other people's words. 'For everyone. But, like I was just saying to Fara, she died in my house. Danielle's family probably blame me for what happened even though I didn't do anything wrong, and that makes it so difficult for me, because . . .'

'Difficult for you?' She slams the book shut and stands up straight. She's so tall. Huge, alien eyes pummelling down into me. 'Difficult for you? How the hell do you think her family are coping?'

Hope wriggles in the pushchair and her cuddly toy falls to the ground. I pick it up and stare into its eyes, hoping that I can stay frozen inside this moment forever. Another sip. I need words. Any words.

'I can't imagine how they're feeling,' I say, returning the toy to Hope. 'It must be awful for them . . . especially when we don't know exactly what happened.'

'What do you mean?' Emily says. Both she and Fara are staring at me.

'To Danielle,' I reply. 'We don't know what happened to her.'

'What are you talking about?' asks Emily. 'She was allergic to nuts and died of anaphylactic shock. You know this.' She places her hand on the table. She's shaking. 'You were there.'

'Was I?' I ask, staring down at the ground.

'Of course you were.' Her voice is shaking too. 'It happened in *your* house.'

'But I didn't buy those biscuits, Emily.' I force my eyes up to meet hers. 'None of the food I bought for the playdate contained nuts.'

'What are you saying?'

'Someone must have brought them to my house. For Danielle.'

'Who?'

'I don't know.' My eyes fall to the ground once again.

'Maybe someone who . . . suspected she may have started to remember something, about Charlotte's death.'

'Charlotte?'

'Yes, because I never believed that she ran out into the road of her own accord.' My eyes finally meet Emily's. 'And maybe Danielle was beginning to question it too. She spoke to Charlotte on the phone that night, didn't she? Maybe she remembered something she heard.'

They're both staring at me. And now at each other. I can tell Emily is angry, but Fara is the one who speaks.

'Beth,' she says gently, taking a step towards me and placing her hand on my arm. 'Listen to me, I'm saying this because I'm concerned, I'm speaking to you as a friend. All this stuff about Charlotte's death, you've got to let it go, because it's all in your head. You're not making any sense.'

'And I'm saying *this* as a friend.' I shake my arm free. 'Because I'm concerned too.' I turn to Emily. 'About Tobias.'

'Tobias?' Emily says. 'My Tobias?'

'Yes,' I reply. 'He was in the car that killed Charlotte. And he thought someone else was there that night too, hiding and watching. What if he saw who it was? What if they come for him next?'

'Beth!' Fara's voice is raised. I've never seen her look so angry.

'I just think you need to be prepared, Emily,' I say. 'Make sure you've got proper protection for Tobias.'

Emily's huge eyes flicker with some emotion I can't place. Anger? Fear?

'Because if someone got to Danielle, they could easily

get to him too.' She's taking a step back, away from me. 'I would never forgive myself if I didn't say anything and then something happened to Tobias. Emily, listen to me. They could do anything to him. String him up by his neck from one of your apple trees. Make it look like suicide.'

'Beth!' Fara's voice is raised. A group of parents standing nearby turn and stare. 'What is the matter with you?' she hisses, her voice lowered. 'Why are you upsetting Emily like this? I don't think this is the right time—'

'When is it going to be the right time?' I ask her. 'Charlotte's been dead for almost a year! Everyone thinks her death is suspicious, when are we going to start talking about it?'

'Everyone? No one else is thinking about Charlotte's death. You're the only one.'

'And why is that? Why am I the only one who cares about Charlotte? Look at this,' I say, pointing at the table. 'I don't remember seeing a shrine for Charlotte after she died.'

'You're not the only one who cared,' says Fara. 'You had so much to contend with after Charlotte's death, that's probably why you don't remember the remembrance table we set up for her, or the book of condolence.'

'What?' I ask, taking another sip from my water bottle. 'I don't remember seeing . . .' My voice trails away as I try to access memories that seem locked away from me. Maybe they're not even mine.

'You've been through so much, Beth,' Fara says, putting her hand once again on my arm. 'But believe me – you're not the only one who cared about Charlotte.'

But am I the only one thinking about you, Fara, I

wonder, staring into her kind eyes. With all her degrees and pashminas, am I the only person who doesn't understand why she's so beholden to Emily?

'I just wish we would talk more about Charlotte,' I say. 'About what happened to her. She was my best friend, and . . .'

'Ten days.' Fara and I turn in the direction of Emily's voice. Emily is hunched over the table. 'Ten days,' she says again, her shoulders shuddering. 'It's only been ten days since we lost Danielle and all you can harp on about is conspiracy theories—'

'They're not theories,' I say quietly. 'It doesn't make sense that Charlotte would leave Leo alone in the house and go out for a run. I believe someone forced her out into the road in the path of that car. I think someone killed her.'

'And how do we know it wasn't you?' she says, her words muffled under the screech of the school bell. 'Because it could have been, couldn't it? You were drunk out of your mind at my Halloween party on the night she died. And you stormed out early, didn't you?' Children are spilling into the playground. 'You could have staggered up the road to Charlotte's house. If you're so convinced someone killed her, Beth, how do we know it wasn't you?'

'I would never hurt Charlotte!' I say.

The remembrance table seems to move towards me and I stumble into it. Photographs fall and I'm falling too, still clutching my water bottle. I lie on the ground next to something silver. The glass is smashing into hundreds of little pieces but at least there's no smudges on the frame. People are starting to gather.

'Mummy!' Jack's face staring down at me. 'What are you doing?'

I reach for the hand outstretched towards me. It's Ana. She helps me to my feet, taking control of Hope's pushchair and the situation, guiding me and my children across the playground. Away from the packs of murmured conversation and stifled smiles and curious eyes.

'Beth, why don't you go to a meeting?' she says quietly into my ear.

I'm staring at the palm of my left hand. It's red and grazed from when I fell over, but not yet starting to bleed.

'There's one starting in ten minutes in the community centre.' Her voice is calm and it's comforting – being with someone who knows what to do. 'Why don't I take the children to the park while you go to the meeting? You can clear your head and then come find us.'

'I don't want to go with them, Mummy!' Freddie looks like he's crying. He's trying to grab hold of my left hand but it's hurting so I brush him away. 'I want to come home with you.'

'We'll have fun in the park, Freddie,' says a little girl, her hair plaited and tied with red ribbons. I've forgotten her name. 'I can teach you how to put your shoes on the right feet.'

'I don't want to, Mummy!' He's still trying to grab hold of my hand. 'Summer's bossy and always saying weird things. Mummy, please! I want to stay with you.'

'It's going to be OK, Freddie.' Ana's voice is so comforting. I feel like I could curl up and fall asleep inside her voice. 'Your mummy's only going to be gone for a little while. Then she'll come and join us and we'll all have fun together in the park.'

Tiny red droplets are starting to appear on the palm of my left hand. Ana is staring at me, and her mouth is moving but I'm not listening any more. I lift the water bottle to my mouth and take a drink. And then another.

31

One day at a time. That's what they tell us at AA. Or is it one step at a time? Those twelve steps they're always talking about, that's what I'm counting to now. One foot in front of the other, getting to twelve and then starting over.

I'm taking one step at a time, but not to the meeting. Because AA isn't going to help me. Nothing is ever going to help me, not until I start untwisting everything that's in my mind. Danielle's death twisted up with Charlotte's – I'm never going to unravel any of it until I know the truth. So, I take one step and then another, and then another towards Pond Street Primary because it's the only lead I have.

And she's there. The red-haired woman, wearing bright green leather lace-ups and talking to some other parents, her son by her side. I approach and then falter. Is this weird? Now she's breaking away from the pack and walking along the pavement towards me. I take a sip from the water bottle and step into her path.

'Hi,' I smile, and she smiles too, automatically. She tries to walk past. 'Hi,' I say again. 'This is a coincidence, bumping into you like this. Do you remember me?' She stops walking and turns to face me. 'We met at the hospital. You,' I say to the little boy standing beside her, 'had just fallen out of a tree and my son had fallen off the climbing wall in the school playground. Do you remember?'

'Oh yes, of course!' she says. 'How is your son?'

'Oh, he's fine.' Two women pushing buggies and surrounded by children are behind us on the pavement, trying to get past. 'I think we're in the way,' I smile, stepping into the road. 'Do you want to go to the park? You like the park, don't you?' I smile at her little boy.

'He loves it there,' answers his mother. 'Mind you,' she adds with a smile, 'I'm not so keen.' She turns to the two women with buggies as they squeeze past. 'Do you remember that time he fell from the top of the big curly slide?'

'Always falling from a height, your Ollie, isn't he?' smiles one of the women. 'I don't know how you keep up with him, you must have nerves of steel!' Now they're standing on the pavement with us, chatting and laughing. Other parents seem very friendly at this school.

'I can walk with you, if you like,' I say, cutting through their conversation. 'I have to go to the park anyway. That's where my children are.'

'On their own?' the red-headed woman asks, as the women with buggies move away.

'Oh, no!' We start walking. 'They're with my friend. She said she'd look after them while I came here to find you.'

'Ollie,' her eyes flicking from me to her son, 'why don't you run ahead, but wait for me at the road, do you hear? I don't fancy another trip to A&E.' He quickens his pace, tripping over his feet near the kerb and almost falling into the road before correcting his footing and catching up with the children ahead.

'What's he like?' I smile. 'So accident prone, isn't he?'

'Why are you here?' she asks, suddenly direct. 'First you said it was a coincidence bumping into me, and now you're saying you left your children in the park to come and find me. What's going on?'

'I'm sorry.' I raise the water bottle towards my mouth, take a sip. 'This is difficult,' I add, swallowing, my eyes on the ground. 'I'm struggling a bit, to be honest. It's been a really tough week.'

'I'm sorry to hear that, but I still don't understand what you're doing here.'

'The truth is, I've been struggling for the last year or so. Ever since my best friend died and my husband left me.'

'I'm sorry to hear that,' she says again. 'But—'

'If that wasn't bad enough, I had a playdate at my house the other week, and one of the mums ended up dead on my kitchen floor.'

'My God.' She stops walking, her hand to her mouth. 'How did she die?'

'Anaphylactic shock,' I reply.

'Nasty.'

'Yeah, so, I'm sorry if I seem a bit weird and desperate but I think you're my only chance of getting to the truth.'

'About what?' She starts walking again.

'When I met you in the hospital the other week,' I adjust my pace to match hers, 'you spoke about being in A&E at Halloween, years ago. You said it was chaotic that night, with a woman collapsing in one corner and a child dying in another.'

'Yes, I remember,' she says, nodding. She's shielding her eyes, staring ahead. 'It was absolute carnage that night,' she adds. 'So many children hopped up on sugar. That's why Halloween is one of the worst possible days to go to hospital. Maybe not as bad as Bonfire Night,' she's getting into her flow, 'but a close second. It's unregulated, you see – the sugar at Halloween, especially if parents aren't keeping track of the trick or treating—'

'Right,' I say. 'But getting back to the child who died that night. Do you remember anything about him?'

'Not really,' she says, turning to face me again. 'I'm not nosy, I didn't want to stare. He was just sitting quietly on his mother's lap. I barely noticed them to begin with, didn't pay much attention at all, until she started screaming. And even then, it didn't register at first because the whole place was so noisy, what with the woman who had just collapsed and all the sugar-crazed children shouting.' She lowers her eyes. 'It was really horrible. He was slumped on her lap and she was screaming that he wasn't breathing, and when the nurses took him behind a curtain, that's all I could hear – her screams. And it was strange because it became quiet then, I remember that now.' She turns back to face me.

'By the time one of the nurses reappeared, it was so silent in the waiting room it was eerie. Apart from her screams.'

We've reached the busy main road and I hold my breath as her son steps off the kerb, right in front of a car. The woman grabs hold of his school jumper with one hand and yanks him back onto the pavement. In addition to nerves of steel, she's got fast reflexes and incredible strength – necessities, I should imagine, with a child like that.

'Ollie,' she says, pointing her finger at him. Her face so angry, she almost looks scary. I don't blame her. He could have been killed. 'You have to start listening to me. I said I didn't want to go to hospital again.' We cross the road together and as soon as we reach the other side she releases her grip on his jumper and he runs ahead again. 'Wait for me at the next road!' she calls.

'Do you remember anything about her?' I ask. 'The mother of the little boy who died.'

'Why do you ask?'

'I think she might be involved somehow,' I say taking another sip of my drink.

'In what?'

'The death of my friend.' She turns to stare at me. 'She was a doctor at the hospital and her name was Charlotte. Do you remember? There was a poster of her on the wall. She used to work in A&E. She was hit by a car and killed last year.'

'Yes, I remember the poster.' She's staring ahead again.

'Charlotte was the doctor on duty that Halloween and she blamed herself for the little boy's death. Never forgave herself, apparently.'

'Why?' she asks, turning to face me. 'She wasn't the only doctor working that night, why was it her fault?'

'I'm not sure,' I reply. 'I just know she felt responsible, and the thing is,' another sip, 'I've never believed Charlotte's death was an accident.'

'I thought you said she was hit by a car.'

'She was.'

'So, you think the driver drove into her on purpose?'

'No. But I think someone chased her out into the road, making it impossible for the car to avoid her.'

'Why do you think that?'

'Because Charlotte wasn't the kind of person to run blindly out into a road,' I say, as we catch up with her son. 'And I'm not the only one who thinks so,' I add. 'Someone else, one of the passengers in the car. He was with Charlotte when she died, and he thought there was someone else there too.'

'So, why aren't you talking to him?'

'I have,' I reply. 'But it was dark that night and he didn't see who it was. The only person I can think of with any motive to kill Charlotte,' I say as we approach the park, 'is the mother of the little boy who died. If Charlotte blamed herself, maybe his mother did too.'

'Ollie,' she says, smiling at her child. 'Why don't you run ahead?' He sprints ahead and she waits a moment before turning back to me. 'Do you mind not talking about this in front of Ollie?' She looks annoyed. 'He's only eight years old. I don't want him having nightmares about murder.'

'Of course, I'm sorry. I wouldn't bother you, it's just that

I'm desperate and I don't have anyone else to ask. Do you remember anything about the mother? Anything at all?'

'Well, like I said – I wasn't staring, and don't forget I was preoccupied with my own kid. Ollie was only a toddler at the time.'

'Of course.'

'And this night you're talking about, it was years ago. I'm not sure what you expect me to remember.'

'Anything about her. Anything at all. Her voice? You said she was screaming.'

Her eyes flick upwards as if she's trying to remember. I look ahead to her child. He's running, already halfway between here and the park, and I see Ana in the distance, lifting Hope into one of the toddler swings. Willow is seated in another, kicking her little legs, eager to get moving. Jack, Freddie and Summer are running towards the big curly slide and Ana's calling out to them, telling them to be careful when they get to the top.

'She was quite young,' Redhead says, and I turn back to face her. 'I can remember that.'

'OK. Anything else?'

'I'm not sure,' she says, her eyes not meeting mine. She looks over to where Ana is pushing Willow and Hope high into the air. 'It was so long ago. If I had to say, I think she had dark hair, quite curly, and she was very pretty. Actually,' she says, still staring at Ana, a strange look in her eyes, 'she looked a bit like that woman over there. By the swings.'

'Who?' I ask, following her gaze. 'The lady in the yellow coat? No, it can't have been her,' I add. 'That's my friend, Ana. She didn't even live round here then.' *Did she?*

'Well, she looks a lot like the mum I saw that night in A&E. Though I could be wrong. It's hard to tell at this distance.' Redhead glances down at her watch. 'Look at the time. Ollie!' she shouts and her son stops running and turns around. 'Come back here! I don't think we can play in the park today after all.' When he reaches us she clasps his hand tightly, protectively, before turning and moving away.

I stumble backwards a little; the ground feels uneven. Green leather lace-ups and black school shoes stretching out the distance between me and everything I thought I knew. It couldn't have been Ana, could it? Banging at Charlotte's door last Halloween? The door of the house she was destined to move into. I close my eyes. Imagine Charlotte opening that door and staring into the face of the woman who still haunted her dreams ... *Why have you come here?*

There are children's voices but I'm no longer sure whether they're real. Imaginary orchards, imaginary friends, my grip on reality – how do we ever know whether anything really exists? Two children in the park running in my direction. They can't see me yet. I stumble into the trees. What's wrong with the ground?

'Come on, Freddie.' She sounds bossy. The little girl with red ribbons tied into her hair. 'I'm going to teach you how to put your shoes on the right feet.'

'No! Leave me alone, I want to play.'

'Come on, Freddie, you're not a baby. You need to learn.'

'If you don't leave me alone, Summer, I'm going to get my big brother.'

'And if you don't do what I say, Freddie, I'll get mine.'

'Why do you always say that? You don't have a big brother.'

'Just because you can't see him, doesn't mean he isn't real.'

'He isn't real!'

'He's a ghost. A ghost that only I can see. And if you don't do what I say, I'll ask him to come and get you.'

'Go away! I want Mummy!' His voice disappears as they run back towards the slide and I'm running too. In the other direction. Tripping on tree roots and fumbling with the lid of my water bottle and drinking whatever remains. Now there's a phone in my hand and it looks like mine but I'm struggling to find her number. It feels strange. I haven't called her for a very long time.

'Hello Beth?' she answers after four rings. 'Is everything OK?'

'Can you come and get the children?'

'What's going on?'

'Jade, can you help me or not?'

'Of course, but why? What's happened?'

'I don't feel well. I think it's a migraine or something. I haven't felt right, since . . . you know, since everything happened. Can you collect the kids for me? They're with Ana in the park.'

'The park?'

'Yes, the one with the curly slide. Can you collect them and take them back to stay with you and Rowan tonight? I don't feel well.'

'Of course, I'll leave now. And I'll collect them from school tomorrow too. We can have them for a few days. Give you a break.'

'Thank you.'

'And Beth, I know a lot has happened between us, but I still care about you and if ever you need to talk—'

I end the call. Then I put my head down and stumble towards home.

The Day After She Died

'Mummy! Your fluffy coat is all muddy.'

'What?'

'Look, Mummy, look at the mud!' He's pushing yellow material into my face, and I'm trying not to gag.

'It's OK, Freddie,' I say, turning my face away. 'I'll wash it later.'

'Or you can be a muddy Big Bird! Did you hear me, Mummy? I said you can be a muddy Big Bird! Have you only just woken up, Mummy? Why didn't you sleep in your bed?'

'Freddie, leave Mummy alone for a while.' The new voice in the living room is quiet, and perfectly controlled. 'Why don't you go outside and play in the garden?'

'OK, Daddy,' Freddie says, as I close my eyes for a moment. Listen to his footsteps scampering from the room.

Rowan passes me a cup of tea and I pull myself up into a seated position on the sofa. I take the mug and a sip, determined to be brave. I know it's my own fault, but the pain in my head is excruciating.

'Have to hand it to Emily,' I say, glancing towards him and forcing a smile. 'She certainly knows how to throw a good party. It was wild, wasn't it? I can't even remember getting home.'

'You stormed out early,' he says, sitting down in the armchair opposite. Keeping his eyes fixed on his own mug of tea. 'I was worried about you, but someone had to stay behind with the children.'

'Of course,' I say. 'I'm sorry—'

'Beth.' His eyes finally find mine. Almost blue, nearly green, shimmering like the ocean. Glistening. Are those tears? 'I need to talk to you about something.'

'I'm sorry,' I say again, my face burning. 'I know I drank too much because the whole night's a bit of a blur. But it's not always a bad thing, is it? To let off steam every once in a while.'

He's staring down at the mug clasped in his hands. 'Something happened to Charlotte last night. Something awful.'

'Was she at the party? I don't remember seeing her.'

'No, she was at home. She went out for a run and . . .'

'What?'

'She was hit by a car. In the lane.'

'Oh my God, is she hurt?'

'She's dead, Beth.' He looks so serious. 'Charlotte's dead.' How is he keeping a straight face?

'Don't be ridiculous,' I say, taking a sip of tea. 'How can she be dead?'

'Beth . . .'

'She's too brilliant to be dead. And too busy. She's got children and the PTA to organise and she's training for a marathon. She doesn't have time to be dead.'

'Beth, I know it seems impossible . . .'

'It *is* impossible.'

'I know you and Charlotte were good friends.'

'Best friends. We were . . . we **are**,' I say, correcting myself, 'best friends. Where's my bag?' I ask, reaching down towards the floor. Picking up the fluffy yellow costume, searching underneath. 'Have you seen my bag?' I push myself to my feet. 'I need my phone.'

Now I'm stumbling through the living room door. Stumbling into the hallway. Stumbling over something unexpected out there. 'What's this?' I turn back to face him. 'A suitcase? Rowan, are you going somewhere?'

'Yes,' he says, still clutching his mug. On it is printed Best Dad in the World. *A Father's Day present from the children. One I chose and paid for and said was from them.*

'Rowan.' My voice is raspy. My throat seems to remember I was shouting last night. 'What's going on?'

'It hasn't been right between us for a long time, has it?' He can't meet my eyes. 'You know it, I know it and then last night . . .'

'What?'

'You guessed . . . that's why you stormed out, why you got so upset . . .'

'Guessed what?'

'That I've been seeing someone else.' Almost blue, nearly green eyes that can't meet mine. 'I'm so sorry, Beth, but I need you to know first, before everyone else finds out . . . we're in love – *Jade* and me. We never set out to hurt you,' his eyes flick briefly up to mine, 'and I'm so sorry about the timing. What happened to Charlotte and now this . . . I'm just so sorry . . .'

I run into the kitchen and slam the door behind me. My bag is on the table, with my phone inside. I slump down into a chair and dial her number, willing her to answer. She's my best friend, I love her but, more than that, I need her. I press redial. Please, Charlotte, please answer the phone.

32

I love you so much, but you know that already, don't you? You're my best friend. Do you know why? Because you're always there for me. You never lie, and you never lecture. But best of all, the thing I love most about you, do you know what it is? You don't smell! That's funny. I'm funny when I'm with you, have you noticed that? My mate vodka, splashing into my water bottle. Splashing onto the floor.

Look at them, hanging around on the street corner. Smoking. Swearing.

'Hello, teenagers. I remember when you used to be little and cute, knocking on the door at Halloween. Trick or treat! What are you doing now? Drugs? Got any for me?'

'*Fucking hell, are you pissed? It's only three o'clock in the afternoon. Where are you going?*'

'St Michael's, my love. Ever heard of it?'

'*Yeah, we used to go there.*'

'Great, can you give me a lift? I don't mind travelling in a stolen vehicle.'

'Do you think it's a good idea, going to the school in this state?'

'I do, sweetheart. I think it's a bloody brilliant idea.'

'But you're off your head—'

'Going to the school and *not* being in this state, *that* would be a bad idea.'

'Why don't I take you home and make you a cup of coffee?'

'Ooh, look at you with your kind face. Can I tell you a secret?'

'What?'

'Last time someone came round to my house for a cup of coffee, they ended up dead on the kitchen floor.'

'I don't think that's a secret and I still think coffee is a good idea.'

'I don't need coffee, my darling; I need a cigarette. Have you got a cigarette? And none of that vaping shit, I need a proper smoke.'

'No, you need to sober up.'

'And you need to lighten up! Why do you always look so worried? You're a young person for fuck's sake, hanging around on a street corner with your mates. You should be having fun, smashing things up or breaking in somewhere.'

'Come on, I'll walk you back to your house.'

'Why? Are you going to rob the place?'

'Of course not.'

'Why not? My house not good enough for you to rob?'

'No, it's just . . .'

'You don't think I've got anything worth nicking?'

'Not at all . . .'

'Do you know what's funny, my darling?'
'What?'
'I *don't* have anything worth nicking.'
'Right.'
'Seriously, in my whole house there isn't one thing worth nicking. Not one. Apart from some Lego. And my dog.'
'Come on, let's get you home.'
'Get your hand off me!'
'I'm just trying to help you . . .'
'Listen to me, you little shit, if you steal my dog, I will hunt you down and I will kill you. Do you hear me?'
'I'm not going to steal your dog.'
'Stay away from my fucking dog! All of you, do you hear?'
'Bloody hell! Stop trying to help her. The crazy bitch is off her head. Leave her alone. She's mental.'
'Yeah, fuck off and leave me alone! All of you. I don't need any help. I don't need a lift. I don't need anyone. I'll walk to school and pick up my kids on my own. Like I do everything on my own. Because that's how I like it. So, fuck off and leave me alone!'

33

Look at them, pushing their babies in buggies like they own the pavement. Walking in groups. Safety in numbers. Natter, natter, natter.

'Oi! Can I ask you something?'

'*Me?*'

'Yes, you. Or you. Or you. Or you. Doesn't matter who, you're all the same, aren't you? Little pack of school mums. Clickety clique. Clickety clique.'

'*Sorry?*'

'Why have you got a yoga mat?'

'*What?*'

'Why are you taking a yoga mat to the playground?'

'*Because we've just come from parent and baby yoga. Sorry, do we know you?*'

'No, you don't, but that doesn't stop you thinking you're better than me, does it?'

'*What are you talking about? Why are you so angry?*'

'Just because you're pushing a buggy doesn't make you special, you know. I've got a buggy too. I just haven't got it with me.'

'*OK.*'

'And I could have a yoga mat, if I wanted. Anyone can buy a yoga mat, you know.'

'*OK.*'

'Stop saying OK. And stop laughing at me. Don't fucking laugh at me. Don't you dare! Yes, that's right, you'd better run. Fuck off, the lot of you, and leave me alone.'

34

'Beth, what are you doing here? I told you I'd collect the kids today. Look, Hope – it's Mummy! This is a nice surprise, isn't it?'

'Bitch.'

'Sorry?'

'Bitch.'

'Sorry, I can't hear what you're saying – that bell is so loud, isn't it?! Are you feeling better? You don't look too good.'

'FUCK OFF JADE, YOU BITCH!'

'What the hell is wrong with you? Hope, don't cry darling, it's OK. Oh my God, are you . . . Beth, are you drunk?'

'Sorry, Hope.'

'You can't be drunk in the school playground!'

'Sorry that Jade makes you wear such horrible clothes.'

'The children will be coming out any minute.'

'What is it with the fucking orange unicorns?'

'Beth, look at me.'

'Why? Are you going to do some emergency reiki? Get your crystals out?'

'I want to help you.'

'By fucking my husband?'

'Stop swearing! Think of Jack and Freddie, it will break their hearts to see you like this. Stay here, I'm going to go and get Ana.'

'Yeah, go and get Ana.'

'She can drive you home, and then I'll take Hope and the boys back to mine. Beth, do you understand what I'm saying to you? What are you staring at?'

'Ana.'

'Oh yes, of course, the tombola. Stay here, I'm going to go and get her. Beth! Stop following me. I told you to stay over there.'

'Fuck off Jade, you bitch.'

'Ana, Beth's really drunk, and she won't stop swearing. We need to get her out of here but she's not listening to me. I don't know what to do for the best.'

'She doesn't know what to do for the best, Ana. What should we do?'

'Beth, come with me. I'm going to drive you home.'

'But wouldn't that be running and hiding? And don't I need to show up for life, Ana? Isn't that what you told me to do?'

'The kids are going to come out any minute. Jack, Freddie, all their friends. You don't want to embarrass them—'

'Will it make them sad?'

'Yes, and—'

'Like you were sad?'

'*What?*'

'Harry said it, didn't he? He said you were sad when he met you.'

'*Why don't we talk about this in the car? Come on, let's go.*'

'I don't want to go. I want to talk about why you were sad.'

'*Why?*'

'Because it's important.'

'*OK, well if it's so important, the reason I was sad was because I'd just left Romania and said goodbye to all my family and friends. Can we go now? The kids will be out any minute.*'

'I don't believe you. I think you were sad because he died.'

'*Who?*'

'Your son.'

'*I don't have a son.*'

'Not any more. But you did.'

'*I've never had a son, Beth. I have two daughters, remember?*'

'Your bossy daughter, the one with red ribbons in her hair . . .'

'*Summer?*'

'Yeah, she talks about your dead son. I heard her.'

'*What?*'

'She said she has a big brother.'

'*And last week she had a pet dinosaur.*'

'What?'

'*She's five. She has an overactive imagination. She's always making up stories and talking about imaginary friends.*'

'She said her big brother is a ghost.'

'*Well, you told her that ghosts are just friends we can't see,* so she probably got that from you. She's obsessed with ghosts at the moment. Last week it was dinosaurs and next week it will be something else. Look, Freddie and Jack are running over, can we go?'

'I've worked it all out, in my head. That's why you looked scared, isn't it?'

'*What?*'

'When I first met you, and I told you I see dead people.'

'*When? In the toddler group?*'

'You thought I was talking about him, didn't you? You thought I could see your dead son.'

'*I didn't know what you were talking about then and I don't know what you're talking about now. I have no idea why you said you could see dead people.*'

'It's a line from that film.'

'*What film?*'

'*That* film! Everyone knows that film.'

'*I don't. Maybe I'm too young.*'

'Nobody's that young!'

'*Beth! Stop shouting, please! Come on, we need to leave right now.*'

'Is that why you hate Fara?'

'*I don't hate Fara. Fara, I don't hate you.*'

'Yes, she does. She was talking about you, Fara. About you sending Tayo to boarding school. He's only eight. That's why she hates you.'

'*I don't hate you, Fara, you have to believe me.*'

'Your son would be eight, wouldn't he, Ana? If he was alive.'

'*I don't have a son. I've never had a son.*'

306

'Is that why you sometimes look so miserable? Because you're thinking about him?'

'*You've been drinking, you're not making any sense—*'

'Sometimes you look so uncomfortable, like you don't belong.'

'*That's because I* don't *belong! I was working in a coffee shop when I met Harry. And now look where I live.*'

'Yeah, Charlotte's house! Because it wasn't enough to kill her, was it? You had to live in her house. You had to take her life. All her life.'

'*What are you talking about?*'

'You blamed Charlotte for your son dying.'

'*Look what alcohol is doing to you, Beth. It's making you think things that aren't real. Making you believe things that never happened.*'

'And not just Charlotte, you blamed Danielle too.'

'*What?*'

'For the death of your son. You found out she was the woman in the hospital that night. Collapsing in a corner, taking Charlotte's attention when she should have been saving your son.'

'*What?*'

'That's why you became so serious, isn't it?'

'*What are you talking about?*'

'You were such a laugh when we first met but ever since you found out Danielle was the woman in the hospital that night, you've completely lost your sense of humour.'

'*That's because I've been worried about you, Beth. I am worried about you.*'

'Bollocks! You became serious as soon as you started plotting another murder.'

'*What?*'

'Danielle's murder. You knew about her allergy. You brought those biscuits into my house.'

'*No, I didn't bring anything. You told me not to. I asked, remember?*'

'And you were with her in my kitchen when she died. You made sure she died.'

'*No! I tried to save her.*'

'You brought those biscuits to my house. You made sure she ate one. You made sure she died. You killed her!'

'*No, no I didn't!*'

'Just like you killed Charlotte!'

'*Beth!*'

'That's why you wanted me to stop working on my project, isn't it? You didn't want me getting to the truth.'

'*No! I wanted you to stop working on it because your project is making you ill, Beth. You're not making any sense.*'

'Who were you going to kill next? Me? Fara?'

'*And who are you going to accuse next? Because first of all, you thought it was Bill, didn't you? Then Jade, then Emily, Fara, Danielle . . . in the short time I've known you, you've accused everyone—*'

'I know it was you, Ana. I know you put those biscuits out when I wasn't looking.'

'*I didn't!*'

'Yes, you did.'

'*I didn't!*'

'*Mummy! It was me!*' Small child. Familiar. '*It was me,*

Mummy! I'm sorry, I'm so sorry. I put the biscuits on the big plate.'

'What?'

'I found them in the cupboard with the big plates and my Rice Krispies and I wanted to help you. I like helping you. You were worried there weren't enough snacks but there were lots of our normal biscuits in the cupboard and we were singing the packet song.'

'What song?'

'Packets to platters. Packets to bin. Packets to platters. Packets to bin. It was fun, don't you remember, Mummy? You were clapping. I like it when you're happy, and I wanted to help you. I didn't know anyone was going to die.'

'Of course you didn't, Freddie, you poor boy, come here.'

'Fuck off Jade, get away from my son.'

'Beth, come on. This is all getting a bit obstreperous now, isn't it?'

'What the fuck does that mean? Fara, if you're going to talk to me, only use words I can understand.'

'Of course. I just think we all need to calm down. Why don't you help me with the tombola? I still need to stick raffle tickets on some of these prizes. You can be in charge of the Sellotape.'

'I don't want to be in charge of the Sellotape, Fara. I want to know why you're so friendly with Emily.'

'What?'

'Someone like you, with all your degrees and pashminas, why are you always hanging around with that ridiculous Queen Bee?'

'She isn't ridiculous, Beth. Or a Queen Bee. And in answer to your question, I'm friends with Emily because I like her.'

'Why?'

'Beth, we're all really worried about you. Are you OK?'

'Don't worry about me, Fara. Worry about yourself; why you're always trying to impress Emily.'

'I'm not! She's my friend and I like spending time with her. That's all there is to it.'

'Why? What do you like about her?'

'Because she never makes me feel bad about myself. Not like you, Beth. I see you, rolling your eyes and judging me behind my back, when all I've ever tried to be is nice. Emily accepts me for who I am and never makes me feel bad about wanting to come into the school to read with the kids or for having a career. She doesn't mock me for wanting the best for my children. She listens to me when I talk—'

'And I want you to listen to me when *I* talk, Fara. I want you to understand about Ana. I want you to understand what she's like. Because she hates you for sending your son to boarding school. She was probably going to kill you next.'

'Why don't we talk about this later? Come back to my house after the tombola, we can get this all sorted out.'

'She's so perfect. Just like Charlotte and Jade. And it's all fake – their friendship with me, because all I am is a phase. I'm just another phase.'

'No, what you are, Beth, is a good person who has had a bad time. Please try to calm down.'

'It's like your jumper, Ana, isn't it?'

'What do you mean?'

'I'm just a phase, aren't I? Like the phases of the moon. And after me, there'll be another phase. And another phase.'

'*You need to calm down!*'

'And then another phase. And another phase. And another phase!'

'*Get away from me!*'

'*Oh my God. Somebody call an ambulance! And the police! Somebody call the police!*'

35

Almost blue, nearly green. The waves of the ocean. Washing over me and leaving me behind on the shore, where it's cold and the sand is gravelly, rubbing into my face. His eyes staring into mine. I want to reach out towards him because I need him to know. I see him too. I love him. I've always loved him. He's close, why can't I touch him? What's wrong with my arms? I can't move my arms. And the gravel is in my mouth, I can taste it. I'm lying face down on the ground with my hands behind my back and it's cold. Why can't I move?

'Rowan, where am I?' My throat hurts. 'Are the children with you? I need to get back to Wilfred. He'll be waiting for his walk. Rowan, I'm cold. Where am I? Why can't I move my arms?'

'You're in the playground.'

'What? No, that can't be right. Jade said she was collecting the boys today, so I didn't need to come to school. I was at the kitchen table, Rowan. I remember sitting there, working through all the clutter. I think I've finally worked it out. I think I know what happened to Charlotte.'

'And what about you, Beth?' His eyes flick away from mine. 'When are you going to work out what happened to you?'

He's staring at something on the ground. The pastel-blue tablecloth. Someone is lying on top of it, perfectly still. Two figures in green are kneeling beside them.

'Oh my God. What happened? I can't remember what happened! Where are you going? Rowan!'

His feet are moving away and there are other shoes next to my face, and hands underneath my arms, lifting me. Dragging me towards the back of a van.

'No! I don't want to go in there. Let me go home. Please, I'm begging you! Get off me! Please, leave me alone!'

36

It's pretending to be homely – this room I've never been into before. Two armchairs are facing each other and there's a box of tissues on the coffee table in between. It almost looks normal, except for the red light up there on the wall, flickering a constant reminder. I'm a person who needs to be watched.

The door opens and my first visitor appears. Bringing part of the old world into the new, and when two universes collide, it's disorientating. I'm glad I'm already sitting down. She moves towards the armchair opposite. Feet shuffling, her gaze on the floor. Lowering herself into the seat, she looks pained. Why is she here?

'Why are you here?' I ask her directly. There's no place for niceties in this world.

'I wanted to check you're OK,' she says, looking around the room. 'Despite what . . . happened . . .'

She's staring at the wall, at the picture. It's an image of a lake. The water is calm. Peaceful.

'I still care about you. I know you're not a bad person. I think you're just lost. Truth is, I think you've been lost for quite a while.'

There's a tree next to the lake. Branches reaching outwards. I close my eyes.

'Ever since she died.'

I open my eyes. She's staring at me.

'But I want you to know, Beth, we all cared about Charlotte.'

Silence descends and I'm beginning to wonder whether it will ever end but I don't think she finds it unsettling. When she finally speaks, there's a reluctance to her words. She's talking, but only because she feels that she should. She glances around the room.

'Doesn't seem too bad in here,' she says, her eyes meeting mine. 'The people out there,' her head nods towards the door, 'they were friendly enough.'

'I'd like it better if I could leave.'

'Right.'

More silence as she studies the picture of the lake and I look down at the itchy scab on the palm of my left hand, inches from that perpetual void encircling my ring finger. An empty space of everything that might have been.

'Why did you do it?' she asks.

'What?'

'Attack her. You shoved her so viciously . . . She hit her head on the ground so hard she was unconscious for nearly ten minutes.'

I start picking at the scab.

'I was drunk. I didn't know what I was doing.'

'But why her? I thought she was your friend. Why did you attack Ana?'

'Because I thought she killed Charlotte,' I reply.

'But that's crazy,' she says, shifting slightly in the chair. 'Nobody killed Charlotte, you understand that now, right? The police investigated and said her death was an accident. That's what the witnesses said too.'

More silence. More staring down at my hands and, this time, I'm studying each bitten fingernail. Counting them inside my head. I'm at six and when I get to ten, I'm going to ask her. Eight, nine, deep breath for courage. Ten.

'How is it?' My voice is shaky. 'At the school, I mean. Do you ever see . . . anyone?'

'It's just the same, to be honest.' She shifts again in her seat. 'Obviously, everyone talked about you for a while.'

She takes a breath and I curl my hands into fists defensively.

'About what happened. But don't worry, they've already moved on to talking about other things now. I see Rowan up there quite a lot, with Jade.' Shots fired. 'And it looks like Hope is properly walking now.'

I'm not sure I can breathe. I taste vomit.

'She's very steady on her feet, toddles into the playground most days. Look, if you're worrying about your kids, Beth – I hope I can put your mind at rest. They all seem perfectly happy with Rowan, and obviously they've got the dog too. I know I wasn't always his biggest fan,' she breaks into a smile, 'but I have to admit, that Labrador seems to be a great support to them all.' Best dog in the world. 'He waits patiently outside the playground and when he sees them coming, well – I don't think I've ever seen so much tail-wagging!' Fatal blow. 'I'm sorry, I didn't mean to upset you.'

'You haven't.' I reach for a tissue.

'It's just that I don't want you to worry about them.'

'That's kind.'

'Because I think you've got enough to worry about.'

'True.'

'Honestly, your children seem fine. Better than fine, they seem happy. Oh no, now you're upset again. I shouldn't have come here, I'm sorry. I'm not sure *why* I came.'

'Please don't leave,' I say, reaching for another tissue. 'I've been here for weeks and you're the only visitor I've had, and it's nice, seeing someone from my old life. Honestly, it means the world to me – please don't go.'

'OK,' she says, 'I'll stay.'

More silence as she studies the picture and I silently dab at my eyes.

'So, Rowan hasn't brought the children to see you?'

'He's been advised not to. Not until I'm feeling stronger.'

'Well, I'm sure you'll see them soon. And I can come again next week,' she says, 'if you'd like?'

'That would be lovely,' I say. 'It will give me something to look forward to.' Another tissue. 'Thank you for being so kind.'

'I'm not here to be kind, Beth,' she says, shifting forward in her chair, leaning towards me. 'I'm here because I want to see my friend.' She places her hand on my knee. 'We used to be friends – you and I.'

'I know. I just . . .'
'What?'
'Felt I could never compete. Not after the divorce.'
'With what?'
'You.'
'What do you mean?'
'You're so perfect . . .'
'No, I'm not! Nobody's perfect.'
'Compared to me, they are.'
'What do you mean?'
'Compared to me, everyone's got everything worked out.'

'Oh, Beth.' She tries to move her chair forward, but I think it's secured in place. 'Nobody's got anything worked out, especially not me.' Huge alien eyes blinking away tears. 'None of us know what we're doing, not really.'

'That's kind of you to say, Emily, but compared to me you *are* perfect.'

'In what way?'
'Your house is spotless—'
'I have two cleaners.'
'Your children are always top of the class.'
'I probably push them too hard.'
'You run the PTA.'
'No one comes to the meetings.'
'You throw the best parties.'
'I get stressed and become a nightmare.'
'You have a separate drawer for Sellotape.'
'What?'
'You've never attacked another parent in the playground and ended up in rehab.'

'No,' she says, taking my hands into hers, 'that's true.' She leans closer, her face inches from mine. 'But listen to me, I saw Ana on the school run yesterday and she's fine. Minor concussion, that's all it was, and obviously very worrying at the time, but she's fully recovered now. I told her I was coming here today to see you and . . .' I flinch. 'She said to send you her love. She doesn't hate you, Beth. Nobody hates you.'

I start to cry. She passes me another tissue.

'We're not enemies, you and me. We never were. After Charlotte died, I was so busy trying to fill her shoes, I didn't think about how you were feeling, not properly. What Rowan and Jade did to you, the lying and the cheating . . .'

'Yes?' I say, dabbing at my eyes.

'It was awful. Truly awful.'

'Thank you, Emily.' I'm crying again.

'I should have been more supportive,' she says, 'because it's tough, isn't it? Bringing up children. All of us trying our best but none of us ever feeling quite good enough. And that's why, when you get out of here, I hope we can have a proper friendship, one where you don't feel you have to stand on your own. Because it isn't good to isolate yourself, Beth. Everyone needs support.'

And now my head is resting down on her shoulder and I'm not dabbing at my eyes any more. I'm letting the tears fall.

37

First school run after three months in rehab. I take a deep breath and walk over to the climbing wall. Jack and Freddie are playing on it, and I want to keep a careful eye on both of them.

'So, you're back then.' Carl the Caretaker shuffles up beside me.

'Yes,' I reply. 'Keeping my eye on my sons.' Jack is at the top of the climbing wall and Freddie is catching up fast.

'Can't be easy for you,' he says. 'What with all the gossips around here.'

'It's OK,' I say, still staring ahead.

'So, what's the plan?' he asks. 'Going to keep yourself to yourself?'

'No,' I say, glancing over towards a huddle of mothers standing nearby. 'I'll join my friends in a minute, just . . .'

'Building up the courage?'

'Letting the boys have a play first.'

'Right,' he says, glancing down at Hope, fast asleep in the pushchair. 'She looks worn out.'

'Yes,' I say, smiling at my daughter. 'We've been playing together all day. It's so wonderful being back home.'

'I bet.' We stand in silence. Both of us staring at the climbing wall. 'I miss her too, you know.'

'Sorry?' I ask, turning to face him.

'Charlotte, I miss her too.'

'Oh, right,' I say, staring straight ahead again. Freddie has joined Jack at the top of the wall.

'She was always good to me,' he's saying now. 'One of the few parents in this place who treated me like a real person. Do you know, one year, she even got me a Christmas present. Gift-wrapped and everything. It was a pen, with my name engraved on the side. I carry it around with me, in my top pocket.' He reaches into his top pocket. 'It's nice to have something with my name on. Look, here it is.'

He holds out a silver pen. I squint at the curly wording. *Carl Hooper.*

'It's the nicest present anyone's ever given me,' he says, returning the pen to his pocket. 'Charlotte was so thoughtful.'

'Yes,' I say, testing my voice. It's croaky but still works. 'She was.'

We stand in silence again.

'The lollipop lady,' I say, clearing my throat, 'I knew Charlotte got her a personalised gift one Christmas, but I didn't know she got you something too.' More silence. 'Carl?' I say, turning towards him.

'Yes?'

'Thank you.'

'For what?' he asks, confused.

'Standing over here and talking to me,' I reply. 'It's very kind.'

'Everyone deserves kindness.'

'Even me?'

'Even you.'

'Even though I'm Sweary Mum who lets her children play unsupervised on the climbing wall?'

'Even you, Sweary Mum,' he says with a kind smile. 'And anyway,' he adds, 'at least you never force your children to jump off it.'

'That's true,' I say. 'At least I never do that.'

Carl is staring at the climbing wall and I'm thinking about something else. Somewhere else. Two armchairs in a visitors' room. A box of tissues on the coffee table in between. A red light flickering in the top corner, and a picture on the wall. Still water. Hidden depths. His last words swirling towards the surface.

'What do you mean?' I ask. 'Why would anyone force their children to jump off the wall? It's so high.'

'Oh, you'd be surprised at some of the things I've seen in this playground over the years.' His eyes flick up to where Jack and Freddie are sitting. They wave at him and Carl waves back. 'There was a crazy mum who used to send her son here and you won't believe this, but one day I watched her tell her kid to scramble right to the top of the wall, and then deliberately jump off. No, not even that, *fall* off! Honestly, I saw it happen! With my own eyes.'

'What mum?'

'Oh, I don't know her name. Traffic Lights Mum, that's what I called her. Forever going on about her son falling from a height. She had red hair, bright green chunky shoes, and always wore a padded yellow coat in the winter. She looked like a set of traffic lights.'

'But why?' Sound from the playground seems to retreat away. 'Why would she want her son to fall?'

'I think she liked all the attention; everyone fussing around her, calling ambulances and whatnot.'

'So, what did the school do about it?' I ask. My voice sounds weird against the backdrop of white noise. 'When you told Miss Lane?'

'Oh, I didn't mention it to her,' he says, 'but I know it got sorted because after I told Charlotte, I never saw Traffic Lights Mum in the playground again. She must have moved that poor boy to a different school.'

That poor boy.

'What do you mean, you told Charlotte? When?'

'Oh, it was sometime last year, on one of those days when the playground is busy with parents standing around gossiping, and nobody in any rush to hurry home. That's probably why she did it.'

'Who?'

'Traffic Lights Mum. I think she liked a big audience – more attention, I suppose. Nobody else noticed, well – you parents do love a natter, don't you? But I watched her, and I saw what she did, and her son, he didn't want to. Far from it. He wanted to play with his skeleton friends—'

'What?'

'All the kids were in costume – yes, now I think about it, it must have been last Halloween. Bloody mess the playground was in, sweet wrappers everywhere. Anyway, he wanted to play with his friends, but she called him away and then forced him to do it. I saw her tell him to climb the wall and when he was at the top, and no one else was looking, she ordered him to let go. He didn't want to, but she pointed her finger at him. Looked quite scary, truth be told. And when that poor kid fell, that was it – suddenly she was the centre of attention. Luckily the kid didn't hurt himself, but that seemed to actually annoy his mum. That's when I told Charlotte what I'd seen because Traffic Lights Mum, well – she was never going to listen to me, was she? Nobody ever listens to me. But Charlotte was a doctor, so I knew she'd know what to do and she went straight over there and dealt with it. I watched her. She had a quiet word with Traffic Lights Mum. Told her she didn't think the fall was accidental and how she'd be taking the matter further, and . . .'

'And?' My mouth is dry.

'Well, I never got the chance to ask Charlotte what happened next because that was the weekend she got hit by the car. But like I say, it must have been sorted out because I never saw Traffic Lights Mum or her son up here again . . .'

'Jack! Freddie!' the voice coming from me doesn't sound like mine any more. 'I'm sorry, Carl,' I say, turning to face him. 'We need to make a move. Come on, boys!' I can't stay still in this moment any longer.

'Of course,' he says, before turning and shuffling away. 'It's nice to have you back.'

'Come on, boys!' I shout again. They're both still at the top of the wall and don't seem to be in any hurry to climb down. I glance over towards the huddle of mums standing nearby. Fara's holding her baby and Ana is staring at me. Poor Ana. 'Jack, please!' I shout up at my son. There are so many children on the wall, they're all blending into each other; a mass of faceless entities. Like the one banging on Charlotte's door that night. Red hair, yellow coat, green shoes – was it Traffic Lights Mum? Bill said Leo kept drawing the accident, even imagining versions where Charlotte was kept safe. But what if it wasn't the lollipop lady or traffic lights in his pictures? What if he wasn't drawing something to protect his mummy? What if he was drawing the person she was running from?

'Come on, boys! Let's go home.' And what about Charlotte? As she lay dying on the ground. *That poor boy.* Perhaps she wasn't talking about a grieving mother from years ago. Was she talking about the son of the red-haired woman? And she kept saying sorry, didn't she? Sorry because she never got the chance to do anything to help him? To tell the police what that woman was doing to Ollie? Sorry because she knew he'd have to keep falling? To keep getting hurt? *That poor boy. I'm so sorry.*

'What did you say, Mummy?' Freddie appears in front of me. 'We have to go home?'

'Yeah, that's right, Freddie, let's go home so I can cook you all a special dinner. Go and get your brother.' He turns and runs back towards the wall and shouts up to Jack and I think about Ana. The blame so easily shifted onto poor Ana.

'Freddie said we're having a special dinner.' Jack is staring up at me.

'Good boys, thank you for getting off the wall. Yes,' I say, turning the pushchair around. 'And I've got something nice for pudding too.'

'Yes!' both boys shout as Freddie flings his arms around my legs and gives me a hug.

'Right, let's go,' I say, pushing the buggy through the playground, towards the exit. That's why she said Ana was the woman she saw in the hospital that night. Because she needed to throw me off the scent. She pointed the finger at the first woman she saw, not knowing that I knew Ana. No wonder she practically dragged Ollie out of the park. She didn't want to stick around to see her lie exposed.

'We'll have a nice dinner and then I'll help you with your homework.'

Truth is, I'll never know the identity of the woman in the hospital, the one whose son died. And she'll never know how sorry Charlotte was.

We're hurrying towards the exit, past all the other parents standing in packs. But I don't believe in safety in numbers, and I think Traffic Lights Mum knew that. I think she knew I was a free-thinker, and that I was getting closer and closer to the truth. Because I don't see things the same as everyone else. Never have. Never will. Other people accept what they're told and follow the crowd, but not me. I stand alone and as soon as the children are in bed tonight, I'll get a new sheet of paper and start writing everything down. New information, new ideas; I'll start working again on my new, improved project.

Then I stop.

'Mummy, I thought we were going home.'

'We are,' I say, turning the buggy, pushing it back into the playground. 'Just give me a moment. We'll be going home in a moment.' And now I'm approaching them, and Emily sees me first. Huge, alien eyes softening with the most beautiful smile.

'Beth!' she says. 'I'm so glad you decided to come over.'

'Hello Beth,' says Fara, gently patting her baby's back. 'It's good to see you.'

'Hi,' smiles Ana, a wriggling Willow in her arms, who reaches down towards Hope in the pushchair, still sleeping.

'Hello everyone,' I say, coughing slightly to clear my throat. 'This is going to sound crazy, but please – hear me out. I think I know what happened to Charlotte.'

Acknowledgements

So many Vipers to thank! Starting with Miranda Jewess – queen of the nest, editor extraordinaire and so ridiculously good at what she does, it's an honour to have her read my words. Thank you, Miranda.

And how much fun is the powerhouse of publicity – Drew Jerrison? Thank you, Drew, for travelling around the country with me, listening to me chatter for hours – making me forget that this writing lark is actually work. Huge thanks also to the extremely talented Rosie Parnham for all her phenomenal marketing ideas.

My superb copy-editor, Rhian McKay, who I've had the pleasure of working with on two books now – thank you, Rhian!

All the other Vipers I've been lucky enough to work with directly – Charlotte Greenwood, Georgina Difford, Rachel Quin, Audrey Kerr , Sian Gibson, Elif Akar – and the rest of the team at Viper/Profile who all work so incredibly hard. I also want to thank Imogen Church for doing such a sensational job narrating the audiobook . . . I could listen to Imogen narrating books all day long!

I'm beyond grateful to the incredible authors who have been so generous with their time and advice, using humour and experience to help me navigate the mysterious world of publishing. Special thanks to Tariq Ashkanani, Tina Baker, David Bishop, Kate Griffin, Janice Hallett, David Jackson, Oskar Jensen, Dan Malakin, Guy Morpuss, James Mylet, Leonora Nattrass, Daniel Sellers, Kate Simants, Alison Stockham and Catriona Ward.

My superstar of an agent, Cathryn Summerhayes and the team at Curtis Brown – Katie McGowan, Annabel White, Jess Molloy and Anna Weguelin – all managing to remain thoroughly lovely human beings whilst effortlessly making the impossible possible.

My family and friends, with special mention to Marie and Laurence Field and their beautiful daughter, Eleanor, who will be forever missed and never, ever forgotten.

Our wonderful dog, Star, who refused to leave my side as I wrote every word of this book but who passed away before it was published. He spent his life living up to his name and we will love him for eternity.

My husband, Marc, our children Grace, Charlie, Lucy, Sam and our dog, Wilfred. You five people, and hound, mean everything to me and there is simply no point to anything without you in the world. Thank you for being my family, for putting up with me, and for pushing me – repeatedly – to that place inside my mind where the only thing that gives me any comfort or solace is writing about murder. Just think, if you tidied up after yourselves every so often, maybe I wouldn't keep plotting the deaths of fictional characters. I love you all very much but seriously, please tidy your rooms.

Finally, to all the teachers and parents I met at my children's primary school over the years – thank you!